The Enchantment
of Lily Dahl

The Enchantment
of Lily Dahl

A   N O V E L

Siri Hustvedt

HENRY HOLT AND COMPANY   NEW YORK

Henry Holt and Company, Inc.
Publishers since 1866
115 West 18th Street
New York, New York 10011

Henry Holt ® is a registered
trademark of Henry Holt and Company, Inc.

Published in Canada by Fitzhenry & Whiteside Ltd.,
195 Allstate Parkway, Markham, Ontario L3R 4T8.

Library of Congress Cataloging-in-Publication Data
Hustvedt, Siri.
The enchantment of Lily Dahl: a novel/Siri Hustvedt.—1st ed.
p.   cm.
I. Title
PS3558.U813E53   1996   96-16514
813' .54—dc20   CIP
ISBN 0-8050-4920-7

Henry Holt books are available for special promotions and premiums.
For details contact: Director, Special Markets.

First Edition—1996

Designed by Jessica Shatan

Printed in the United States of America
All first editions are printed on acid-free paper. ∞

10 9 8 7 6 5 4 3 2 1

For Liv, Astrid and Ingrid Hustvedt

The Enchantment
of Lily Dahl

1

She had been watching him for three weeks. Every morning since the beginning of May, she had gone to the window to look at him. It was always early, just before dawn, and as far as she knew he had never seen her. On that first morning, Lily had opened her eyes and spotted a light coming from a window across the street in the Stuart Hotel, and once she had moved closer, she had noticed him in the shining square: a beautiful man standing near a large canvas. Stripped down in the heat to only his shorts, he had stood so still for a minute that he hadn't looked real to her. But then he had started to move, using his whole body to paint, and Lily had watched him reach, stoop, lunge, and even kneel before the canvas. She had watched him pace the floor, rub his face hard with his hands, and smoke. The man smoked little cigars, which he held between his teeth whenever he paused to think. And sometimes, when he was just quietly smoking, he would nod at the painting as if it were talking to him. Lily had studied the lines of his muscles and the light brown color of his skin and the way it gleamed in the light, but she had not seen what he was painting. The front of the canvas had always been hidden from her.

Division Street was wide and treeless. The man's room was at least twenty yards from Lily's, and she had never been closer to him than that. Exactly what she expected from watching him she didn't know, but it hardly mattered. The truth was that she couldn't look at the man enough, and on those days when he didn't go to bed but stayed up and worked through the dawn, she had to force herself to close her curtains and turn away from the window.

On this particular morning, however, it was raining hard and Lily couldn't see him clearly. She stuck her head out the window and squinted in his direction. Rain pelted her face, and water was streaming down his closed window, so all she could make out was a blurred, waving body behind the glass. And then, before she understood what was happening, he walked to his window, jerked it open and leaned out into the rain. Lily ducked beneath the sill and squatted on the floor. Her heart was beating fast and her cheeks turned hot as she listened to the noise of water running in the gutters. She had taken a terrible risk leaning out that way. Before that moment, she had scolded herself a little for spying on him, but the thought that she had been discovered filled her with sudden, acute shame. She had been so careful, too, always crouching beside her window with only her eyes above the sill, making sure no light was on in her room, and every time she did turn them on to shower and get dressed for work, she had kept her curtains tightly closed.

Lily knew that the man's name was Edward Shapiro.

Although they hadn't exchanged a single word, she had gathered several facts about him and had heard a lot of gossip. She knew for certain that Edward Shapiro had spent a year as "artist in residence" at Courtland College. She knew that instead of returning home to New York City at the end of his last semester, he had decided to stay on in Webster, and that was when he had rented the room in the Stuart Hotel. She also accepted as fact that sometime in March, his wife, who had been living with him in faculty housing, had packed her bags and left him. The rest was rumor. A lot of people wanted to know what he was doing in a fleabag like the Stuart, a hotel so crummy that it didn't even take women. The five or six old codgers who lived there were a sad bunch, and Lily knew most of them. The hotel's restaurant had been closed for as long as she could remember, even though they had never taken down the sign for it, and just about every morning, one by one, the men would shuffle across the street to eat their breakfasts at the Ideal Cafe, where Lily waited on them six days a week. She had heard that Edward Shapiro was poor, that he gambled his earnings at the college on baseball games, and she had heard he was rich but was too cheap to rent a decent place. She had heard his wife left him because he gambled, and she had heard she left him because, as Lester Underberg put it not a week ago in the cafe, "he couldn't keep his pecker at home." Lester had it "on good authority" that Shapiro had "nailed" a beautiful redheaded student in his office while playing Verdi at full tilt. According to Lester, Shapiro had received dozens of young opera fans in his office while he was at the college, but the truth was that Lester couldn't be trusted. He collected dirt on everybody and anybody, and on a couple of occasions Lily had caught him telling out-and-out whoppers. Lester was right about Edward Shapiro's love for opera, however. There had been nights in the past weeks when she had heard music coming from his window, and twice the voices had been so loud that they had woken her from a deep sleep. The story about the redhead stuck in her mind nevertheless, and Lily kept adding details to it that Lester had left out. She imagined Shapiro and the girl, saw her lying with her legs open on a desk, her skirt pulled up around her waist and the man standing over her, completely dressed except for an open zipper. Over and over, she had played out the scene in her mind, had seen papers scatter and books drop from the desk as the man grappled with his student. Lily had watched for women to appear in the man's window, but if they visited, they never stayed the night. The narrow iron bed that stood in the far right-hand corner of his room had been empty twenty-two mornings in a row.

Lily balked at moving, but very slowly she peeked over the sill. Shapiro's window was dark, and she felt her shoulders sink in relief. When she closed her curtains, she heard footsteps from the apartment next door. Mabel's up, she thought. Mabel Wasley slept very little, and the wall between the two rooms wasn't thick enough to muffle even the smallest noise. Day after day, Lily listened to the old woman walk, rustle papers, open and close cupboards and drawers, clink dishes, cough, mumble, flush her toilet, and all afternoon and far into the night she listened to Mabel type. Exactly what Mabel was writing had never been clear to Lily, although the woman had once explained it. The enormous manuscript was an autobiography of some kind that included dreams and how they mixed into everyday life, but whenever Mabel talked about the book, she went on and on and used words Lily didn't understand, and sometimes when she was particularly excited, her voice would get very loud until she was almost shouting, so Lily didn't like to bring up the subject. For nine months Lily had lived above the Ideal Cafe alone. She had rented her room only a few days after graduating from high school, and when Mabel arrived in early March, Lily had welcomed the company, even though from time to time, she had the impression that Mabel was hiding something. No one knew much about her, although she had taught at Courtland College for twenty years. There were rumors that she had been married several times before she came to Minnesota, but Mabel had never mentioned a husband, and although she was very friendly, she was also stiff, and that stiffness forbade prying.

Lily sat down at her table where she ate and put on her makeup and did anything else that required sitting. She had hung her mirror above it and looked at her own tired face in the reflection and at Marilyn Monroe's face behind her on a poster she had fastened to the wall. Boomer Wee had once said she looked like Marilyn, only dark, and even though Lily knew this wasn't true, she liked the idea. She leaned toward the mirror, lowered her eyelids, parted her lips and pushed her breasts together to make a long cleavage over her white bra. She glanced at Marilyn again and then heard a knock at the door.

"It's open," she said, her voice hoarse with sleep.

Without turning around, Lily saw Mabel enter the room in the mirror. The old woman walked quickly, her long robe sweeping the floor, and stopped when she reached the chair.

"I'm sorry to bother you, but I wanted to catch you before work and ask you how the play was going and tell you that if you're still having trouble with the part, I might be able to help. You know I taught *A Midsummer Night's Dream* for, well, close to thirty years, and it struck me last night that I could coach you. Hermia's a wonderful part, really, and you're perfect for it. What do you think?" Mabel delivered this speech fast and with few breaths, addressing Lily's reflection in the mirror, all the while waving her hands for emphasis, and once her fingers brushed the top of Lily's head. Then she let her hands fall and rested them lightly on Lily's shoulders. They were both silent for several seconds, and Lily stared at their faces in the mirror and at Marilyn's between them, and she thought that the three of them looked strange together. Mabel's small heart-shaped face, with deep wrinkles on her forehead and around her eyes and mouth, had an intense expression that could have been either defiance or concentration. Marilyn wasn't smiling either, but her lips were parted to show teeth, and her fingers indented the flesh of her right breast. There was something too perfect about the way the three of them were framed in the mirror, and it bothered Lily. It created an annoying stillness that made her think suddenly of things that were alive and things that were dead, and she shrugged her shoulders to release herself from Mabel's touch.

"Monday's good after work. I need help. I remember my lines, but half the time I don't know what they mean."

The woman clasped her hands. "We'll have tea first."

Mabel's happiness irritated Lily for some reason, and she said nothing more.

Mabel left the room. She didn't say good-bye. Instead, she recited some of Lily's lines from the play: "Dark night, that from the eye his function takes." Lily saw Mabel put a finger to her ear. "The ear more quick of comprehension makes; / Wherein it doth impair the seeing sense, / It pays the hearing double recompense."

The woman's voice was thin and old, but her delivery had a nuance and understanding Lily knew she lacked completely. That's why she did it, she thought, to show me how natural and good she is. Isn't that what Mrs. Wright had been telling her in rehearsal? "Just speak in your natural voice," and Lily had thought to herself: But what is my natural voice?

The early customers who straggled into the Ideal Cafe were all men, all regulars, and none of them had much to say. Between five and six the place was pretty quiet. The men who came in during that first hour didn't have wives or girlfriends, but every one of them would have had a story to tell if he'd chosen to tell it, a story about the accident, death, bad break or quirk of personality that had turned him into what he was now: a solitary character who arrived at the crack of dawn to eat his breakfast alone in a room full of other solitary characters who were eating their breakfasts alone.

Pete Lund usually arrived first, after chores on his big farm east of town. Pete's wife had died of breast cancer a couple years back, and he had taken to eating his meals out. A year ago when Lily first started working, he had placed his order aloud, and it still stood: a cup of black coffee, two eggs, scrambled, and three pieces of white toast with strawberry jam, not grape jelly. After that, he hadn't bothered to speak. When Lily approached him, he nodded at her, and she put in the order. Harold Hrdlicka, who had bought the old Muus farm, took his eggs sunny-side up with hash browns, and Earl Butenhoff from the Stuart Hotel ate a bowl of Wheaties before his eggs—once over easy—and finished off his meal with a fat, usually half-smoked stogie that he carried around in his shirt pocket. By five-thirty that morning they had all arrived, each one sitting in his own booth waiting for food. Pete was staring over the counter at Vince's collection of "semiantique" windup toys. Harold was reading the *Webster Chronicle*, and Earl studied the tabletop between repeated throat-clearings—during which he spat gobs of yellow mucus into a huge, stained handkerchief that he pulled in and out of his pants pocket. From the kitchen, Lily could hear Vince singing "Anything Goes" in a low voice. She could hear the rain outside and smell bacon and sausage on the grill, and from the street came an odor of wet pavement, grass, and what she supposed were worms crawling onto the sidewalk, and as she moved from table to table with her pot of coffee, she felt happy and hummed along with Vince under her breath.

Martin Petersen walked into the cafe around six, took his usual seat in the booth by the window and started staring at Lily. Every time he came in for breakfast, he stared. She was used to it, not just from Martin, but from lots of people. She had suffered through braces on her teeth, breasts that wouldn't grow and a reputation as a tomboy, but the year she turned fourteen, it had changed, and now after five years she had grown used to her looks and the staring that went with them. Sometimes she liked it, and sometimes she didn't, but she had learned to pretend that she didn't notice. Martin, however, was different. He always studied her calmly and deliberately as if it were his job to look at her, and because she couldn't penetrate what he meant by those long stares, Martin's eyes made her a little uncomfortable. But at the same time, she felt oddly drawn to him. Martin was mysterious. She had heard rumors that he was gay and rumors that he was a person who had no interest in sex. Linda Haugen had once whispered to her in confirmation class that Martin had been "born both" and that "they took the girl half away." But this had to be nonsense. The secret of Martin wasn't his body, but it wasn't his mind either. He gave off something peculiar—an air of hidden knowledge or intuition that sometimes made Lily feel he was looking at her from a great distance even though he was only inches away.

Lily couldn't remember not knowing Martin Petersen. The house where Martin lived as a child and where he still lived wasn't far from Lily's own childhood house on the outskirts of town, and she and Martin had sometimes played together in the woods or near the creek. He had stuttered even worse then than he did now. A couple of times, she had taken Martin home with her to play, but Lily had never gone to Martin's house. There had been something wrong with his father, and whatever it was, it had made Lily's mother nervous enough to leave it unexplained. When Lily was eight, Martin's father, Rufus Petersen, had killed his dog—a bitch about to give birth. He shot her and left the bleeding carcass down by the creek, where Lily's father had found the poor mutt and buried her along with her unborn pups. Lily remembered the blood on her father's shirt from the dog, and remembered that he had cursed Rufus Petersen with uncommon violence. She had played with Martin less often after that, but he rode the same school bus that she did, and she remembered he was teased mercilessly for his stutter. Once Andy Feenie and Pete Borum had beaten up Martin behind Longfellow School, and she remembered him coming around the brick building, bawling loudly as blood poured down his shirt from his nose. In high school, Martin had kept mostly to himself, and he and Lily hadn't talked to each other much, but she had felt connected to him anyway, and sometimes they had run into each other at the creek, where Martin fled his house to read books and be alone. His father had left the family by then, and his young mother who didn't look young was sick with leukemia, and his older brother and sister were fending for themselves and, some said, running wild. Mrs. Petersen died during Martin's last year of junior high school, and there had been a mess with the welfare people. Hard knocks, Lily thought, one after the other. The other Petersen kids had left town, but Martin had stayed on in the family house and was working as a handyman. The word was that he was very good at it. Reliable and honest, they said, and people were calling him all the time to fix this or that, to do some painting or small carpentry work, and Lily had a feeling that life was better for him now that he was grown up.

Martin always wanted the same breakfast—poached eggs on toast—but unlike Lily's other early customers, he had never been happy with silence. It wasn't enough to say to him, "The usual?" and let him nod. He wanted an exchange, so instead of Martin stammering out an order and getting flustered, he tapped out a little rhythm on the tabletop with his fingers, rat-tat-a-tat-tat, and Lily answered him with two raps of her own, tat-tat. The tapping had started soon after Lily began working in the cafe and had made them friends again, after a fashion. No one else was in on it. Those beats were a little language all their own, and Martin seemed so happy to order his breakfast in code, it made Lily happy, too.

That morning they went through the routine again. Martin rapped the table.

Lily slapped her index finger twice against the edge of the table and said, "You've got it, Cobweb."

Martin had landed the tiny part of Cobweb in *A Midsummer Night's Dream*, and Lily thought it would be friendly to acknowledge it, although she wondered if Mrs. Wright hadn't taken charity a little too far by casting Martin in any role, no matter how small. She hadn't rehearsed with Martin yet. So far practice had been limited to the actors with big parts, but it was hard to imagine Martin as any kind of actor, much less a fairy.

When she gave Vince Martin's order in the kitchen, the fat man leaned across the stove and said, "Where's the funeral? It's so quiet in there, you'd think I was cooking for a bunch of stiffs."

Lily grinned and shook her head. "You say that every morning, Vince. It gets noisier in an hour. You know that."

"This is one dead little burg, baby doll. It's big-time excitement around here when one of them old Lutherans lets out a fart."

Lily smiled at Vince. He was in a good mood this morning, and she felt grateful. "Go back to Philadelphia then, why don't you, if it's so perfect there," Lily said and picked up the plate of French toast for Mike Fox. "Must be great, people shooting each other in the streets, muggers, pickpockets. I read the papers, Vince. Sounds like paradise." Lily backed through the swinging doors.

Vince pointed his spatula at her. "At least people talk to you before they shoot you!"

With Mike's plate in her hands, Lily paused behind the counter. She could feel Martin watching her and glanced over at him for an instant. His sober face was measuring hers. Maybe he does have a thing for me, she thought, and laid Mike's plate on the counter beside the six cigarettes that he had already lined up in front of him on the Formica surface.

"You're food's here when you're ready, Mike," she said.

He looked up at her and pushed a strand of long blond hair behind his ear, before he stuck a fresh cigarette between his teeth. Lily watched him light it. Six days a week for a year, she had watched Mike go through the same ritual. The job called for a whole pack of Kents, and when he was finished, Lily would find a row of twenty cigarettes on the counter, each one smoked just a hair shorter than the one before it. Looking at Mike, she felt sure that he was counting his puffs, but she knew he couldn't be dragging too hard on it either or the butt would burn too fast. Mike lowered the cigarette to the black ashtray and began to snuff it with a gentle turning motion of his wrist and fingers. The first time Mike had left that perfect slant of Kents on the counter, Lily had been scared to throw them away. But Bert had said, "He doesn't care about it once it's done. Just sweep the masterpiece into the garbage. He'll make another one tomorrow."

Lily walked back to the kitchen to pick up Martin's food, and Vince started in right where he left off. "And because there's no talking in this goddamned place, there's no real sex. Ever think of that, doll? Look at the women in this town, hardly a single one with a speck of 'cha-cha.' In the winter they're all covered up with those god-awful down parkas and in the summer they wear dresses that look like bags. Lipstick's a sin. Jewelry's a sin." The man's face was red. He had big jowls that shook when he moved his head.

Lily grabbed Martin's plate. "There's plenty of sex in this town, Vince. Don't be a dummy."

"Yeah, but it's not *fun* sex. There's a big difference."

Lily groaned. "Come on."

"You haven't been around, baby. I'm telling you." He held his arms out at his sides and wiggled his enormous hips back and forth. "Sex is shmooze in a dusky bar with a jazz band and a girl who looks like she likes it. Oh, honey, the nights I spend dreamin' about Sandra Martinez," the man groaned.

"What you don't know, Mr. City Man," Lily said, "is that a cornfield can be just as sexy as a jazz club. You just haven't been around." Lily rolled her shoulder at him.

Vince opened his mouth and pretended to be shocked. "Why, Lily Dahl," he said. "You little devil."

"Don't ever tell *me* I haven't got cha-cha," Lily said on her way out, and she heard Vince muttering something under his breath.

The rain had stopped and Division Street looked brighter. When she put down the plate in front of Martin, he looked up at her with his serious face and his wide eyes, and she remembered how light his irises were—pale blue—a color that made her feel she could look right through them. As she left the table she felt a vague spasm in her abdomen, heard the screen door open and, turning toward the sound, saw the Bodler boys shuffle into the cafe. She sighed, but not loudly enough for them to hear it, and watched them walk toward the booth in the back just outside the bathroom with the sign Vince had put up that said "EITHER/OR." If only they weren't so dirty, Lily thought, as she looked down at the trail of mud on the floor behind the two men. If only it was just their boots that were dirty, and not their arms and legs and heads and butts and every square inch of their whole selves. Lily stopped in front of the Bodlers' table and took out her order pad. She looked from Filthy Frank to Dirty Dick and back to Filthy Frank. The old coots were just as grimy as ever, only moister. She could see drip lines on their cheeks where they'd been rained on. Lily tapped her toe and waited. Frank would order. He always did. Dick never said a word. The Bodler boys were identical twins who over many years had turned out different. Nobody had the slightest difficulty telling them apart. Dick's body echoed Frank's but didn't repeat it. Punier, balder, blanker, Dick had become a diluted copy of his brother.

Everything they touched turned black. Lily looked down at Frank's hands. She could already see smudges forming on the white table.

"Well, what'll it be?" she said.

Neither man moved or even blinked.

She leaned closer to Frank and raised her eyebrows. He smelled like clay.

The man opened his mouth, showing brown teeth interrupted by several holes. Then came the guttural rumble: "Two eggs, scrambled, bacon, toast, coffee."

"Coming up." Lily turned away and looked over Martin's head into the street. The weather was clearing steadily. Martin was reading now. He usually brought a book with him and read for a while before leaving. As far as Lily could tell, Martin read everything. He seemed to like history books, especially books on World War II, but he also liked novels— cheap ones and highbrow ones—and science fiction books and how-to books. She remembered him reading *Anna Karenina* in the cafe for several weeks, and when he finished with that he had started in on a book called *A Hundred Ways to Make Money in the Country*. Still, Lily figured all that reading had to do some good. He's probably pretty smart, she thought, and then on her way to the kitchen she considered the fact that Martin had turned twenty-one and was most likely a virgin. She liked this thought, liked the idea of innocence in a young man. At the same time, she felt sorry for him.

Only a few minutes later, when Lily was serving the Bodlers their breakfast and pouring them more coffee, she noticed a brown grocery bag sitting beside Frank in the booth and asked herself what the dirt twins might be hauling around with them. Then she watched Frank grasp his cup and looked down at his thumbnail—a thick, yellow husk—and staring at the fat, dirty nail started her thinking about Helen Bodler.

No one doubted anymore that old man Bodler had buried his wife alive back in 1932, but at the time people thought she'd walked out on him and the twins. Bodler drank. His small farm, like a lot of other farms, was in bad trouble and the theory was he went mad from the strain. Lily remembered her grandmother telling her the story, remembered how she had leaned over the oilcloth on the kitchen table, her voice tense but clear. "Helen wouldn't've left them two little boys and gone off without a word to nobody. She wasn't that kind. I knew her, and she wasn't that kind. Mighty pretty woman, too. People said she ran off with the peddler, Ira Cohen. Talk about rubbish. Cohen had a wife and six kids in St. Paul. Where'd he put her? In the back of the cart? The whole thing stank to high heaven from the start."

They found Helen's body in 1950. The twins and another man, Jacob Hiner, were digging up the old outhouse on the property and unearthed her skeleton near it. Bodler had already been dead for eleven years. His two sons had fought in Europe, had come home and started up their junk business. Lily didn't know exactly when they had stopped washing. The army enforced cleanliness, so it must have been sometime after 1945 that the Bodler twins became Filthy Frank and Dirty Dick. Had they married, the gruesome story of their parents might have aged faster, grown distant with children and grandchildren, but there were no more Bodlers. What the two brothers had felt when they discovered their mother's bones frozen in a position of panic, a position that showed she had tried to claw her way out of her grave, was anybody's guess. Illegible as stones, the two walked, ate and snorted out as few words as possible.

Then, as she looked up, Lily saw Edward Shapiro standing on the steps outside the Stuart Hotel. Even from that distance, she could see that he was rumpled, as if he had just climbed out of bed. Lily walked toward the window and stopped. She watched the man scratch his leg, and at the same time, out of the corner of her eye, she saw Bert waltz into the cafe and let the screen door slam behind her. After tying an apron around her waist, Bert sidled up to Lily and said, "So how's the Ordeal this morning?" Without waiting for an answer, she surveyed the booths, nodded at the twins and groaned theatrically.

Lily nodded and moved her head to the right so she wouldn't lose sight of the man on the steps. Bert followed Lily's eyes and the two women watched him together.

"Absolutely, definitely cheating material if I ever saw it." Bert gave her wad of gum a snap. "It's not often I get the urge to sneak out on old Rog', but that one . . . ," and without bothering to finish the sentence, Bert shook her head. Then she whistled and turned to Lily. "Poor Hank, he's in for it."

"I'm not married to Hank, Bert."

"Oh yeah, I thought you two were engaged."

"Not really," Lily said and held out her left hand. "No ring, see. Anyway, who says I'd have a chance with a guy like that. He must be at least thirty, and he's an artist, and—"

"Honey," Bert interrupted her, "with a bod like yours

you've got a chance with anything male and breathing." She paused. "Well, what d'ya know, Mr. Tall, Dark and Mysterious is coming over."

"Nah," Lily said. "He never comes in here."

But Edward Shapiro was striding across the street toward them, and Lily grabbed the coffeepot off its heating coil and began to pour coffee into Clarence Sogn's cup, even though it was nearly full already, and once she had done that, she wiped her hands on her apron for no reason and felt her heart beating and told herself not to be stupid. She didn't see him, but she heard him come through the door, and at the sound she straightened her back and pulled in her stomach. Just as she turned to look at him and saw him sitting at the counter, she felt a slow, warm sensation between her legs and knew it was blood. Shit, she thought. I never keep track. She stared at Edward Shapiro from behind. He was leaning forward and the fabric of his blue work shirt had tightened across his shoulder blades. She moved her eyes down the back seam of his jeans that disappeared into the red covering of the stool, and she could almost feel his weight. The man was lean, but the idea of his heaviness aroused her. Even if he did see me, he'll never recognize me, she said to herself and watched Bert pour him a cup of coffee. She wished she were on the other side of the counter with the coffeepot. She wished she didn't have to run upstairs to her room for a tampon. She waved at Bert, mouthed the word "curse," raced to the back of the cafe and through the door to the stairwell.

Sitting on the toilet in her apartment, Lily felt grateful to be off her feet. Her jeans and underpants were lying on the floor, and she was looking down at the blood stain on the white material of her underpants, its red brilliant against the denim and the dull blue floor tiles. She didn't want to move, but after several seconds she reached for her tampons, unwrapped one and pushed it inside her. She glanced down at the blue string between her legs, at her bare knees and the lines of their bones, and had one of those sudden, curious feelings, more sensation than thought, and more familiar to children than adults, that she wasn't really there in the room at all, that she had been blown out of her own head somewhere else, and that every thing she was looking at was no longer itself, but a kind of inanimate impostor. Lily changed position to get rid of the feeling and then changed into a fresh pair of underpants and jeans.

She opened the back door to the cafe slowly. She wanted to look in on Edward Shapiro at the counter, but he was gone. Instead, she saw Martin only three or four feet in front of her, standing beside the Bodlers' booth, and at that very second, he was handing Filthy Frank two twenty-dollar bills. Half a minute later, she would have missed the whole transaction. Frank took the money, picked at his greasy shirt pocket and tucked the bills inside. Then he handed Martin the bag. It was the way Martin took the bag that gave Lily a start. As he reached for it, his fingers trembled with expectation, and his eyes rolled upward so that for an instant his pupils disappeared and all she saw was white. His lips parted, and she heard him exhale. Lily didn't know what she was seeing, but whatever lay inside that dirty grocery bag, it had affected Martin in a way that embarrassed her. She suffered for him, for his oddness, for his not knowing how to act, for that horrible expression that was much too private for a cafe. She pushed the door open, and in her hurry to get past him, accidentally brushed his elbow. Damn, she said to herself as she confirmed that Shapiro had really and truly vanished. She felt a light touch on her shoulder, turned around and saw Martin staring down at her. He stuttered out her name and said, "I'm leaving something for you on the table."

She glanced down at the bag that Martin was holding in his left hand. "A present for me?" She knew perfectly well that it wasn't. The question was prompted by irritation with him, and she heard an edge in her voice.

He shook his head, and Lily turned away from him to avoid his face.

She hurried over to Bert and said, "So, what's he like?"

Bert looked up. "To whom are you referring?" she said with an artificial sniff.

"Ah, cut it out. Give me the dope."

"He came and went like lightning, but for the minute he was here, I'd say he was real class, real nice and not stuck-up at all."

"Yeah?" Lily said. She slid behind the counter and poured Matt Halvorsen more coffee. "Did you talk about anything?"

"He said he'd take a doughnut."

"That's deep," Lily said.

"I said, 'Which one?' and pointed at the case. Then he said in New York you don't get to pick 'em, and I said, 'Well, this ain't New York,' and he said he knew that, and that he'd take the one without the hole, more for your money. He swilled down his coffee in three seconds flat, grabbed the doughnut and ran out the door."

Lily pressed her lips together. "His eyes are kind of unusual, wouldn't you say? They go up a little. Did you notice?"

Bert nodded. "Almond shaped. That's uncommon, at least around here."

"He's uncommon, all right."

Lily and Bert turned their heads to spot the eavesdropper.

Ida Bodine walked toward them, carrying her coffee cup. The tiny woman wore her hair in a towering beehive to compensate for the missing inches.

"Gossip radar," Bert said to Lily in a low voice.

"He's got somethin' goin' up in his room," Ida said. "I've been hearin' things."

"What kind of things?" Lily said.

"Bangin', creakin'. More than once I've had to tell him to cut the racket—opera music blarin' till it busts your eardrums. It's my job as night manager to keep things runnin' smooth-like, and that one's made my job a regular hell."

Night desk clerk, you mean, Lily thought to herself. "Doesn't sound so bad to me," she said aloud. "A little noise."

Ida sipped her coffee, her eyes on Lily. "That ain't all. I seen people goin' in there when I start work at six, and they don't go in the front door neither, go in the back from the river side and stay in there with him for hours. And they ain't what you call 'nice' folks neither." Ida nodded.

"I think a man's got a right to see anyone he pleases," Bert said.

Ida looked straight at Bert, cocked her head to one side and smiled with false sweetness. "Tex?" she said.

Lily looked at Ida, who had put down her coffee cup and folded her arms across her chest. It did seem unlikely. Lily conjured an image of the big man—six feet five with long red sideburns, a nose bent from too many fights and a big beer belly hanging over his pants. Vince had banned him from the Ideal a couple of years before Lily started as a waitress, and she rarely met up with him, but Hank knew Tex from the city jail, where he sometimes spent the night in one or the other of the two cells. Hank's summer job as a dispatcher at the Webster

Police and Fire Department had made him an expert on the big redhead's misdemeanors. It was true that his crimes usually didn't amount to much more than disturbing the peace, but he disturbed the peace at a pretty regular clip and drove the officers batty. Tex's last offense had taken place last Thursday, when he barged through the doors of the Jehovah's Witness Kingdom Hall out on Highway 19, howling like Tarzan as he loped down the aisle dressed in nothing but a pair of leopard bikini underwear, a ten-gallon hat and cowboy boots.

"I'd say Tex must've paid that Shapiro fellow eight or nine visits, and the last time I seen him, he was comin' out of the room buttonin' up his shirt." Ida's face puckered in disgust.

Bert gaped at Ida in mock horror. "Why, Ida Bodine," she said. "If the man's a fruit, I'm a five-eyed alien from the next galaxy."

Ida sniffed. "I'm just sayin' what I seen, nothin' more."

"Come on, Ida," Lily said. "Edward Shapiro taught at Courtland. He had a good job there—"

Ida interrupted. "His wife left him, didn't she? It's gonna be divorce." She hissed the last consonant. "Tell me this, if he's so hoity-toity, big professor and all, what's he doin' in the Stuart?"

Lily glanced at Bert, then back at Ida. "I think he's painting." Her tone had more vehemence than she had intended.

Ida raised her eyebrows. "You know what they say about the paintings, don't you? They're pictures of Webster, and they ain't none of our beauty spots. I guess he's done the grain elevator and the tracks and the dump and made 'em real ugly to show all of us here that we're a bunch of hicks."

Lily had only seen the backs of Shapiro's paintings, but she wondered why he would paint outdoor scenes inside.

"Now where did you get that information?" Bert said.

"Around." Ida narrowed her eyes.

Lily leaned over the counter toward Ida. "And what law says he can't paint whatever the hell he wants?"

Ida moved her head back from Lily. "Well, la-di-da," she said. "If you aren't takin' this personal." The woman retrieved a Kleenex from her purse and dabbed either side of her mouth with it. It was a gesture of absurd, extravagant femininity that made Lily want to laugh. Ida lowered the napkin and clutched it in two hands. "What I'd like to know, Lily Dahl, is what's that New York Jew to you?"

Lily glared at Ida but said nothing. Bert gave Lily an uneasy glance. Then Ida crumpled the napkin in one fist, lifted her coffee cup from the counter and walked back to her stool.

"Windbag," Bert said.

"He's Jewish," Lily said, observing the fact aloud.

"Shapiro," Bert said. "It's a Jewish name."

"Oh," Lily said. She felt herself blush and wondered why Bert knew such things when she didn't. She looked at the clock. It was pushing seven. Soon there'd be another rush when the downtown merchants came in for a bite before opening their stores. Lily surveyed the room. She had missed the Bodlers' exit. "God, Bert, you cleaned the scuz booth."

"So you owe me." Bert picked up a stack of dishes, then motioned with her head toward the door.

Hank Farmer walked in and smiled at Lily. His face looked a little swollen, but then all night at the police station would clobber anybody. He gave Lily a quick kiss on the cheek, and instead of straightening up, he kept his head level with hers and said, "I'm going home to sleep, but I'd like to see you later, okay?"

Lily looked into his handsome face. He was so close she could see the faint scars of adolescent acne. A piece of dark blond hair had fallen onto his forehead. She didn't answer him but looked past his cheek at Martin's empty booth and studied the inverted letters of the neon sign in the window. She leaned back a couple of inches. "Call me," she said. "I feel a little low. My period."

Hank nodded and kissed her again. She watched him bound out the door and across the street. He moved beautifully, and she thought to herself that he looked better from a distance. She stared through the window and fiddled with the pad in her apron pocket.

Bert addressed Lily's back. "I know you're juggling love interests right and left here, Lil', but you better get that fanny of yours back to work."

Lily didn't bother to turn around. She wiggled her hips at Bert and said, "It's seven. I'm going to play something before you-know-who gets there first." Lily looked over her shoulder toward the jukebox and saw Boomer Wee coming through the kitchen doors.

"Cut him off at the pass!" Bert yelled, flinging an arm toward Boomer.

Lily made a dash for the jukebox, but Boomer was too fast for her, and by the time she reached it, he was leaning over the selections. His T-shirt had hiked up his back, exposing his white skin and bony spine. "Don't you dare play that song. Get back to the dishes!" she hissed at Boomer, trying to elbow him away from the box. "You're going to kill me with that song." But Boomer blocked her and she heard the rattle of the quarter, the click of the machine and then Elvis started singing "Blue Suede Shoes."

"You little skunk," Lily said to Boomer, who was smiling innocently on his way to the kitchen. I loved it, too, before I heard it 6,458 times, Lily thought, and walked over to Martin's booth to clear it.

The dirty plate, silverware, coffee cup and saucer had been stacked and pushed to one side of the table, but lying squarely in the middle was a white napkin, and on it, written in large, cursive letters was the word "mouth." That was all. Mouth? Lily thought. A thin ray of sunshine eked through a hole in the cloud cover and lit the table at a slant. Lily picked up the napkin and stared at it. Could this be what he was talking about, the thing he was going to leave me on the table? How weird. The ink had bled into the soft paper. Lily shook her head, and then, without knowing why, she glanced around to see if anyone had seen her reading the napkin. No one was showing the slightest interest. Lily brought her hands together, crumpled the paper, and quickly stuffed it into the back pocket of her jeans. Then she lifted the stack of dishes from the table and headed for the kitchen.

Lily told Hank not to come that night. When she heard the disappointment in his voice, she felt bad, but *Some Like It Hot* was on TV that night, and she wanted to watch Marilyn alone. Hank had teased Lily about Marilyn, had said she was dizzy on the subject, and once when Lily had tried to articulate her feelings about her, Hank had grinned through the explanation. After that, she had stopped talking about Marilyn to Hank or anyone else. The Marilyn story had started with *Bus Stop*. Lily was still living with her parents then. That was before her father's cancer operation, before they moved to

Florida to get away from the winters, and she had stayed up watching the movie until two o'clock in the morning. The coat in the very last scene had clinched it. The cowboy had taken off his jacket and put it around Marilyn's shoulders, and when she snuggled into it, her whole upper body had moved and trembled as if she were being kissed on her cheeks and neck and shoulders, and when Lily had looked into Marilyn's face on the screen, she had felt she was seeing a wonderful and dangerous happiness that was so strong it was almost pain. The scene had made her want to act more than anything in the world, and the next morning she had told her parents that she wanted to be an actress. They hadn't said much. Her mother told her in a gentle voice that high school plays and real theater were two different kettles of fish, and her father said a B.A. prepared you for everything. But Marilyn had made Lily think about acting in a new way, and she started wondering if it wasn't a way of being very close to the heart of things, that maybe acting actually brought you closer to the world rather than farther away from it.

After *Bus Stop*, Lily found Marilyn Monroe everywhere: in magazines, tabloids, comic books, on T-shirts and stickers, on posters and flags. She noticed little statues of her in ceramic and metal and rubber and saw her face and body emblazoned on ashtrays, mugs, pencils and clocks. But for Lily these icons were no more than crude approximations of the person on the screen, cheap leering versions of something intimate, almost sacred, and she avoided them. She had her poster, which she had chosen carefully in a store in Minneapolis, deciding against the famous one from *The Seven Year Itch* of Marilyn standing over the grate, her skirt billowing out from her thighs, for one less well known. She had bought a biography then, too, and had started it eagerly, searching among the details of Norma Jean's life for the secret she had glimpsed in the movie, but after about a hundred pages, she realized it wasn't there and stopped reading. As she lay in bed that evening watching *Some Like It Hot*, Lily laughed out loud at the men dressed as women and listened to Marilyn's voice, to its halting rhythms and breaths, and near the end, she studied the dress Marilyn was wearing. It was like part of her body, she decided, hardly clothes at all, a magical movie dress Lily imagined herself wearing, not in Webster, of course, but in a faraway city, like Los Angeles or New York or Paris, where women went slinking into clubs and bars in next to nothing. She smiled to herself and took bites of the Milky Way she had bought especially for the movie.

When it ended, Lily tried to sleep but couldn't. Edward Shapiro's windows were dark, and she wondered where he had gone. Through the wall, she heard Mabel blow her nose and start typing again. A copy of *Glamour* lay on the night table, and Lily picked it up. She turned the pages and stared at the clothes she couldn't afford and then stopped to read a headline: "What Does a Man Want in a Woman?" It was a survey. Lily threw aside the magazine and began to recite her lines in a whisper. "So is Lysander." She closed her eyes. "I would but my father look'd with my eyes." She paused. "I do but entreat your grace to pardon me. /I do not know by what power I am made bold." A breeze blew in through her open window, and the fresh air aggravated her restlessness. I could walk over to Rick's and have a beer, she thought. She remembered Hank, felt troubled, and then after putting her hand down inside her jeans, she held her genitals for comfort and, still dressed, fell asleep.

Once in the middle of the night, she woke up and thought she heard voices singing far away. Then she fell asleep again. At nine o'clock, she heard the church bells from Saint John's and opened her eyes. Lily had been dreaming, and the Sunday bells had mixed themselves into the dream, which she had forgotten except that it hadn't been pleasant, because the repeated clang bothered her. She could almost hear the congregation's murmuring, that hollow, haunted tone people use to speak to the unseen, interrupted only by the occasional cough or a baby's cry. As she pulled herself out of the muddy dream, she saw Pastor Carlsen's face with its permanently sincere expression—an indistinct blend of pity and remorse. His face had always irritated her, not because she thought it was hypocritical, but because she knew it was real.

Lily never consciously decided to take the route that passed the Bodler place, but she found herself pedaling her bicycle in that direction and dreaming of the car she could buy with the money she had in the bank if she didn't have to use it for college. Her father's medical bills had eaten up the savings put aside for Lily's education, and when Vince offered her a job at the Ideal Cafe and the room upstairs, she took it without complaint. Lily had told herself she needed time to think anyway. She needed to plan. Hank had a plan for himself and for her, but whenever she thought about the imaginary house in Minneapolis and the imaginary children and Hank Farmer forever, a part of her balked. So far she had managed to save $3,476.32 from her job, and that money promised her a life after Webster. Watching Edward Shapiro paint had launched new fantasies about New York, a place she had seen only on postcards and in the movies. Before he had moved into the Stuart Hotel, she had dreamed mostly of Hollywood and California, but watching the man in the window had turned her eastward, and now she imagined herself walking in crowded streets beneath towering buildings on her way to an audition, a script tucked under her arm. Lily pedaled harder with the wind in her face and looked out at the cornfields, the stalks still short but growing taller in the wide, flat fields. The sky had cleared since yesterday, and the sun was hot on her face. When she came to the end of the driveway that led to the Bodlers', she stopped, climbed off her bicycle and looked at the ruined farmstead turned junkyard.

The Bodler place was such a spectacular eyesore, it was almost gorgeous, a sight that made people whistle in disbelief if it didn't stun them to silence. A mountain range of refuse had formed in the front yard, great heaps of junk so high they hid the house, garage and fallen barn behind them. These multi-colored towers that included parts of bicycles and cars, old appliances, wires, pipes, lumber and innumerable moldering somethings never failed to impress Lily. She remembered searching for toys in the piles when she came here with her father as a child. She remembered feeling both exhilarated and uncomfortable as she dug in the mounds of junk. That was before she had heard the Helen Bodler story, and yet she had known that the old farm with its two dirty men was a place apart. She had never been inside the house. Her father used to go in to speak to Frank, but he had always asked her to wait on the step, as though he didn't want her to see what was inside. Once, after her father had left her in the yard, she had walked around to the side of the house and pressed her face to a windowpane. She had seen hazy piles of objects and furniture, and then out of nowhere she had seen a face—an enormous, only vaguely human face, its great mouth hanging open, its tongue flickering like a snake's, and Lily had run gasping from the window. She did not tell her father about it. She did not tell anyone about it, and only years later did she assume that she had mistaken Dick Bodler for a monster.

The brothers' old green truck wasn't parked in the driveway today, and there wasn't a junk picker in sight. Lily listened to the sound of her feet scraping against dirt and pebbles in the driveway and looked up suddenly when she heard a crack above her. A loose piece of canvas from a baby stroller had caught the wind, and she heard it crack again. Otherwise the place was very quiet. Birds chittered, the grass rustled, and she could hear car motors in the distance. When she reached the garage, she paused and looked in through the open doors. The sun cut a sharp rectangle on the earth floor, but beyond that light the interior looked almost black. She could make out a chaos of boxes, old tools and farm equipment, and she inhaled the odor of mildew and cold, damp earth, two smells she liked. Lily had no intention of going inside. The sun and air had made her slow and a little sleepy. But then she saw a suitcase lying on a crate, one corner of it illuminated by sunshine, and she walked toward it. Feeling only vaguely curious, she touched its cracked leather surface, then tugged at its handle. It felt full, and its unexpected weight attracted her. Lily dragged it into the light, hesitated for a second and opened it. The bag was filled not with odds and ends as she had anticipated, but with neatly packed clothes, as if someone had planned a trip, never taken it and then forgotten about the suitcase altogether. The clothes inside had belonged to one woman. They were all the same tiny size, and whoever she was, she hadn't worn them for a long time. Lily couldn't date them exactly, but examining a long shapeless dress, she guessed it had been fashionable during the twenties or thirties. Lily seated herself on the dirt floor and pulled out a threadbare camisole with a liver-colored stain. Although she knew it was childish, she pitied the stained garment, pitied it the way she would an unhappy child or whining animal. She folded it, replaced it carefully in the suitcase, and then noticed a fabric pocket under the lid that bulged with something. She slid her hand inside and took out a pair of white shoes. These had held up better than the clothes. Only slightly scuffed, they looked like shoes their owner had saved for church and going to parties. Lily guessed they would fit her. Her mother had always said she had Cinderella feet: size five. Lily pulled off her sneakers, slid one bare foot into a shoe, then the other. The shoes had no tongue, only laces. She tied them quickly and stretched out her legs, examining her feet in the old-fashioned shoes. She liked the curve of their stacked heels and the softness of the leather. They fit snugly. In fact, they pinched, but the tightness around her feet gave her pleasure, a sensation that was almost erotic—tense and warm.

As Lily sat on the dirt floor of the garage, looking at her feet in somebody else's shoes and pondering that satisfying pressure on her toes, she thought she heard a step outside the garage, then a person breathing. She stopped breathing herself to listen. A car with a broken muffler passed on the road, and she listened as its loud rumbling faded away. Was there someone in the grass outside? Did she hear footsteps again? Lily shook her head. No, she thought. She reached forward to untie the shoes, and when her fingers touched the laces, she was struck by the thought that these were Helen Bodler's shoes, that she had packed her suitcase all those years ago to run away from her husband. With a shiver of excitement Lily removed the shoes and in that same instant decided to take them. After closing the suitcase and returning it to its original place, she found an old paper bag, dumped the nails out of it and dropped in the shoes. Then she dug in her pockets and came up with two dollar bills, a quarter and a dime. I'll leave this as payment, she thought.

The heavy inner door to the house stood open. Lily looked through the screen door and into the kitchen. She could hear flies, a low uneven buzz, and inches inside the dim room she made out long rolls of flypaper hanging from the ceiling, crusted black with insects. The room smelled strongly of mold, and when she looked down at the floor, she thought the cracked linoleum squares were oozing liquid. It's just wet, she thought, from yesterday's rain. The house probably leaks like a sieve. A couple of feet inside the dark room, Lily could see a table. To run in, slap down the money on the table and rush back would take seconds. Still, Lily hesitated. She listened. The house was silent. Her eyes had adjusted to the murky room within, and she could see a rifle resting against the wall. I'll count to fifteen, she said to herself, and then run. This method had never failed, because Lily had never cheated on herself. The numbers changed according to the degree of the challenge, but they always worked. The silent count had been responsible for her eating that worm on a dare when she was eight during recess at Longfellow School, for prompting her over the cliff into the ice water of the quarry in May when she was thirteen, and for her greatest triumph—that night only four years ago when she lay down on the railroad tracks in front of an oncoming train, and then, only seconds before it hit her, rolled out of the way. Bert had been furious, but the boys had all shaken her hand and beat her on the back. The count helped her face more mundane trials, too: like getting out of bed at four o'clock in the morning to go to work. Lily counted, pushed on the screen door, took a step, heard the noise of a car in the driveway, turned her head and slipped. She fell half in and half out of the door, her left arm flat in a pool of cold slime. Coins rolled across the kitchen floor, and she sat up as fast as she could to look at the driveway. With relief she saw that it wasn't the twins' truck, but an old blue Chevy with a bashed fender. The floor had left a yellow film mixed with dirt on her arm and Lily wiped it with the bottom of her T-shirt. Then, holding the bag of shoes behind her, she walked down the steps and paused for a second. She saw a dollar bill float over the grass as it caught the wind. I must have dropped it on the step when I fell, she thought. It blew further away. Lily let it go, and began to invent a story for the person driving the car, in case the person wanted to know why she had been sprawled in the Bodler's doorway. She would say she was leaving money for a purchase and fell. It was true, of course, but also wasn't.

The Chevy stopped, and Lily watched an obese woman slowly ease herself out the car door. "Give your brother half of that one, Arnie, or I'll smack you," she said to the backseat. The woman's hair had been bleached to a crisp. Lily stared at her enormous belly and thighs in double knit bermudas. She took three heavy steps and puffed. When Lily passed her, the woman said "Hi," in a dead voice, and Lily said "Hi" back. She glanced into the car and saw two remarkably similar blond boys sitting in the backseat. One was clearly older, but both tanned faces were streaked with tears, snot and Oreos. Lily moved beyond the car, heard its door creak open and the woman say, "Truce, babies. Come and give Mama a hug." Lily looked back for a moment to see the boys climb out of the car and fling themselves into the flesh of the now squatting woman. When the woman's arms closed around them, Lily turned back to the road and started to run toward her bicycle.

Mabel's room smelled of dust, perfume and the paper of old books. She owned hundreds of them, and they crowded the apartment, bulging from shelves that lined several walls in the living room, bedroom and even the bathroom. Lily breathed in that odor again when Mabel opened the door for her Monday afternoon. Stale and dry, Lily thought, like dead bugs. Mabel was talking, but Lily didn't listen to her. Mabel's living room had always made her feel funny. There were two things that didn't seem to belong in the room. One was a miserable old table that Mabel didn't dust. The other tables were dusted, but the rickety pine table with those old keys lying on it was never touched. And then there was a bird's nest that was little more than a pile of refuse. If Mabel had not told her what it was, she never would have known. The rest of Mabel's furniture was adorned with silk and velvet pillows and woven pieces of cloth. The floor was covered with a beautiful red and blue Oriental rug—the leftovers from her big house on Orchard Street. Lily remembered Mabel saying that she had kept only those objects that had "personal meaning" whether they were valuable or not, and that the apartment was a "storehouse of memory." Once, Lily had mustered the courage to ask Mabel about the undusted table, and it was then that she had discovered that Mabel could answer a question without answering it. For five, maybe ten minutes, she had prattled on about Cicero and some other guy whose name Lily couldn't remember, and when she stopped, Lily didn't know a single thing more than when she'd first asked.

"Lily." Mabel sang the name.

Lily looked at Mabel.

"You're lost in thought."

"Sorry."

Mabel brushed the sleeve of her black tunic. Expensive, Lily thought. She probably bought it in one of those stores in Minneapolis where they look you up and down before they let you in the door. I wonder where she got her money. Professors don't make that much.

Mabel poured Lily a cup of tea, her hands trembling as she held the pot in the air. The woman always looked cold. But the room was warm, and Lily had gotten used to Mabel's tremors and quakes and her constantly moving hands. She wasn't sick. She was nervous, so tightly strung that Lily half expected to hear the woman's body hum from the strain. Lily held the translucent teacup and imagined its thin sides breaking in her hand.

A copy of *A Midsummer Night's Dream* lay on Mabel's lap, and she drummed it with her fingers. Then she leaned forward, stared at Lily and said abruptly, "I've always liked the idea of changelings."

Lily didn't know what to say. It wasn't a question, so she said, "Why?"

"Because the older I get, the more certain I am that you can't know who's who or what's what." Lily examined the layer of pale powder coating Mabel's face. It ended at her chin. "You never get down to the bottom of it. Never."

Lily didn't ask why again, although she wasn't sure she agreed with this. The "changeling" in the play didn't have a goblin double or anything like that. She turned her head toward Mabel's bookshelves and noticed a small drawing propped up between two of the volumes. Japanese, she thought. When she looked at it more closely, she saw with a start that it was a picture of a man with his penis halfway inside a woman. The penis was finely detailed and was unusually large, as were the woman's genitals. Lily looked away. How could Mabel have such a thing out in the open for people to see? An old lady like her? Lily stared at her knees. The picture reminded her of one of those distorted sexual dreams, and its image lingered: the woman resting on her side with her legs open, her head thrown back, and the man leaning over her, their loose robes falling from their bodies. In spite of herself, the Japanese lovers aroused her, and Lily squeezed her thighs together in the chair.

"I'll cue you," Mabel was saying.

Lily looked up. "Fine," she said. The window lit Mabel from behind and whitened the wisps of gray hair on her head. She moved, and the halo disappeared.

"How old are you, Mabel?" Lily tried to make her voice sound quiet and polite.

Mabel laughed. "Too old to be coy. I'm seventy-eight. I'll be seventy-nine in February." She smoothed back a strand of hair. "There's fifty-nine years between us." She didn't calculate. She had the number ready.

Lily sneaked another look at the drawing. "You don't act that old, you know."

Mabel stood up. "Well, my inside never caught up with my outside." She took a deep breath. "Now, stand up. Your voice is important, but so is your body. We have to find Hermia's posture, her walk, her physical expression."

They worked together that afternoon for two hours almost without pause, but it took just minutes for Lily to sense that

Hermia would never be the same. It wasn't only that Mabel knew the play well and could quote long passages from it by heart or that she could explain words and phrases that Lily had never made sense of before, it was that Mabel's voice changed when she spoke Hermia's lines. She didn't sound young exactly, but she didn't sound like herself either, and Lily could almost feel the presence of a third person in the room. At one point, she stopped Mabel and said, "Did you act?" And Mabel answered, "My whole life." And then, before Lily could question her further, the woman had continued, "Remember this," she said. "Hermia is no more and no less than the words on the page. To speak them is to be her. It's that simple. How good you are, however, depends on your ability to embody the language. And that"—Mabel shook a finger at Lily—"is spiritual."

Until then, Hermia's verse had been as remote to Lily as a song in another language she could memorize but not understand. But that afternoon, she discovered that by watching Mabel closely, by adopting her tone and posture, she felt more when she spoke the lines. In fact, it seemed to Lily that the emotion came from Mabel's voice and gestures rather than from inside herself, and this made her a little uneasy. Mabel barked orders at Lily, corrected and scolded, and then, all at once, Lily discovered that she meant what she was saying. She meant it as much as she meant anything. It was as if the old woman had cast a spell over her, a magic of comprehension and belief. A couple of times she burst out laughing for no reason and had to start a scene over again. And once, after Lily gave a particularly fiery speech to Mabel's Helena, the old woman hugged her, and Lily hugged her back. They had never embraced before. Under the black cloth of Mabel's tunic, Lily felt the woman's sharp little bones. She's just a stick, Lily thought, no flesh at all.

That night at rehearsal, Mrs. Wright told Lily that she had made a "major breakthrough."

Riding home on her bicycle from the Arts Guild, Lily looked up at the moon in the darkening sky. Clouds as thin as smoke passed over its white surface, and below it she could see the silhouette of the grain elevator rising above the squat buildings of the town. Her bike jolted over the railroad tracks, and then, crossing the bridge, she breathed in the smell of the Cannon River—carp and rust and underwater weeds. She turned down Division Street, glanced up at Edward Shapiro's window in the Stuart Hotel, saw that his lights were on and felt a surge of hope.

Inside her apartment, Lily walked to the window without turning on her light. Edward Shapiro was talking on the telephone. He sat in a chair with his legs apart and was jiggling his right knee as he talked. Then he stood up and paced the floor with the receiver clamped between his raised shoulder and chin. Most of the other windows in the hotel were dark or covered. A television flickered beneath a half-drawn shade in a window on the first floor, and the lobby glowed behind the glass door. Ida, who no doubt sat behind the desk, was invisible. Lily looked up at Shapiro and saw him stare at the receiver for an instant before he put it down in disbelief or resignation—Lily didn't know which. Then she remembered Hank and unplugged her phone. When she turned around, she saw the paper bag lying on the floor, reached for it and took out the shoes. She looked down at the two pale forms in her hands and asked herself why she had taken them. In the garage she had believed that these shoes had belonged to Helen Bodler. In her room, this idea seemed far-fetched. Why would she want a dead woman's shoes, want them enough to steal them? She hadn't left the money and that made it stealing, didn't it? "I'm a thief," Lily said aloud. Then she kicked off her sneakers and put on the shoes.

When she stood up, they hurt. I'm bad, she thought, and at that same moment, she knew what she was going to do. Lily turned on every light in her apartment and yanked open her window so violently that she saw Shapiro turn his head and look toward her. Good, she thought. Good. He walked toward his window and leaned out. Mabel was typing urgently next door. Lily heard the woman pause, then beat the keys again. Lily walked straight to the window and faced Shapiro. She reached for the band that held her ponytail, undid it and shook her hair onto her back. She looked straight at him, although his face was hidden in shadow, and unbuttoned her blouse slowly. Then she threw it on the floor, ran her fingers over her naked shoulder and bit her bottom lip hard, rolling the flesh inward. This is wonderful, she said to herself, and unbuttoned her cutoff jeans. She turned to one side and wriggled out of the tight shorts. She could feel the stiff material slide down her buttocks, and that sensation, along with the fact that she knew he was looking at her, prompted an image of herself as someone else—a party girl crashing a strip show, a girl who never said die and who could bump and grind with the best of them. She had to hold on to her underpants to keep them from gliding down with the shorts, and she did this as gracefully as she possibly could. Then she hurled the cutoffs in the direction of her blouse, tossed her head and smiled.

She hoped he could see the smile. All she could make out of Shapiro now was his silhouette—the line of his head and shoulders in the window. Lily unhooked her bra. She was glad she had worn the one with a front clasp so she didn't have to struggle with the back. She let it fall down her arms and then crossed her hands over her breasts and rolled her shoulders. These were borrowed gestures, but that was part of the pleasure. For an instant she thought about Marilyn, took the bra in one hand and flung it across the room. The bra sailed higher and farther than she had intended. On its way down, it caught the TV's On/Off button, and there it remained, hanging several inches off the floor. Lily stared at the bra. It was gray. I've got to go to the Laundromat, she thought, and looked down at her breasts, then at her feet. Red marks had formed where the laces rubbed into her skin. She felt naked. For an instant she considered making a dash for the bed and rolling herself in the blanket, but instead she covered her breasts again. Oh my God, she thought. Her heart was beating fast now, and she took a long breath before she took off her underpants. You can't stop now. It would look really dumb, like you lost your nerve. But the sight of her pubic hair sobered her even more—a triangle of dark hair, more poignant than erotic. Lily didn't touch the shoes, even though they were pinching her toes like vises. Standing at her window wearing nothing but the shoes, Lily looked across the street at Edward Shapiro. He left the window. For a moment she stared at the back of his canvas, at the chair and the black telephone, and she almost cried. But she held back the tears, walked to the window, and after wrapping herself in the curtain, sat down on the sill. She could smell lilacs in the air. The scent probably came from the bushes outside the library at the end of the block. Their last days, she thought. And that was when Lily heard the music. A man started singing in a language Lily didn't know, and after a short time a woman answered him. Edward Shapiro came back to the window, and Lily looked at him and listened to the man and woman singing together. She leaned back against the window frame. The crackled paint scraped against her shoulder bone, and she adjusted the curtain to protect her skin. It was a duet from an opera. That much she knew, but it was much simpler than she had imagined that kind of music could be. She thought it was the prettiest song she had ever heard, and she wanted it to go on and on because she knew it was his way of talking to her without talking to her, and she didn't feel like crying anymore. Listening to the voices of those two people, she imagined that the real adventure of her life was beginning now, that after this, anything could happen, anything at all. When the song ended, the man left the window to turn off the record and returned for a second time. Lily looked into his dark face. They could have called to each other or waved, but they didn't. They continued to look at each other for what seemed like a long time, but maybe it wasn't. Lily heard the sound of a car up the street, the wind in the tree branches at the end of the block, and then running footsteps in the alley behind the Stuart Hotel. She looked toward the sound, but saw nobody, and then the footsteps stopped. She realized that Mabel wasn't typing anymore either. Lily took a last look at Edward Shapiro, and then she stood on tiptoe in the painful shoes and slowly closed the curtains.

When Lily walked into the hallway at five-fifteen the next morning, dressed and ready for work, she heard Mabel's door open, saw the woman's head push through the opening, and heard her say in a loud voice, *"Don Giovanni."*

"What?" Lily whispered to signal a lower tone.

"Didn't you hear it?" Mabel brought her voice down a few notches. "The duet from *Don Giovanni* blasting from across the street about ten-thirty, eleven o'clock." Mabel narrowed her eyes. "You'd have to be deaf not to have heard it."

"I heard it," Lily said. *"Don Giovanni."* She addressed the wall. "I didn't know what it was."

"Mozart," Mabel said.

Lily nodded, then turned to the steps.

"He stood in that window like he'd been turned to stone."

Lily was tempted to look back at Mabel's face but didn't. "Who?" she lied.

"Our neighbor from across the street. Shapiro. If it were possible to die standing up, I'd have said that fellow went into rigor mortis right then and there."

Lily said nothing.

"By the way, how was rehearsal?"

Lily stopped and turned to look up the stairs. Mabel was standing on the landing. Her hair had been pinned into a loose bun. Little wisps flew out all over her head. "It went great," Lily said. "Thanks to you."

Mabel looked down at Lily and smiled. "Shall we work again today or tomorrow?"

"Tomorrow," Lily said.

Mabel said, "Good." She turned to the door and opened it, her back rod-straight and her arm bent at a graceful angle. Lily knew this was an exit meant to be seen. The door closed with a click, and Lily wondered why Mabel was so interested in her. The woman's loneliness was palpable, and that explained part of it. No children, she thought. I hope I can have children, at least one, and if it's only one, I want it to be a girl. Lily had been an only child. It wasn't that her parents hadn't wanted more children, it had just turned out that way. Outside the door to the cafe, Lily stopped. She remembered the day she drove home with her father from the lumberyard. He had explained the weather to her in the car, the way it blew through the Dakotas and arrived in Minnesota a day or two later. She remembered walking through the door and calling for her mother, but her mother hadn't answered her, and she remembered her father picking up a note that lay on the kitchen table. She remembered the stricken look on his face, which she wasn't meant to see. Mrs. Daily had driven Lily's mother to the hospital. The doctor had told her that after three miscarriages she shouldn't get pregnant again. As a child, Lily had often thought about those children that were never born. She had even named them: Reginald, Alexander and Isabella. The names belonged to nobody Lily had ever known. She had stolen them from English novels for children, but the names reverberated even now, as signs of what never was. She remembered her mother telling her that she couldn't have more children, that she felt lucky to have her Lily, and then she never spoke of it again. Maybe I'll have two children, she thought, revising the number. She wondered why Mabel hadn't had children. She wondered why she had moved to Division Street. She had said the house on Orchard Street had been too much for her, but of all the places to come to, why this little brick building with warped floors and bad plumbing? The woman wasn't poor. And now she had seen Edward Shapiro standing in the window. Mabel Wasley was no dummy. She might be old, but it was obvious to Lily that the woman's brain was as sharp as ever. Lily had the uncomfortable notion that Mabel might suspect what had been going on last night. At the same time, unless Mabel had hung herself out her own window, she couldn't possibly have seen into Lily's. Of course Mabel knows the name of the damned opera, she said to herself and pushed open the door.

As she moved in and out of the kitchen from table to table, the memory of herself naked in the window filled Lily with awe. Every few minutes, she glanced over at the Stuart Hotel, shabby in daylight, and recalled the way it had looked only hours before—the illuminated window, the light of street lamps on the dark brick—another place altogether. He's asleep now, she thought, and paused for a moment. She was standing with her back to the counter, a plate in her right hand, a coffee cup in her left, when an image of Edward Shapiro's shoulders and chest shuddered through her. The plate tipped and a sausage rolled to the floor. Lily ducked behind the counter, picked up the little wiener and plopped it back on the plate. It looked fine. She set the plate in front of Elmer Esterby.

Lily was pouring coffee for Mr. Berman of Berman's Apparel and still thinking about the man in his bed across the street when she felt a hand on her shoulder. She didn't turn to see who it was until she had finished pouring. It was Hank. His face looked heavy and tired. Lily supposed he hadn't slept after his shift but had come straight to the cafe. He spoke to her in a low, tense voice. "We had a date last night, remember? To see each other after your rehearsal and before I went to work. I called and called. Where the hell were you?"

She didn't answer him. She looked into his face for a

couple of seconds, then turned away. Hank was holding her right arm, then he grabbed her left arm and squeezed. Lily knew he wanted her attention, wanted her to look at him, to be sorry, but she wasn't, and his tight grip on her made her feel stubborn, then indifferent. In response to his grip, she could feel herself go limp. I don't care, she thought. Her head bobbed forward and her spine collapsed.

"What the fuck?" Hank muttered.

He clutched her upper arms harder to hold her up. If he let go, she knew she would fall. I don't care, she thought again, and looked up at him with a dead expression. She knew what he saw when he looked at her: the face of an unruly schoolgirl who goes blank when scolded, and it gave her a sensation of defiant pleasure. I'm bad, she said to herself, and with that thought she smiled. Before she knew what she was doing, she was smiling like an idiot into Hank's outraged face. He started to shake her. Lily's head flew backward, then whipped forward again. She lost her footing and stumbled forward into Hank, who continued to shake her. His fury amazed Lily, and she heard herself cry out in surprise.

Mr. Berman stood up. "That's quite enough, Hank," he said.

The paternal command worked like magic. Hank's hands flew off Lily. She scrambled to regain her footing, stood up and watched him glance at his raised hands as he turned to the door. His cheeks looked shiny, and Lily bit her lip. On the sidewalk Hank broke into a run before the screen door slammed behind him. The noise felt like a signal that the drama was over. Lily heard muttering, felt people staring at her and took a deep breath.

"Are you all right, Lily?" Mr. Berman said.

She avoided his gaze. "I'm fine." She shrugged. Her

cheeks and forehead burned. She pulled her order pad out of her pocket and pretended to read it.

Bert walked up to Lily and put her arm around her. "Holy shit! What's *his* problem? I thought you were going to come sailing over the baked goods any second!"

Lily talked to Bert's feet. "Forget about it. He was pushed."

Bert angled her head downward to meet Lily's eyes. Lily lifted her head, looked at her friend and chewed her lip.

"Listen to me, Lil'. Even if you said you were going to hack off his dick, chop it up in little pieces and eat it for supper, he doesn't have the right to lay a hand on you. That's the law. Got it?"

Bert uttered these words in a voice so musical and tender, Lily had to smile.

"Just so we understand each other," Bert said. She moved her arm in feigned slow motion and pushed a fist gently into Lily's shoulder.

Thoughts of Hank came and went during the remainder of Lily's shift. She remembered how old he had seemed in high school, a senior when she was a freshman, and how all the girls had wanted him, and then when he came home from the university last year and she saw him at Rick's in his letter jacket, and he had asked her to dance, what had she felt, exactly? Flattered, she thought, and safe—after Peter. Peter was the college student she had met in the Courtland Arboretum when she was fifteen. He was twenty, and Lily still remembered the way his pale fingers clutched the book he carried around with him everywhere: *Beyond Good and Evil.* The title alone had excited her, and she remembered the conviction in his voice when he read to her about dancing and happiness and weak, sickly Christians, and how he kissed her in the damp grass and unbuttoned her shirt and talked about Nietzsche while he was doing it. Peter was thin and white, and Lily could see his naked body perfectly when she wanted to—a hairless boy's body that smelled of soap and perspiration at the same time. He wrote poems that didn't make sense to Lily, but she remembered there were lots of exclamation marks and ellipses. Her meetings with Peter had been a secret from everyone but Bert, who could keep all secrets. Eight times she had met Peter Lear in the woods of the arboretum. The ninth time he didn't come. Lily had waited by the tree for an hour and then gone to his dorm room to find him. It was his roommate who talked to her. Phil knew about Lily, and he had sat her down on one of the narrow beds and told her he thought she looked like a good kid, and he didn't want her to get hurt, but Peter had a serious girlfriend. He was with her at that very moment, and that he, Phil, didn't approve of Pete's exploitation of girls. That was the word he used—"exploitation." He had gone on about it for what seemed like an hour, and Lily had listened until he stopped. "Are you done?" she had asked him. After he had said yes, she had left the room, walked down the hallway to the stairs and out the front door. She had cried as soon as she felt the air. The humiliation had lasted much longer than the sadness. What she remembered most was Phil's enthusiasm when he talked to her, the gush of words that made his face hot. She could still see the freckles all over his face, his orange eyelashes, and how he kept looking at her bare legs while he talked. Afterward, Lily had invented speeches for him and for Peter, but she never had the opportunity to deliver them. A month later, Peter Lear graduated from Courtland College and went home to Chicago. During the following year, Lily had turned down every date and pushed away the boys at dances and parties. Kathy Finger had started the rumor that Lily was a lesbian, and she hadn't shut up about it until Hank came along. Lily had only seen Hank on weekends and during his vacations from the University of Minnesota, and she realized now that it had suited her just fine. She had told herself it would be nice to have Hank around all the time, but instead she felt lousy. In fact, the more she thought about it, the more she realized that although she had wanted Hank, she hadn't wanted him for the same reasons she had wanted Peter. She may have wanted Hank because of Peter. But the truth was that until she saw Edward Shapiro in the window, it was Peter Lear she imagined beside her at night. Peter was a physical memory—his delicate fingers between her thighs and his tongue in her ear.

Around noon, Ida stuck her head through the screen door of the cafe and peeked around it. She gave Lily an extra-long look. She knows about me and Hank already, Lily thought, and pretended she didn't see the midget clerk with the big hair. Stupid town, she said to herself, full of long noses sniffing for dirt and loose lips yakking about it once they've found it. Well, they sure as hell aren't going to see that I give a damn one way or the other. When she left the Ideal Cafe half an hour later with eleven ninety-five in tips in her pocket, Lily straightened her back and lifted her chin and made a dignified exit for anybody who might have bothered to look.

That afternoon, she wandered up and down Division Street for a couple of hours, looking in store windows and watching the kids who were hanging out on Bridge Square. She bought *Don Giovanni* on tape and a pair of pink underwear with lace around the legs, and when she walked out the door of Berman's Apparel with the little bag in her hand, feeling relief that she hadn't run into Mr. Berman, she paused, looked up at the clouds and realized she had decided to get unengaged from Hank Farmer.

At six o'clock, Lily walked into the Webster Police and Fire Department. From the driveway, she saw Hank's head through the wide window over the dispatcher's desk. She had no speech ready. The conversations she had invented earlier in the day had all sounded like people talking on *Secret Storm* or *As the World Turns*.

"I didn't think you'd come," Hank said.

Lily seated herself on the long desk in front of the window and let her legs dangle.

He looked at her evenly.

"Well, here I am," she said. Lily stared at her newly painted nails. A piece of hair fell across her cheek. She pushed it away.

"Why don't you tell me what's going on?"

Lily avoided his eyes. "I don't know," she said.

"That's not an answer."

"I know." Lily looked through the glass window behind Hank at two uniformed officers who were drinking coffee. Lewis Van Son's feet were propped up on the desk. Lily waved. Lewis nodded.

"So," Hank said. "Is there somebody else?"

"Not really," she said.

Hank sighed. "What the hell does that mean?"

Lily looked Hank in the eyes. "It's my fault, not yours."

"Okay," he said. "And?"

"I'm confused."

"About what?" His voice was aggressive. He leaned back in his chair, and it rolled with the motion.

"Well," Lily said. "I don't know what I want."

Hank opened his mouth. The telephone rang. "Webster Police Department." He used his official voice. "Yes, Mrs. Klatschwetter." He listened, puckered his mouth and shifted in the chair. "Are your sure?" Hank rubbed his forehead. "Could you see clearly? Okay, I'll send someone right away." Hank recorded an address, repeating it aloud as he wrote. "Highway 19 to Old Dutch Road, left across the creek. Yes, they know the way. Uh-huh, bye." Hank hung up and lifted his right hand to signal the officers.

"What was that all about?" Lily said.

"Rita Klatschwetter's got trespassers again, or so she says. Last week it was some guy dragging trash across her field. Now it's some guy with a body."

"A body? Jeez," Lily said.

Hank tapped his index finger on his temple. "They've never found a thing out there. She's called in the sheriff, the highway patrol and us, and insists on giving me the address every time. As if we don't know it by heart."

"That's the big farm out by the Bodler place, right?"

Hank nodded.

Lewis walked through the door, winked obscenely at Hank and grabbed the piece of paper with the address on it. He glanced at it. "Not again," he said.

"This time it's a corpse."

Lewis raised his eyebrows. "Right," he said.

Lily remembered the garage, saw her fingers disappear behind the thin fabric of the pocket under the suitcase lid. She closed her eyes for a second, opened them and watched Lewis leave the room. He waddled toward the door, the stiff cloth of his blue pants making a noise as his thighs scraped together. He's really gotten chubby, Lily thought. Carrying a gun in Webster seemed to authorize fat but not violence. No officer in her memory had ever pulled a trigger, unless you counted the tranquilizer gun they shot that poor moose with in the Courtland Arboretum. A man from the Sheriff's Department had driven the unconscious beast miles north so he could wake up at home. From behind her Lily felt the light change as the sun sank in the sky.

Hank touched Lily's hair. "Why are you doing this to me?" he said.

Lily arched her back and felt her bra tighten under her arms. Hank laid a hand on her knee, but Lily didn't uncross her legs. "Stop it," she said.

He leaned forward to kiss her. His lips parted. The handsome face looked too eager, too hungry.

"Not here," she said.

"Come on, Lily." She heard a whine in his voice and edged backward on the desk.

"Forget it." Hank's pale brown eyebrows moved together for an instant, then he exhaled loudly.

"You think that call could have something to do with Filthy Frank and Dirty Dick?"

Hank made a face. "What?"

"What Mrs. Klatschwetter saw?"

"I don't know." Hank spoke quickly in an annoyed voice. "It could've been anybody, or better yet, nobody. What do you care?"

Lily worded her answer carefully. "I went by there yesterday on my bike—"

Hank cut her off. "By the Bodler place? What the hell were you doing out there? Were you alone?"

"Of course I was alone."

"Lily, you shouldn't go out there by yourself. Those dirt-bags aren't normal. You know that. They almost killed Pastor Ingebretzen, or have you forgotten?"

"That was years ago, Hank. People go out there all the time to look at the junk. Why shouldn't I?"

"Because they're lecherous old coots, that's why." Hank massaged his left hand with his right.

Lily covered her mouth to hide a smile. "Those funny old men? Come on."

Hank didn't smile. "Dolores pays a weekly visit out there. Did you know that?"

Lily shook her head. The woman came into the Ideal from time to time. She drank. Lily remembered overhearing Gary Hrbek telling three other guys that she charged five bucks a tumble.

"Probably does them both at once."

Lily shifted her position and looked out the window into the dusk. "Who cares," she said. "Everybody needs sex."

"That's right," Hank said.

Lily turned to look at him. His face had fallen and his eyes were closed. She leaned forward and was about to embrace him when he opened his eyes and sneered, "You know who else she visits?"

"No." Lily edged further back on the desk until her head rested on the glass.

"That guy in the Stuart, Shapiro, the one who taught at Courtland. Ida called the other day, screaming prostitution. She saw Dolores coming out of his room, stuffing bills into her bra. Ida ought to know we don't bother with Dolores. It's catch as catch can for her. But that guy?" Hank shook his head. "And I heard he had a great-looking wife, too, or used to anyway. It doesn't add up."

Lily stared at Hank. "And you believe Ida, windbag of the century?"

"And why not?"

"Because she's a one-woman gossip factory, that's why. She churns out hot air faster than anyone can breathe it."

"And what's your problem?" Hank squinted at her.

Lily continued to look at him. She pressed her lips together as she paused. "It's over, Hank," she said. That's what people said didn't they? It's over. It's raining. It's snowing. The weather has changed.

"What?" His mouth opened. He lifted his hands.

"I'm sorry, Hank."

"You're sorry?" His chin bobbed in a series of shallow nods.

The phone rang.

"I'm going, Hank."

He held up a hand, a signal for her to wait. His face looked red.

Lily pushed herself off the desk and stood up.

"Webster Police Department."

She put her hand on the door and turned around. Hank's hand was still in the air. He shook his fingers at her and mouthed the word "Wait." "Yes, Mr. MacKensie, when did you notice it was missing?"

He paused. "Color?" Hank put his fingers to his forehead.

"No, Mr. MacKensie, not all yard deer are brown. We had a blue one stolen a few months ago. Right."

Lily walked through the door and down the driveway under the streetlight. She expected Hank to come after her, to call from the door, but he didn't. This surprised her a little, and as she took a step from the pavement onto the sidewalk, her ankle buckled and sent a pain through her calf. For a few steps, she hobbled, but then it was all right.

Rick's was slow. Lily ordered a hamburger and a Coke at the bar and talked to Rolf, or rather Rolf talked to her. He was on the Jesse James Days Committee and gave her an earful of plans. "They want to change the name to 'The Defeat of Jesse James Days.'"

"Why?" Lily looked at her fingers through the glass. She moved them to examine the distortion behind the dark liquid.

"They think it gives kids the wrong idea, turns Jesse James into a hero. I told them it was stupid. Doesn't sound right: Defeat of Jesse James." Rolf popped a cracker into his mouth. "I'm Frank in the reenactment this year. Plugged right here." He pressed his index finger into his chest.

"Yeah," Lily said. "I've seen the postcard. Don't you think it's a little tacky to sell those photos of the dead gang members, Rolf? And at the Historical Society?"

"Here's Frank." He pulled a bent postcard from his back pocket and slapped it down on the bar.

Lily looked at the grainy black-and-white photograph of the dead Frank James. For some reason he wore no shirt. She guessed they had stripped the corpse for the picture to expose the bullet holes in his chest. His eyes were open.

She shook her head. "Remember when we used to play in the caves, Rolf?"

Rolf leaned his elbows on the bar. "Old Jesse found one hell of a place to hide out. He must've known about those caves before the robbery. I'll bet it was part of the gang's plan." Rolf gave himself a Missouri accent. "If it all goes to shit, Frank, I'll meet ya in them caves outside of town." Rolf smiled and looked Lily straight in the eye. "Remember the rope swing? That was a gas. Out and over the creek and back again. Daredevil Dahl, remember that?"

"Are you kidding?" Lily said. "It's my claim to fame." Lily bit into her hamburger and chewed. "I wonder if you could get in there now?"

"The Jesse James Caves?" Rolf shook his head. "After that boy died, they boarded them up."

Lily nodded. "What was his name again?"

"Larry Lofti."

"That's right," she said. "Larry Lofti."

The following morning Lily spotted the wig in the Bodlers' truck. She was watching the twins leave the cafe, and when Dick opened the door on the passenger side to climb up beside his brother, Lily noticed a dark shape on the seat. At first she thought it was a dead animal, but Dick slid his hand inside the hair, and she saw the tresses dangling down his arm. After he was seated, he laid the thing carefully on his lap and slammed the door shut.

"Probably ripped it right off the head of some cancer victim," Bert said when Lily mentioned it to her. "They watch the obituaries, those two, and whenever someone croaks, they come sniffing around to horn in on the pickings the relatives don't want." Bert paused. "Do you think it was real hair?"

"I don't know." Lily hadn't thought about it. The best wigs were real hair. She knew that, but on somebody's head, all wigs were fake. Real or synthetic, it's dead hair. Still, Lily thought, maybe all hair is dead, and maybe that's why I didn't like seeing it—unattached.

When Lily looked for the pornographic drawing of the Japanese lovers in Mabel's room the following afternoon, it had disappeared. In its place was a black-and-white photograph of a handsome young man wearing the loose pants of the forties and a white shirt. He held a cigarette between two fingers.

"Do you think your book will be finished soon?" Lily stared at the huge manuscript on Mabel's desk.

"I'm beginning to think I'll never finish. I'm beginning to think I can't finish, or that it will end up finishing me. Do you understand?"

Lily shook her head. She turned to the keys on the pine table. "What are those keys to?" As soon as she said it, Lily regretted the question.

Mabel was silent. Then she said, "They're the keys to a place where I once lived. I keep them there to torment myself." She smiled.

Lily narrowed her eyes. She didn't believe Mabel was insincere, and yet this speech had a prepared quality to it. "You know," Lily said, "sometimes you talk like a person in a book."

Mabel eyed Lily for a second, then laughed. "That's what happens when you read too many." She paused and said, "I dreamt about the play last night, that I auditioned and was given the part of Bottom the Weaver."

"Bad casting," Lily said.

"Well, that's what I thought in the dream, a part of me

rebelled, thought it was unfair and ridiculous. Then I decided it was a good part, and I'd make the best of it. It was one of those wandering dreams, you know, with hallways and stairs and doors that go on and on."

Lily nodded. "I've had those."

"I was carrying around the Ass head. At first it was very light, and then it got heavier and heavier."

Lily imagined the papier-mâché head she had seen Mickey Berner working on in the prop room for Oren Fink, and she saw the unpainted form in Mabel's arms.

"Then it started to bleed."

"The head?"

Mabel nodded.

Lily changed the image in her mind to a real donkey head with fur. "Was it horrible?"

"No, it was just a fact." Mabel removed her reading glasses and let them hang from their chain around her neck. "You were in the dream," she said. "You were in one of the rooms. I didn't know which. I couldn't find you."

Lily didn't meet Mabel's eyes. She felt embarrassed for some reason and stared at the bookshelf. After a couple of seconds she said, "Sometimes I remember a little thing, like a picture or part of a conversation, and I think it really happened, and I try to remember, and then I realize it was a dream."

Mabel straightened her gray blouse and began muttering to herself. "Lost youth, of course, bottom, blood. It's absurd, really, no subtlety at all."

Lily had no idea what Mabel was talking about. The woman leaned back in her chair. "There was a man standing outside Berman's for a long time last night. He was under the awning in the shadows, so I couldn't get a good look at him, but he parked himself there and didn't leave for a long time."

"I heard someone," Lily said.

"I was sitting by my window, as I often do when I can't sleep or work, just staring out into the street. Usually there's not much to see, a few drunk kids, a car or two, that deaf man riding by on his bicycle, but last night this man was there, holding vigil under the awning, and I couldn't help thinking he wanted something. He looked up at me several times, or so I thought. It's a wide street. I never saw his face. Then I fell asleep in the chair. When I woke up, he was gone, but our neighbor was there, standing in his window just like the other night, without the musical accompaniment. He stood there for, oh, five minutes, and I thought to myself, something's finally happening on this street, not an event, exactly, but the preamble to an event—two men just watching and waiting. There's something in it." Mabel looked at Lily intently for several seconds. "He's very good-looking, isn't he?" She paused. "Our neighbor."

Lily stared back at Mabel to see if the comment was directed at her or was just a general statement. She couldn't tell. "I guess so."

Mabel smiled at Lily. "I've always cultivated male beauty. I don't discriminate. I never had a type. I liked them short and tall, thin and stocky—not fat, although there was a fat man once I found very sexy. Of course he was brilliant, really brilliant, and bulk suited him, like Ben Jonson—a big brain in a big body. Dark, light, bearded, shaven, muscular or smooth and skinny." Mabel sighed. "I've fallen for them all. In general, I suppose, stupidity has always alienated me, but there was a stupid boy I met in an elevator many, many years ago that made me weak in the knees."

"How did you know he was stupid?"

"I found out, my dear."

Lily opened her mouth at Mabel. "Were you in love a lot?"

"I was always in love."

Lily laughed. She looked at the manuscript. "Is it in the book?"

"Yes."

"Will you let me read it sometime?"

"If you're very good," Mabel said.

"Last night," Lily said. "Did he see you looking at him?"

"Which one?"

"Either one," Lily said.

Mabel smiled. "Why?"

"I don't know, just because."

Mabel laughed. "Because why?" she said. Mabel laughed more, and when she laughed, she wrinkled her nose and her eyes looked very small.

Lily laughed, too.

"Why are we laughing?" Mabel choked out the words.

"Because why," Lily said and laughed harder.

Mabel laughed until she coughed and gasped.

Lily stood up and pounded Mabel on the back. "Are you okay?"

"I'm fine. It depresses me to think this old carcass can't even stand up to a good joke. It's pathetic."

"It wasn't good. It wasn't even funny," Lily said.

"Oh, it was funny. We just don't know *why* it was funny." Mabel moved her eyebrows up and down.

"Don't start that again," Lily said.

The two remained silent for about a minute. It would have

seemed overlong had they not laughed so hard together, but Lily liked that pause. The room was warm, and the heat seemed to make Mabel's perfume stronger. Its sweet smell mingled with the dust, and the sun shone through the open curtains onto the coffee table. She concluded that Edward Shapiro had gone to the window to look for her, and this made her glad.

Lily heard a sound, looked over and saw that Mabel had slumped down in her chair. Lily leaned toward her. The woman's eyelids fluttered. She gasped and looked wildly around her. Her hands trembled. "Help me!"

"My God, Mabel!" Lily grabbed the woman's shoulders. "What's the matter?"

"Lysander, help me!" Mabel cried. "Do thy best."

Lily let go of the woman's shoulders. "Jesus, Mabel. You scared me to death!"

Mabel straightened up in the chair and adjusted her blouse, which had slid up around her waist. She pressed one lock of hair behind her ear, and then with an expression both prim and satisfied, she said, "Good, now you scare *me* to death."

Lily looked up at the roof of the Arts Guild and added a steeple where there wasn't one. The real steeple had been missing for as long as she could remember. Maybe it had been blown off in a tornado, or maybe someone had decided that acting and actors did not belong in a building that looked like a house of God even if it wasn't, and had hacked off the spire along with its cross. Running up the steps, Lily heard talking, hammering and laughter coming through the open doors.

Then someone shouted, "Quiet," and the noise stopped. In the vestibule Lily looked toward the stage and saw Martin Petersen sitting under a spotlight that turned his blond hair white and erased the color of his eyes. He looks happy, she thought, happy to be the center of attention even for a moment. Then Martin noticed her and his expression changed. He stared hard at her for several seconds and then nodded, as if she should know what he meant by this, as if they had some secret understanding, but Lily ignored him and looked away. "Thanks, Martin," someone yelled from behind her. The spot switched off, and the room returned to ordinary, dull brightness.

The place was hot, and even with all the windows open, the heat weighed on the cast. Amy Voegele lost a tooth and was so excited, rehearsal was delayed for several minutes while everybody ran around looking for a container the girl would accept. In the first scene, Lily noticed that Mr. Dugan had poison ivy all over his legs and had smeared the welts with calamine lotion, stiffening the long hairs on his calves into a pink forest. When Jim spoke Lysander's lines and held Lily's hand, she saw large sweat spots under the arms of his shirt that she found distracting, but Mrs. Wright told Lily she was finally "natural." Lily couldn't help thinking that she had stolen, or at least borrowed, that "natural" performance, that what looked natural wasn't, and even though Lily felt Hermia's every emotion as if it were her own to feel, she worried that her performance was somehow counterfeit, that she had no right to be as good as she was. Mabel Wasley inhabited the role, and Lily was enacting Mabel, or rather Mabel as Hermia.

She didn't notice or think about Martin again until the beginning of Act II, when she was standing offstage fanning herself and listening to Puck. Susie Immel, who had been yawning loudly for several minutes, pulled a rubber lizard out of her pocket and burped loudly. With each noisy, artificial burp, she made the lizard jump. While Lily was hushing Susie, she noticed Martin standing a couple of feet away, waiting to go on. She saw him in profile, his head and shoulders bent, his eyes closed. He breathed in deeply. His preparation struck her as ridiculous—too much for too little—but then he raised himself and walked onstage with the other fairies, and Lily saw that he had changed. Martin Petersen, dressed in his short-sleeved plaid shirt, stiff jeans, thin vinyl belt and sneakers— the staples of his limited wardrobe—moved like somebody, no, Lily thought, something else. Martin towered over the other fairies in the train, all of whom were children, and yet there was nothing overgrown or clumsy about him. He didn't mince or prance like some of the younger boys.

Jim tugged at Lily's sleeve and said, "Get a load of Petersen!"

Lily nodded but didn't answer. She studied Martin's body, trying to discover what it was that transformed him, but she couldn't isolate the elements. His posture, his motion, his expression—all of these were different from the Martin who ate breakfast in the Ideal Cafe. Mrs. Wright was watching him, too. And when Martin spoke in Act III—"And I," he said, "Hail!" and "Cobweb"—he didn't stutter. Not a single tic or grimace passed over his face, and Lily felt she was witnessing a miracle—like the invalid in the Bible who picked up his mat and walked. And she wasn't alone. She felt everyone's amazement. Later, when she met him offstage, she looked into his eyes and hugged him. "You were wonderful," she said. "Better than that!"

Martin smiled.

And then Lily kissed him. She kissed him on the cheek because she was happy for his success, and she kissed him because she felt guilty for expecting him to fail, and she kissed him because she imagined he would like it. But at the same time, it was a meaningless kiss, and Lily would have forgotten it instantly had she not noticed his expression as she pulled her face away from him. He didn't smile or blush or look pleased with himself. Pale and solemn, he opened his mouth as if he were about to say something, then closed it tightly.

"Are you all right, Martin?" she said.

He nodded, and studying him for a moment, Lily asked herself why Martin never responded in the way she expected. She wished he would stop looking at her in that meaningful way, but she shrugged off her discomfort and walked away from him.

After rehearsal Mrs. Wright took a champion's pose, arms above her head, hands clasped, and spouted encouraging nonsense at her actors like "A good start" and "We'll iron out the wrinkles." Mothers arrived to fetch their children, and the room emptied fast. Lily was heading for the door when she felt a light touch on her shoulder. When she looked, she saw Martin. He signaled for her to follow him outside and then pointed at the steps. From inside she heard Mrs. Wright say something to Mrs. Baker about "wing wire." Martin eyed the two women quickly, then turned back to Lily. His lips quivered and he stuttered over an initial *D*.

Lily tried to hide her disappointment.

"D-d-did you get it?" he said.

Lily looked over at him. "You mean the napkin, Martin?"

He nodded.

"I got it. I can't say I understood what you meant by it, though."

Martin shook his head and stuttered again. "It's what it says, that's all." He stared at Lily and moved his face close to hers.

"Is my face dirty or something?"

He shook his head, then stared at his hands.

"What did you mean by it?" Lily said.

Martin talked to his fingers. "W-well, it can only work with that word, you see."

"Mouth?" Lily said.

Martin jerked his head up and stared at her. "S-s-s-say it again?"

Lily felt her face go hot. "Jeez, Martin. I don't get this at all."

He looked at her. "I, I, I wanted your mouth to say the word 'mouth.'"

Lily wrinkled her nose. "What?"

Martin pressed his two index fingers together. He turned his face away from her. "Because," he stammered, "the two come together perfectly, the word and what it means."

Lily was silent. She thought about it. "So?" she said.

Martin looked over his right shoulder. The sound of Mrs. Wright's key in the lock made Lily glance behind her, and she saw the director and Mrs. Baker step quickly past them. At the bottom of the steps, they paused, and Mrs. Wright waved. "You two were both great tonight. Keep it up!" she said.

"Thanks, Mrs. Wright! Bye, Mrs. Baker," Lily called after them as they walked to a car parked down the block.

Lily watched Martin's profile. He opened his mouth and started talking. He stuttered badly at first, but then he seemed to gain momentum and spoke quite fluently. She could hear a lilt in his voice and suspected the music helped organize his speech. "I'm looking for the way in," he was saying. "I want to find an opening."

"To what?" Lily said.

"Do you ever feel that nothing's real?"

Lily looked at him. "Well," she said slowly, "sometimes I think ordinary things are kind of strange . . ."

Martin nodded vigorously. "It's, it's like there's a skin over everything, and if you could just get under it, you'd, you'd get to what's real, but you never can, so you've got to look for a way to cut through it. You see?"

Lily didn't see at all. She felt uncomfortable. "No," she said. "I don't."

"W-w-well." He turned a pale face to Lily. He pushed out the *M* after several tries. " 'Mouth.' The word isn't real, but, but you use your mouth to say it, and then the two meet . . ."

"Martin," Lily said, and shook her head.

"F-f-fakes," he said loudly.

Lily looked at Martin. She didn't like the word. "Fakes?"

"W-words are fakes—just sounds for something, right? Pictures are fakes, the play is a fake. But maybe, if you push them onto the real thing—they can open each other up." Martin looked triumphant.

Lily just stared.

"But it has to be right. You have to look so hard that your eyes hurt from looking. Most of the time, it's wrong. But you can't stop looking." Martin paused. "Say it again."

Lily leaned away from Martin. She shook her head at him and looked into the street. The low branches of big elms darkened the pavement and sidewalk. She could see the night sky between their branches and looked up at it. She felt tired and wanted to be somewhere else. "It's too weird."

Martin whispered in her ear, "Cobweb." Lily turned sharply toward him. "What?"

"Hermia's father is going to put her to death."

His abrupt change of subject confused her, but she answered him. "He doesn't do it, for heaven's sake. It's a comedy, Martin." Lily gestured with her hands. "It's funny, remember? People are supposed to laugh."

Martin rubbed his hands and then he pressed his two index fingers together. They trembled under the pressure, and Lily took his silence as a chance for her to leave. She stood up and started walking toward her bicycle.

"Will you come and visit me, Lily, come to my house?" he said to her back.

Lily didn't turn around. "Someday," she said. "Sure."

Martin was walking behind her, and suddenly she didn't like having her back to him.

"Professor Wasley," he said. Martin seemed to want to cover all territories at once. "She's your friend." He said this loudly and clearly in a voice that wasn't quite his own.

Lily put her hand on the bicycle seat. "Yes, she's my friend. Why?"

"She's got the nerves of a bat."

"What?"

Martin didn't answer.

Lily grabbed the lock on her bicycle and began to turn the combination. To locate the numbers she had to bend very close to the tiny wheels, and again she suffered from a feeling that her back was vulnerable. She tugged at the lock. It didn't open. Very slowly, she repeated the combination. The lock clicked, and she pulled it open. She could hear

Martin breathing behind her. She turned toward him. "Bye," she said.

His shoulders moved up toward his ears and he waved his hands in front of his chest as he began to stutter out a word that started with a *Th*. She felt sorry for him. But enough is enough, she thought, and she wondered where a stutter came from. It must be like wearing a muzzle.

Then he moved his lips close to her ear and whispered, "The Bodler place."

Lily resisted the temptation to pull away from him, then released the kickstand with her foot and threw her leg over the bicycle. She could feel her heart pounding and hoped Martin wouldn't sense her agitation.

"B-b-b." Martin worked the *B* for a long time. "Before you go, say it again."

Lily started pedaling. "No!" she said. The "no" seemed to resound in the air and then, in a matter of seconds, she felt her bicycle tires bouncing over the railroad tracks. She wanted to look back at him, wanted to see his dark form standing alone in front of the little building, but she didn't. Why had he mentioned the Bodlers like that? It was the way he had whispered it that made her feel funny. Almost like he knows about the shoes, Lily thought. She remembered the stillness of the place, the sound of the wind, the big sky, and then the barn, its roof collapsed inward, moss growing between the stones. Had Martin been outside the garage? Had he been the one she'd heard? And then she asked herself whether she would have stripped for Edward Shapiro if she hadn't put on the shoes. She saw the Bodler farm again, just as it had been that day. A man who looked a lot like Filthy Frank was standing on a mound of newly dug earth. Where were the boys when it happened? Lily asked herself. Were they in school? Suddenly, the story seemed wrong to Lily. The town had turned Helen Bodler's murder into legend, but what about the details? How could a woman disappear the same day her husband digs a huge hole near his house without making the neighbors suspicious?

2

Lily could see Ida's hair but not her face through the glass door of the Stuart Hotel. For almost a minute she had been telling herself to open the door, but every time she reached for the handle, she stopped. It's now or never, Lily said to herself, and decided to count to ten, but when she got to seven, Ida Bodine looked up from the book she was reading, and Lily opened the door and walked into the lobby.

Ida cocked her head and opened her eyes wide. A spider plant was hanging above her, and its myriad offshoots framed her face like a mad wig.

"Hi, Ida," Lily said. She heard false friendliness in her voice.

"Isn't it a little late to come callin'?" Ida's face stiffened into a mask of vivid makeup.

"Depends on the hours you keep," Lily said and headed for the stairs.

Lily looked straight ahead. She held the railing as she

walked, feeling she needed it for steadiness. Halfway up, she peeked at Ida, who had returned to her book, a story that must have been engrossing if it kept Ida from snooping on Lily. The woman was leaning forward in her chair, the book propped on the edge of the desk. Its pink cover, embossed with gold lettering, showed a swooning woman who had fallen over the arm of a man with a scabbard and sword around his waist. The sleeves of her gown had slipped down over her shoulders to reveal breasts that looked like they'd pop out of the dress any second.

When Lily arrived at the second floor, she stared down the long hallway. She'd never seen it before. All these years I've lived in Webster, and I've never seen the second floor of the Stuart Hotel. Well, it's just as dumpy as I thought it'd be. What remained of a brown carpet had buckled away from the walls, and a smell that reminded her of the high school cafeteria filled the air—the smell of pallid green beans and mashed potatoes on a tan plastic tray. A single light illuminated the hall—a peculiar fixture shaped like an elk head with a weak bulb screwed into its scalp. Lily counted doors to orient herself. She stopped in front of the fourth, lifted her fist and prepared to knock, but she didn't. I can't, she thought. Lily breathed so loudly, she worried that the man might hear it. Stay calm. You can do it. But Lily lowered her hand to her side. Then, after a couple of seconds, she knocked. When she withdrew her hand, it felt very cold.

The door opened. Edward Shapiro looked out at her and smiled.

Lily tried to smile back but found she couldn't. Her mouth had stiffened with anxiety.

"Hello," he said.

Lily could smell him—paint and cigars. His eyes had long, very black lashes, two tiny ones at their inside corners, and she saw that his irises were mixed colors—green, gray and ocher. He was wearing a white T-shirt streaked with paint, and blue jeans.

"Hello," Lily said. Her voice sounded normal.

"Would you like to come in?" He smiled again.

Lily didn't try a second smile. Instead she swallowed loudly and stepped inside. The room was smaller than she had thought, and when she looked toward the paintings, she saw that they had been turned to the wall.

"We haven't met formally," he said and extended his hand. "I'm Edward Shapiro."

Lily put her hand in his, and after his warm fingers had closed around hers, she saw a spot of blue paint on his third knuckle. "Lily Dahl."

"Well, Lily Dahl, would you like a glass of wine?"

She nodded.

He waved at a canvas chair. Lily sat down on it, and staring at her bare legs under her cutoff jeans, she noticed a faint bruise near her kneecap. Her legs were newly shaven, however, and she felt glad that she had repaired her toenail polish that afternoon after deciding to wear sandals. She crossed her legs and watched the man bend over a tiny refrigerator. Quickly, she pinched her cheeks to redden them. He turned around, handed her a glass of white wine and said, "You like your job at the cafe?"

"You saw me there?" Lily said and felt herself blush.

"Of course I saw you." He looked at her evenly and sat down in a chair opposite her.

Lily looked at the floor. "It's okay, I guess."

"It seems like a nice place—the real thing."

"How do you mean?" She looked up at him.

He smiled and reached for a cigar tin that lay on the floor. "Well, I guess I mean it's a real small-town cafe— unpretentious." He lit the cigar.

Lily laughed. "The whole town's pretty much like that, in case you hadn't noticed."

He looked at her but didn't speak. He brought the cigar to his mouth and blew the smoke to his right.

Lily sipped the wine. It had none of the sweetness she expected. She waited for him to say something, and when he didn't, she said, "Everybody's talking about you." She hesitated. "In town, they're all talking."

The man leaned back and smiled. "Is that so?"

Lily took a breath. "Well, it's natural to gossip about a stranger."

"I'm still a stranger, huh?"

"Well, compared to most people, sure."

Edward Shapiro lifted his glass and motioned with it toward himself. "To the strange," he said. Then he tipped his glass toward Lily. "And the not so strange."

Lily lowered her glass to her knee. She stared at her fingers around the stem. "I didn't mean strange like that."

They were silent. Lily didn't look up. She saw where his jeans ended and examined the tops of his bare feet in a pair of moccasins.

He spoke then, his voice just above a whisper. "I think we should drink to Division Street at night, to its silence and its music, to its darkness and its light."

Lily lifted her eyes to his, and they clinked glasses. Lily spoke slowly and carefully. "I didn't mean to say that you were strange, but that people around here are curious about a person they don't know."

He nodded. His eyes were attentive.

Lily sipped her wine and spoke more quickly. "You see, in Webster there are folks who yak their heads off all day to anybody who's bored enough to listen, and they're not all that concerned about what's true and what isn't." She leaned forward a couple of inches. "Some of them, the worst ones, might even blab to the police." Lily gave Edward Shapiro a meaningful nod.

The man cocked his head and narrowed his eyes. Lily watched his ash drop to the floor. Then one side of his mouth moved up in an expression of amusement. "Are you referring in your own discreet way to my friend downstairs, Mrs. Bodine?"

Lily nodded.

"And Mrs. Bodine has been so distressed about my music that she's called the police?"

"Not the music."

"Not the music," he repeated with mock gravity. "What then?"

Lily looked at him. "Dolores."

His eyes wrinkled as he said, "Dolores Wachobski?"

So that's her last name, Lily thought.

The man made little circles near his ear with his right hand, a signal for her to get on with it. He held the cigar stub between his thumb and index finger, and Lily watched the smoke dance.

"I don't really know how to say this," Lily said.

He widened his eyes in encouragement.

"Well, Dolores has kind of a bad reputation." Lily looked

out the window. "She takes money." She paused. "From men." Then she turned back to him.

All humor had left the man's face. "I see," he said. "I know Dolores. I'm painting her."

Lily stared at him. She bit her lip as it quivered for an instant under her teeth.

"Let me show you," he said. "I haven't finished, but it's getting there."

Lily looked away. She heard him stand up and felt his hand on her arm. She had to brace herself against his touch because she felt an urge to collapse into him. She let him guide her toward the wall without looking up at him or speaking, but she felt his hand move to the small of her back, and when they neared the paintings, he reached across her to take hold of the canvas and his thumb grazed the button of her jeans. Lily breathed in through her nose a little too loudly, she thought, and stepped backward. He turned the large painting toward her.

A life-size Dolores Wachobski stared straight out at Lily. The woman straddled a stool, her hands gripping the seat between her parted legs. Dolores leaned forward with a face that was both fierce and sober. She wore a black-and-white polka dot dress, cut low enough in the front to expose at least half of her formidable breasts. Across the top of the canvas was a series of three boxes with drawings inside them that reminded Lily of the funny papers. The figures inside them looked drawn rather than painted, and when compared to the realism of the portrait below, they seemed even more like cartoons. Lily took several steps toward the painting, stood on tiptoe and examined the boxes. In the first box, she saw a little girl crouched behind a small shed or outhouse. It was night, and above the child was a crescent moon, drawn so simply,

Lily thought it should have a face. "What's this part?" Lily asked, pointing at the boxes.

"It's the story part," he said. "Everyone I paint chooses a story to tell with pictures inside the portrait. You see, I always collaborate with the person I'm painting. We talk during the sitting, and before it's all over, he or she decides what story to tell in the narrative series."

"The little girl is Dolores?"

"Yes."

Lily peered at the second frame. The child was sleeping behind the shed with her head on her arm. In the third box, a woman had appeared and was grabbing the girl by her shirt with one hand. The other hand was extended as though the woman was about to smack the child. "Who's that?" Lily pointed at the woman.

"Her mother."

Lily didn't say anything for several seconds. "Was she afraid of her mother?"

"I don't think so. Dolores used to hide from her though. I think she liked being found." He spoke in a low voice, deliberately pronouncing each word.

Lily searched his face, but she saw no clear emotion in it.

From outside Lily heard a car, hoots, and then the sound of rattling metal. The car screeched and then skidded away down the street, its sound dying slowly. Lily stared at the child in the last frame, huddled against the imminent blow. "She must trust you," she said. "It's pretty private."

She heard the man sigh. The sound aroused her. "And the others?" Lily said, looking at the three remaining canvases.

He walked to the next one and turned it around for her.

Lily gave a long whistle and grinned. "Holy moly," she said. "It's Tex."

The man, all six feet and several inches of him, stood before her—stark naked. The red hair on his head repeated itself in his pubic hair. His bloated white belly was speckled with moles. Lily looked closely at his penis. It looked like any other. Standing on tiptoe, she tried to get a better view of the three boxes above the man's head. In the first box a man waved his hat from a bucking bronco.

"I didn't know Tex rode rodeo. I used to go to the local shows, and I never saw him."

"Actually, I don't think he does. You see, the stories don't have to be true. It's what he wanted, so that's what he got. I don't interfere."

"How come he's naked and Dolores has her clothes on?"

Shapiro grinned. "He wanted to reveal his 'true self.' That's a quote."

"You think that being naked is any more your true self than having clothes on?" Lily didn't turn to look at him but kept her eyes on the boxes. After she had said it, she blushed.

"No," he said. "I don't."

In the second frame, a male figure stood above a female figure who was kneeling on the ground. The man held a gun to the woman's head. "Oh," Lily said. It wasn't so much a word as a vowel of exclamation. She faced Shapiro.

The man looked at her. "I think it's another fantasy, more sinister than the first."

"Is the woman someone special? I mean . . . "

"He didn't say."

"But I thought you said you talked to everybody when they're posing for you."

"I do, but he wouldn't say. He just told me what to draw."

In the third box a dead man was hanging by his neck from a tree. "Is that him, too?"

"Yes, I think it is, but when he talked to me, he explained every particular in the drawing, but he never used the word 'I.' He said 'he.' I think we both knew 'he' meant 'I.' What I admired about him was his certainty. He knew. Howard never wavered."

"Howard?"

"Howard Gubber."

Lily smiled. "Wow! That's a wuss name if I ever heard one. I bet you're the only guy in Webster who knows his real name, except his mother, and she's probably pushing up flowers in Urland Cemetery."

Lily pointed at the third canvas, and Shapiro obediently turned it toward her. It was smaller than Tex's.

"Why, there's Stanley," Lily said. "Stanley Blom. He eats at the Ideal quite a lot. He's a sweet guy." Lily moved her head to one side as if she could see him better that way. The little man sat on a chair and looked straight out. His bent body was somewhat disguised in that position, and he was dressed in a suit he must have saved for church. He certainly didn't eat breakfast in it. His narrow, wrinkled face was unmistakable, however, a mass of brown spots and cysts. Lily looked at Stanley's boxes. In the first there were two boys running together, one ahead of the other. In the second was a large, long house with lots of windows. "Who lived here?" Lily said.

"It's a sanatorium," he answered and stepped close to her. "That boy"—he pointed to the second child in the first frame—"was his brother. He died of tuberculosis in 1925. 'I've only got one big story,' he told me, 'and this is it.' His brother's name was Henry."

Lily turned her head to the last picture. It showed a room with a window and an empty bed. The baseboard of another bed could be seen in the frame, but the bed with nobody in it stood at the center.

Lily felt the man's hand on her shoulder. "Henry died before one of the family's visits. When Stanley and his parents walked into the room, the boy was gone."

"You mean they didn't get to see him?"

"Not that day, not alive. The empty cot was the way he knew his brother was dead, and that's how he tells the story."

Very gently, the man turned her toward him. She looked up at his eyebrows and large eyes, the straight nose and small mouth, and she thought, God, it's a beautiful face. Before he kissed her, she said, "How old was he? Henry, I mean."

"He was nineteen."

Lily's shorts were unsnapped and the man's shirt was off before she remembered she was menstruating. She knew she had to say it. She clamped her fingers around his wrist and said in a tense voice that embarrassed her, "I have my period. Does it matter?"

He shook his head.

"I'll be right back."

Lily watched her nearly bloodless tampon disappear down Edward Shapiro's rust-stained toilet. Blue, green, yellow and brown paint streaked the sink basin. Before she left the bathroom, she opened the medicine cabinet. Inside, on a filthy glass shelf, lay a slender black razor—nothing else. Lily checked her face in the mirror. She thought it looked a little red, but otherwise good. When she shut the bathroom door, she consciously acknowledged that she had no doubt. She felt nothing that might make her hesitate.

He wasn't shaven, and his whiskers rubbed her cheek

when he kissed her, and she smelled turpentine from his hands, but what she liked was that he didn't seem to worry about himself. She could feel the relaxation in his arms and legs. He wasn't passive, but he wasn't in a hurry either, and Lily had the sudden thought that both Peter and Hank had watched themselves making love to her, and this man didn't. She felt the coarse hair on his chest, and she moved her fingers to his navel and touched the skin around it, and then she kissed that spot and felt the muscles in his thighs that she had looked at so closely through the window. She touched his knees and his calves, and he kissed her neck and shoulders and back, and he kissed her behind her knees and he kissed her ankles, and he didn't touch her genitals for a long time, and Lily thought that if she hadn't loved him before, she loved him now. Then he surprised her. He gripped her inner thighs with his hands and pulled her toward him, and she thought, It's like he knows, knows all about me, and she let her head fall back on the mattress. Through the thin sheet she could feel a small hard button pressing into the back of her head as he lowered his body onto hers. He fumbled with a condom for a couple of seconds, but she closed her eyes and listened to him breathe. She clutched his back tightly. They were both sweating on top of the white sheet, and Lily imagined herself in the window as though she were looking at herself with his eyes, and again she saw herself pulling down her shorts, and she bit his neck, not hard, lightly. While they made love she talked to herself silently, telling herself what they were doing, and this aroused her more, and when she felt her orgasm, she yelled out, but she didn't know how loud she was and didn't care, and seconds later, she looked up at his face and saw the pupils of his eyes move upward toward his lids and felt the faint tremor of his orgasm and then the weight of his body on top of her. She smelled his hair—shampoo and cigars. In the dim light, she looked at the skin on his shoulders, at the tiny bumps and discolorations. She ran her finger over them and thought that he was like nobody else.

When he asked her how old she was, she lied to him and said, "Twenty-one." The addition of those two years seemed significant, and she promised herself to tell him the truth later.

They talked for hours that night, and Lily found out that he was born in Newark, New Jersey, and went to art school in New York, but he had studied art history, too, and that before he found a gallery, he had made money copying old masters' paintings and selling them to rich men, mostly in Texas, who wanted a Caravaggio or a Renoir or a David for their wives and girlfriends. Shapiro was thirty-four years old, and he said that he had only recently "found his real work." So far, he had sold four "real" paintings, but he was feeling optimistic. And Lily told him about acting and about playing Hermia in a *A Midsummer Night's Dream*. He didn't say it was an impossible business and much too hard to get into, or what made her think she could do that? He listened to her talk and smoked his cigars and asked her questions about why she wanted to be an actress and how she felt when she acted. She told him about Marilyn then. He didn't even smile. He said he had loved Marilyn in *The Misfits*, and that what he had liked about her was that she seemed so alive, more alive than a lot of actors, fragile and vigorous at the same time. It made Lily very happy to hear him talk about Marilyn, and when he paused, she kissed him all over his face, and told him he was beautiful, and they made love again.

In the morning Lily woke for work without an alarm. She had slept only two hours, and after she had carefully lifted the man's arm off her waist, she sat up and put her feet on the floor. Her legs trembled with exhaustion, but when she looked at the sleeping man, she said to herself, I was lying there beside him. She dressed quickly and penned him a note. There were many things she would have liked to have written in that note: "I love you. I adore you. I think you're the most wonderful person in the whole world," but these sentences would have been unwise, so she wrote: "Dear Ed"—it was nice to call him Ed—"My telephone number is: 645-1133. Lily." She studied her handwriting for an instant, fearing it looked childish, but she let it go, and tiptoed down the stairs past Ida. The woman was sleeping with her head on the desk, a jowl mashed by her right arm. Her makeup had faded during the night, and Lily thought her face looked softer and prettier than it had the night before.

Division Street was empty and just beginning to turn gray with the dawn. She walked halfway across it and stopped. She looked past Berman's and Tiny's and Willy's Shoe Repair to the Ben Franklin on the corner and told herself to remember exactly how the street looked on this Friday morning, June seventh, the summer after she turned nineteen years old. Then she headed across the pavement, and the same instant her left foot touched the curb, Lily saw the lights in the Ideal Cafe go on.

At five twenty-five, Martin Petersen pressed his face against the cafe window. Lily was certain of the time. She had just glanced up at the minute hand on the clock because Vince wanted the cafe doors opened "on the dot." Martin's nose was flattened snoutlike on the pane, and Lily would have laughed at him if he had appeared any less suddenly. But no sound had preceded his arrival—no engine in the street or feet slapping the pavement. Part of setting up for breakfast in the cafe was listening to Webster's early-morning noises, and when she turned her head and saw Martin, dressed in the same clothes he had worn the night before, she jumped.

He motioned to her.

Lily unlocked the door and spoke to him through the screen. "What are you doing here so early?" she said.

Martin walked toward the door and held out a piece of paper. "I-I-I," he stammered, "brought you a map."

"What for?"

"To, to get to my house."

Lily waved her hands at the sides of her face. "Martin Petersen," she said in the voice of an aggravated schoolteacher. "I know where you live. My parents' old house is a quarter of a mile away, and I lived in that house for seventeen years."

Martin walked up the single step and pushed his face into the screen. It made a dull pop as he increased the pressure, pushing his forehead, mouth and chin against the wire netting as if he wanted to burst it.

Looking at Martin, she saw that the tiny crosshatch pattern of the screen was etching itself into the skin of his face, and she also saw that he didn't care. Stubborn, determined and blind, Martin refused to follow the rules that came automatically to most people, and Lily felt an urge to plow her fist straight into that big, white face that distorted the shape of the screen. Behind Martin she saw Pete Lund stepping out of his blue Ford.

"Cut it out!" she whispered to Martin. "You'll break it."

Lily unlatched the screen door, let Martin inside and held the door for Pete, who nodded at her.

After Martin had looked around the cafe suspiciously, like

a kid playing Cold War spy, he handed Lily a little square of folded paper. He stuck his now-checkered face close to hers and whispered, "S-s-say it again."

Lily stepped back and shook her head. She could feel the edge of the folded paper cutting into her palm.

Vince spoke from behind her, his voice commanding but not yet angry. "A customer, Lil'."

"Coming," Lily said.

"Say it again," Martin was whispering.

"Dollface!"

"I'm coming, Vince." Lily looked behind her. Vince looked redder than usual. She turned back to Martin. His eyes were enormous, blue and desperate. She didn't want to look at those eyes anymore. She hated that mooning, pleading face and wanted it to vanish. "Mouth," she said. Then she said it again more loudly, "Mouth." She leaned toward him and growled, "Mouth! Okay?"

Martin smiled. Lily thought it was the smile of a drunk—loose-lipped and giddy. She turned away from him and walked toward Vince.

"Is that a customer or not?" he barked at her, pointing at Pete Lund.

"Relax, Vince," Lily said. She glanced at the clock. "It's five thirty-four." Pete Lund was quietly reading the *Chronicle*. "Does he look upset? Is he demanding my attention? You know what he wants to eat. I don't even have to take his order. Go in the damned kitchen and cook it. I know you. You're mad about something else. Probably Boom. Is he still living with you? He doesn't want to go back to his mom, does he?"

The man folded his arms across his chest and stared at her. "How come I hired the only two girls in this little shit-hole town who talk back?"

"Because you hate wimps, Vince, that's why. And sensitive types quit on you. Remember Cindy? She ran out of here bawling after three days."

"Aw, get off it, that little broad couldn't take a joke."

"Come on, Vince, that wasn't a joke. It was a filthy, disgusting story, and you told it to shock her." Lily smiled. "Is Boomer driving you nuts?"

"That kid doesn't know whether he's coming or going. I'd throw him out if it weren't for that goddamned woman."

"What's her problem?"

"When he's with her, she doesn't want him, but when he's not there, she does."

"So she doesn't," Lily said.

Vince shook his head. "And he can't stay away. He's like a lush sneaking a drink. She kicked him out, but he won't blame her, takes it out on the husband—not that he ain't a first-class sleazeball." Vince paused. "What was that all about?" He pointed with his thumb at the door.

Lily looked at Vince. "I don't know," she said, and she meant it. "He's beginning to get on my nerves, but what it's all about, I couldn't tell you."

After serving her first four customers, Lily took a break behind the counter and pulled the map out of her pocket. One glance told her that whatever Martin might have said about "directions" to his house, he had something much more complicated in mind. When she looked more closely, she saw that what Martin had given her wasn't a map so much as a drawing representing two unfolded maps, complete with creases where the imaginary, not the real, paper had been folded. The maps had been drawn in such a way as to give an illusion of depth, as if one transparent map were floating on top of the other. The uppermost map showed Webster and the area around it and the map below showed Athens and the fairy wood from the play. Division Street was boldly labeled, as were the Ideal Cafe and the Stuart Hotel, but no stores. Beyond the town she saw the Bodler place, Heath Creek, Heath Woods, the Jesse James Caves, and up in the far right-hand corner Martin had drawn an arrow and written "To your Dahl Grandparents." Not far away from the arrow was the Overland farm marked with a large star and a drawing of an oblong box or chest. Her grandparents were both dead, and there was nothing left of their farm, so the notation struck her as odd. The Overland place was still there, only minutes from where her grandparents had lived, but she hadn't thought of it for a long time. She had never laid eyes on the children who lived upstairs in that house, and she tried to remember what was wrong with them. They couldn't speak. Her grandmother had told her the two girls rocked back and forth for hours and hours, each in a corner. But what did that box mean? The drawing irritated her. She sensed Martin was speaking to her again in that roundabout way of his, hinting at things she couldn't grasp. And then, right before she lifted her eyes from the paper, she noticed that around the edge of both maps, Martin had written the word "Sleep." Lily puzzled over it for a couple of seconds, looked up at the red booths and then over at Clarence Sogn's sunburnt head, and wished she hadn't said the word for Martin. It had been wrong to say it, but why? It was because he had looked so satisfied. When she remembered it, she felt sick.

Around twelve-thirty, just before her shift ended, Lily cut two pieces of lemon meringue pie for the old Moss sisters.

"It's hives, dear," Leonora said. "I've had them a hundred times. It's that new detergent you used on the sheets."

"I'm afraid it's shingles," Bessy said.

"Nonsense, dear. I had shingles just after the war, you remember. They don't look a thing like hives."

Just after Bessy had leaned forward and hissed the words, "Hives don't crust!" Edward Shapiro walked into the Ideal Cafe. He gripped the counter, and with his nose an inch from Lily's, he said in a low but clear voice that Bert must have overheard because she dropped the cover to the pie case on the counter: "I missed you." Lily forgot Martin Petersen then, and she forgot to say good-bye to Bert and Vince and Boomer, and she forgot to take off her apron. She followed the man out the door and onto Division Street, where he took her in his arms and kissed her in full view of every customer in the cafe as well as half a dozen people on the sidewalk. Then he put his arm around her and walked with her up the steps into the Stuart Hotel.

That afternoon, Lily asked Ed a question she knew she shouldn't ask. She hesitated, understood it would be smarter not to give in to her curiosity, but the desire was strong, like wanting to pick at a scab that's bound to bleed if you touch it.

"What's she like?" she said to the ceiling as she lay on the bed.

"Who?" Ed turned to look at her. He had been standing in front of his canvas.

"Your wife."

He looked at her and smiled. "Maybe you should tell me. It seems that my life is an open book."

"No, I just know you have a wife and she's not here."

"No, she's not here."

"Okay," Lily said. "I take it back."

"No," he said. "It's all right." He walked over to the bed and sat down. "I was married for five years." He paused. "It fell apart. She's a painter. Her work is very different from mine. She does these tiny little paintings." Ed traced a rectangle in the air with his fingers about as big as a postcard. "They're pretty abstract, but once in a while you can make out a little object in them—a pair of scissors or a hat or a pillbox." He paused. "I always respected her work, but I don't think she ever liked mine. She never said it, but I got the feeling she thought my stuff was oversized and vulgar. She always seemed surprised when other people showed interest in it."

"But what's *she* like?"

"I thought I was telling you." He leaned across the bed and took her hand. "Maybe not."

"How could you marry someone who didn't like your paintings?"

Ed pressed his lips together and was silent. "I guess I didn't know until later. We met when we were eighteen, and I think I found her mysterious. I never understood what she was about really, and I ran after her for years."

"She must be beautiful, though."

Ed smiled at Lily. "Why do you say that?"

"Because you said she was mysterious and you chased after her, and I think men see pretty women, and they imagine all kinds of things inside the prettiness before they even know the person, and then they're stuck running and running."

"Are you speaking from experience, Lily Dahl?" He looked at her tenderly with his eyes narrowed and then grabbed his T-shirt, which was hanging from the iron rail at the end of the bed.

Lily leaned back and looked at him. "You're the third."

Ed gave her a surprised look. "Is that what you thought I asked you?"

"I'm telling you. There were two others. I broke up with the second guy the day before yesterday."

Ed pulled the T-shirt over his head and reached for his jeans. He forgot his boxer shorts, which were lying beside them, and pulled the jeans up over his naked thighs. "Is this for the record, or are you telling me something else?" he said.

Lily bit her lip and looked at him. She looked for her shirt, the same one she had worn yesterday. I have to change, she thought. Then she said, "I guess I just like things to be clear. Do you know what I mean?"

He walked over to the window and looked out. Lily studied his back and wondered if he was hiding some emotion. She thought that if she were in her own room now, she might be able to see his face.

"It's rare, isn't it, for things to be clear?" He didn't turn around. Lily thought he might have been looking into her window across the street, and thinking this made her sad. They were silent for at least a minute. Lily dressed quickly, grabbed her crumpled apron from the bed and walked to his door.

"I'm going home now," she said. "Good-bye, Ed."

He turned then and walked toward her. He kissed her hard on the mouth and said, "I'll call you later."

Lily lifted her face to his. He likes me better when he knows I'm leaving, she said to herself.

"What's that look?"

"What look?" she said.

"That look, that look of irony and smugness."

"Guess," she said. Then she turned around and walked out the door.

There were no sounds from Mabel's apartment, and Lily supposed she was either out or asleep. Mabel often slept better during the day than at night. Lily closed her curtains and thought about Ed. I shouldn't have asked about her. "Elizabeth." She said the name aloud to hear it. Not Eliza or Liza or Liz, not Lizzie or Beth or Betsy or Bess. She wondered why anyone would want to paint nothing, and then she decided to straighten her room. She tossed a T-shirt and a pair of dirty jeans into her bathroom hamper, walked back into her room, saw the toe of one of the stolen shoes sticking out from under her bed and leaned down to pick it up. In the filtered light that passed through the curtain, she made out the shadow of a foot inside. She didn't remember this imprint. She knew it wasn't her foot because hers had a high instep and whoever had worn these shoes before had flat feet. Somehow she had missed that, and she had a sudden, irrational thought that the shoes were changing on her, that traces of their former owner were slowly beginning to appear on them. The shoes did look worse to her, no question about it, more creased and soiled than she remembered, but then maybe she had seen wrong in that dingy garage. Lily brought the shoes close to her nose and sniffed. The Bodlers' garage smelled like her grandmother's root cellar, and the odor brought back a memory of lying beside the open door of the cellar, inhaling that good earthy smell, and she saw the small white house in her mind. Her grandfather had stopped farming during the depression when the bank took back most of the land, and that must have been when the place went quiet. Even the house had made no noise. There was no plumbing, so it had never hummed or gurgled as her own house had, and the cows and pigs and chickens that had once been there, animals Lily knew by name, because her father had told her about them, had never been more than thoughts for her. Lily glanced at the night table and saw the book Mabel had given her. She was planning to read it. *Middlemarch*. The last time she was inside her grandparents' house was after the vandals had ruined it. She remembered feeling glad that both her grandparents were dead by then and that nobody lived there anymore. She and her father had walked through the door to find smashed mirrors and windows, broken furniture, crockery in pieces on the floor, and that same uncanny silence in the house.

Through the wall came panting and then a short, breathless cry. Lily sat very still and listened. Was Mabel sick? A nightmare? She heard the woman sigh; then her footsteps sounded on the floor. Not long after that, she heard the typewriter. Lily had grown used to that old typewriter. It had come to mean sleep for her. I'm so tired, she thought. She remembered the chicken coop at the Overland farm. She decided she would look at Martin's drawing again and fell asleep.

Lily woke up to the sound of the phone ringing.

It was Ed. She heard his voice on the telephone for the first time, and the sound of it seemed to make her body warmer. She suddenly felt conscious of her own voice and spoke softly into the receiver, trying to sound unconcerned, as if she wasn't all that glad, but when he invited her out to dinner at Rick's, Lily said yes right away and laughed, which probably undid all the studied nonchalance that had gone before.

They sat at a table in the corner, and he told her more stories about his life. After art school he had worked as a plumber's assistant for a year and learned the inner workings of sinks and toilets, a job he said he never regretted, and then he took the money he earned and moved to Amsterdam, where he read and painted and worked at odd jobs like designing sets for plays and painting a brick wall and ten windows for an art movie he never saw. Lily liked the way he talked to her. He didn't presume she knew Amsterdam, but he didn't presume she knew nothing either. She liked the way he ate his lasagna. He seemed to enjoy it without paying great attention to it. She liked his neck above the rim of his white T-shirt and his thick hair and his eyes that didn't wander. Lily didn't eat much. She looked down at the red, white and brown dinner and couldn't bother with it. She didn't feel hungry, and besides, she felt reluctant to chew in front of Ed. Rolf looked over at them several times, not unkindly, Lily thought, but she knew he'd tell Hank, and even if he didn't, someone else would. Hank was bound to find out anyway. After Ed had paid the check, she told him she was really nineteen, not twenty-one, and he raised his eyebrows.

"I didn't want you to send me away," she said, "so I added a couple of years."

"I see," he said. Ed breathed loudly through his nose, and then after throwing his napkin on the table, he stood up.

They met Denise Stickle on the way out the door. Lily introduced her to Ed very quickly, pretending she didn't see the startled look in the girl's eyes, and said, "See you at rehearsal."

Out on the street, he said, "You don't like that girl, do you?"

"Denise?" Lily said. "You can tell?"

"Yes."

"Denise is all right. I've known her forever. We both went to Mrs. Lodenmeyer's dance school when we were kids, and now she's back from college for the summer and she tried out for Helena and got the part. At least her looks are right for it. She's one of those girls that always rubbed me the wrong way. You know the type—cheerleader, technical virgin."

Ed gave Lily a puzzled look.

"Does everything *but*, at least in high school. I don't see the difference."

Ed sighed.

Lily was silent. She stopped walking and looked up at him.

He stopped, too, looked down at her and frowned. "You seduced me," he said. "You started it."

"I know," Lily said. "And I'm proud of it." The word "seduced" sounded beautiful to her. She closed her eyes and breathed in the air. It smelled good. She opened her eyes and looked up at the half-moon and noticed how perfectly half it was.

Hours later, when Rick's and the Corner Bar had closed for the night and the bus for Des Moines had come and gone, Lily and Ed were still talking in his room. She told him about Hermia and about Mabel helping her with the role, and she told him about playing Maria in *West Side Story* in the high school play and how she had loved singing and dancing onstage. Then Ed asked her for a song. At first Lily said no, but when he insisted, she gave in and ended up singing "Diamonds Are a Girl's Best Friend." And because he looked like he was enjoying it, she didn't hold back but belted out the words as she strutted across the floor. When the song ended, she winked at him.

He clapped. "You've got a strong, clear voice." He looked at her. "Marilyn was wearing a pink dress in the movie when she sang that song. I'd love to see you in that dress."

"You think I'd look good in pink?"

He nodded.

Lily thought about Marilyn. Then she said, "It's a funny thing about Marilyn. Nobody would be very happy if she were alive, except maybe me. You know how in the tabloids they're always finding Elvis and JFK alive and living in South America or something? But they never find Marilyn, even though she's just as famous. Well, they don't find her, because they wouldn't want to find her old." She climbed onto the bed with him. "Your ears are beautiful, did you know that? They stick out a little bit, but they're really nice." Lily sat back and studied his hair near his neck. Then she reached out and touched his cheek. She liked talking to him, liked saying whatever popped into her mind, liked the way he looked when he was listening. "Sometimes I wish my parents hadn't moved," she said to him. "My Dad got a rare and bad cancer in his leg. They saved the leg, but it's no good. He was a great carpenter. Everybody knew it." Lily stared at the wall. "He could've died, could've lost his leg. They couldn't really stay, I guess. The winters, you know." She looked back at Ed and lowered her voice as though she were telling a secret. "So they sold our house outside town and moved to Florida—Tampa. It's nothing like here. A lot of the old folks I grew up with are dead now—my grandparents, their friends. It's been one funeral after another these past five years. I guess the place didn't hold them. My parents, I mean."

"Does it hold you?" he said.

Lily looked at him. "I never really thought about it. I've always been saying I'm going to leave, and I will, too. I don't want to be here my whole life. But I feel close to this place anyway. It must be in my bones."

Ed didn't speak for several seconds. Then he said, "The series of paintings, the ones you saw. You know what I'm going to call them?"

"No."

"*Webster.*"

Lily nodded.

"You think it's a bad name?"

"No."

"Then what?"

Lily paused. "I think it's okay because you've got those boxes with the stories in them, and that brings in part of the place. It's not just pictures of the people."

"Even if the stories aren't all true, like Howard's."

"This place runs on stories that aren't true. My grandfather used to say, 'One man's fool notion is another man's truth.' "

"A relativist?" Ed said.

Lily was puzzled. "No," she said. "He was a socialist. Thorstein Veblen was his hero."

"Really?" he said.

"Don't you approve?" Lily said and grinned.

"Are you kidding? I've got an uncle who's great claim to fame was that he licked envelopes for Emma Goldman."

Lily paused. She wondered whether she should ask who that was, but before she could decide, Ed said, "They were all on the same side, Lily. They looked up at the same stars."

"Did all this start with your ears?"

"No," he said. "With Marilyn Monroe."

The man was in the street that night again, watching and waiting. Lily slept through it, but Ed told her the next morning that someone had been outside, pacing back and forth in the alley and muttering to himself.

The next day the wind shifted. The air turned clear, warm, dry. The new weather sharpened the outlines of every building, every tree and bush and fire hydrant and crack in the sidewalk. Lily thought the edges of every person and object she saw had a clarity that almost hurt and that this hard daylight corresponded to her high, aching happiness with Ed. Before she left work she told Bert what she never would have told Ed, that she was terribly in love with him and could barely stand it. Bert had squeezed Lily's hand and said, "You're sure, then? And Hank?" Lily had told Bert the truth—that she didn't think much about Hank. It was awful, she knew it, but that's how it was. And Bert had looked at her and said, "Well, heaven wouldn't be heaven if you remembered your friends in hell."

That same afternoon, Lily walked in on an agitated Mabel. Pale and shivering, she greeted Lily with outstretched arms and said, "You're here! Thank God! You wouldn't believe the night I've had. It was a torment, Lily. I haven't recovered." Mabel sat down in a soft chair and looked up at Lily. "Sit," she said.

Lily sat. "What happened?"

A flush of red appeared on the old woman's cheeks very suddenly. She leaned forward in her chair and said, "He was here." Mabel pointed downward with her finger. "In this building last night."

"Who?"

"I don't know who, but I'm sure it's the man"—Mabel lowered her voice and motioned with her head toward the window—"who's been holding vigil outside."

"How do you know?"

"I felt him, Lily. You weren't home, were you?"

Lily shook her head.

"I thought it was you at first, returning from, from your revels."

Lily wondered if this was an indirect accusation. There was a quality in Mabel's tone that made Lily feel responsible for having left the old woman alone all night.

"I called out your name, but there was no answer."

"Maybe Vince was in the hallway, checking on the lights or something. He does that, you know."

"Never at that hour. It wasn't Vince. He always lets me know, and besides, he sounds like a herd of elephants on those stairs. This was someone with stealth. He was in your room."

"My room?"

Mabel nodded. Her face flushed deep red and a vein stood out on her forehead. "He was whispering and muttering to himself. I heard him through the wall, but I couldn't make out a single word, and you know how every sound passes through these walls. I should have been able to understand something." Mabel rubbed her arms and looked at the ceiling. "Babble. Don't look at me like that, Lily."

"I'm just trying to understand it."

Mabel rubbed her hands and looked at the floor on either side of her. "Every once in a while, not often, I've had 'auditory hallucinations,' strange term I admit, but that's what it's called, and that voice coming from your room was both like it and not like it."

"You're sure it wasn't that?"

Mabel touched her lips for a second. "No," she said quietly. "When that happens, it's someone I've known, usually Evan. My husband. And what's said is clear and short. He died many years ago of a brain hemorrhage." She turned her head and stared at the keys on the pine table. "One morning, he complained of a headache, and two hours later he was dead." Mabel took a short breath, pursed her lips and said, "Anyway, it happens that I hear him say, 'Help me.'" Mabel looked back at Lily. "He never said that in life, but it's as if I carry the imprint of his voice in my brain and sometimes it comes back to me. Sometimes I hear my mother calling my name." The woman rubbed her thighs. "I don't mind."

Lily put her hand on her forehead. She didn't speak.

Mabel looked straight into Lily's eyes. She spoke slowly, emphasizing each word. "It wasn't that last night, you see. But it was almost like that man knew about my experiences, a couple of times I thought he imitated them."

"That's impossible," Lily said.

"Yes," Mabel said. "And yet I felt it like that. Did you notice any change in your room?"

"I haven't been home yet."

"Let's look," Mabel said.

Lily walked with Mabel into the hallway. She studied the woman's face and wondered if she was living next to someone who was slightly deranged. Mabel turned the knob slowly and then pushed open the door fast. It slammed against the wall inside.

There was nothing to see. As far as Lily could tell, her room was exactly as she had left it. With Mabel beside her she felt glad she had pushed the white shoes under her bed.

Lily turned her palms upward and smiled. "It looks just like it did when I left."

Mabel turned to Lily. "You do believe me, don't you? You don't think I'm crazy, hearing things, an old, senile woman who can't distinguish between what's real and what isn't?"

"No," Lily said slowly. "Ed heard him last night in the street. He even said he was talking."

Mabel nodded. Her expression made it clear that she

knew exactly where Lily had been last night and had no intention of pretending surprise. She also looked relieved. "I'm a highly rational person, Lily. I know that I give a scattered, high-strung impression, and I don't deny I'm that way, too, but those very qualities that"—she hesitated—"that may annoy you, allow me to feel what many people don't. It's like a scent or a strain of music that emanates from another body, and I pick up on it." Mabel eyed Lily significantly. "That man who's been lurking under the awning and in the alley . . . he gives off something high-pitched, almost a scream." Mabel hesitated. "I think you should lock your door."

"Jesus, Mabel," Lily said aloud.

Mabel turned her head from Lily and looked over the bed toward the window.

Lily eyed Mabel's thin shoulders under her floating blouse. Who could have been in her room? Lily hoped it had been Hank. He's stayed here enough to feel like it's part his, she thought. I've still got some of his shirts and underwear in the drawers. I wasn't too nice to him, either. I didn't even give him a chance to tell me off. But Hank would have been loud and defiant, not quiet and secretive. Lily thought of Martin, but she didn't mention him. I might be all wrong, she thought. Sunlight shone through the closed curtains, and Lily stared at Mabel's narrow pants and gold sandals and changed the subject. "You know, I think you'd like Ed. I already told him about you, and I think the two of you have a lot in common. You'd like to see his paintings, wouldn't you?"

Mabel turned around. She seemed to relax by increments, her expression first, then her neck and shoulders. "Yes," she said, her voice still tense. "I would like that."

Lily smiled. "Okay, I'll talk to him, and we'll make a date."

After Mabel left, Lily walked slowly from one end of her room to the other and looked for signs of an intruder. Hank's shirts were undisturbed. Lily wasn't fastidious, however. Any number of objects might have been moved without her noticing, and this thought prompted her to look under the bed for the shoes, although why they seemed more vulnerable than any of the other things, she couldn't explain. But the shoes were there, lying under the bed, and after she had grabbed them, she walked to the mirror and held them up in front of it. Looking at them, it occurred to her that maybe Helen Bodler had had a lover, after all, and then, as if it followed from the first thought, Lily remembered the name of Mabel's husband: Evan. He was probably the handsome young man in the photo. She laid the shoes on her table and looked at their reflection in the mirror. I wonder how old he was when he died, she thought. A breeze stirred the curtains and blew them up and into the room. Lily watched them flutter aloft for a couple of seconds before they dropped back to the floor. Then she stuffed the shoes into her canvas bag, ran out her door, down the steps and into the alley, where she jumped on her bicycle and began to pedal down Division Street under a sky so blue and cloudless, it made her want to sing, which she did. By the time she was within a quarter of a mile of the Bodler place, she had sung several show tunes and a couple of her favorite hymns.

The Bodlers' truck was parked in the driveway. Lily rolled her bicycle into the ditch, climbed the embankment, and at its crest she lay down on her stomach in the tall grass and looked across the field toward the little house, the garage and the mountains of junk. Smoke rose from a rusted metal bin only yards from the garage, black then gray as it caught the wind. She noticed the fender of a second truck and heard voices. The speakers were invisible, and the wind distorted the sound—unintelligible rumblings followed an isolated word or phrase that carried over the field oddly charged and amplified. She heard the word "rope" very clearly, then "burn" or "barn." A figure emerged from behind the trucks. It was Frank, carrying a large black garbage bag in his arms, and at his heels Lily saw an old cane wheelchair come rolling forward from behind the truck. Dick was pushing someone. At first Lily thought it was a tall girl, but then after two or three seconds she realized it was Martin Petersen. He leapt up out of the chair, said something to Dick, and the two men lifted it into the back of the hidden truck and then began to secure the wheelchair with rope. Martin was standing in the back of the truck, his upper body visible against the sky as he leaned forward to receive the bulky black bag from Frank. Lily edged over in the grass to get a better view of them, but she kept her head low. Martin jumped down from the truck. She wished she could hear what they were saying and crawled forward in the grass. The three men were now standing close together. She saw Dick's head turn to one side. He seemed to be looking over the field directly at her. Lily hugged the ground, and then she realized he couldn't have seen her because he turned back to Martin. Frank must have been negotiating a price. He held out five fingers of one hand, and with the index finger of the other he touched each finger once. Martin had his back turned to her now, but Lily saw him dig into his pocket. The wind blew her hair into her face and flattened the grass in front of her. Frank talked, but Lily couldn't hear the words. She heard Martin's voice—an initial stutter that he quickly overcame—and then he said, "Private business, Frank." Martin rubbed his face, and the gesture looked like one of Frank's. He might not know it, she thought, but he's imitating Frank. They shook hands and Martin clapped Dick on the shoulder. The touch seemed to rouse Dirty Dick from his stupor—his head bobbed up and down in acknowledgment—and he fumbled for Martin's hand, which he didn't shake so much as hold for several seconds. The physical contact among the three suggested an intimacy Lily couldn't understand. Few people touched the Bodlers. Her father had, hadn't he? Yes, he would shake hands with Frank at the door. Lily put her head down in the grass and closed her eyes. She imagined Pastor Ingebretzen bolting from the house, his black robe flying as Frank chased him into the road with an ax. Then she changed the image. No, the minister wouldn't have worn vestments, just a black suit with his collar. She remembered old Pastor Ingebretzen. He had been a serious little man who quoted Scripture on every occasion, even to the Sunday school kids who rarely understood a word. He had been prone to pointing for emphasis during sermons, and once he had pointed his short, white finger at her, Lily Dahl. He had singled her out among all the children in the Sunday school class. "Stand in awe and sin not; commune with thy heart upon thy bed, and be still." Years had passed before Lily figured out that the man must have pointed at random, that he hadn't looked into her heart and seen smudges of sin, but had merely picked out a young face that looked particularly bored and punished it. At the time, Lily thought Pastor Ingebretzen had read her soul and knew that in her bed at night she suffered not only from guilt, but from awe. She had dreaded God, Satan, the Holy Ghost, and angels equally and had prayed that she be spared the appearance of each and all of them. She had even used the word "spared," because it sounded biblical. At the sound of Martin's truck, Lily picked up her head and watched him back out of the driveway. The wheelchair rolled and jumped once under its constraint as the truck left the gravel and turned right onto the highway—away from town and toward the little road he had drawn for her on the map. As she watched the truck grow smaller, she saw in her mind the delicate lines of the web he had drawn beneath his house, the inexplicable box at the Overland's and the arrow to her grandparents' house. It was like pointing at nothing, except maybe heaven.

Filthy Frank and Dirty Dick lingered in the driveway. They didn't speak to or even look at each other. They stood inert and blank for a long time. Lily had hoped they would climb into the truck and drive away, but she understood that wasn't going to happen when she saw Dick wander over to the fire. He reached up, picked a soft bundle from the nearest junk mound and dropped it into the bin. Whatever it was, it excited the flames and they rose high. Dick lifted his chin and stepped away from the heat, but when the blaze subsided, he moved close again and repeated what he had done before. This time, when he backed away from the leaping fire, Lily saw that he was laughing or that his expression suggested a laugh, but she heard no noise. It could have been that the crackle of the fire in combination with the wind hid the noise from her, but Lily was surprised that she heard nothing at all. He lifted his shoulders, threw his head back and opened his mouth wide as his head bobbed in silent hilarity. Then he drew something white from his pocket and threw it into the fire. The white thing had little effect on the flames, but Dick laughed the noiseless laugh anyway, as though a burnt bit of cloth were the most uproarious thing he could think of. Lily saw Frank shuffle toward his brother, stop beside him and raise his fist above Dick's head. She braced herself for a blow, but instead of hitting his brother, Frank let his arm fall slowly in front of Dick's face. Then Frank turned toward the house, and his brother trailed after him. The screen door slammed and Lily thought to herself that it was now or never.

She made a run for the garage. When her feet hit the driveway, she heard the gravel shift under them and thought, I'm making too much noise, but she didn't stop until she arrived panting inside the garage, where she backed against the wall to hide herself. She listened for the house door. Nothing. She moved quietly in the direction of the suitcase. She remembered exactly where she had left it and guessed she could open it, return the shoes and shut it in a matter of seconds. Standing in the middle of the garage, she crouched down to reach out for the suitcase, which should have been wedged between two rain barrels, and found that it wasn't there. She pushed aside cans, boxes and an old rake, expecting to discover it, but the suitcase wasn't in the garage anymore. Lily paused, clutched the bag with the shoes in it to her chest and wondered what to do. Then she heard the screen door slam and the sound of footsteps. She ducked behind a large wooden crate and squatted on the floor. Through the slats of the crate she saw Dick shuffle past the garage toward the fire and stop beside the bin. Lily looked at the dark, motionless figure, his face blurred by the rising smoke, and waited. Behind him, she could see the Klatschwetter barn and silo. She noticed that the sky had clouded over and that the sun had sunk lower than she would have thought. Suddenly she worried about making rehearsal on time. But Dick was in no hurry. Lily sat down. She removed the shoes from her bag and laid them on her lap. She would have to leave them here in the garage. What choice did she have? The damp earth floor began to seep through her jean shorts and underwear, and she lifted her buttocks off the ground to adjust her position. As she moved, the shoes slipped. Lily turned to grab them, smashed her nose into the edge of a rusted wheelbarrow behind her, and then, reaching for her face, slammed her forehead into the tine of a garden rake. With a short gasp, she put her fingers to the spot, and removing her hand saw that it was covered with blood. "Oh shit," she whispered to herself. She touched the gash in her forehead; it wasn't deep. Then looking down she noticed spots of blood on her thighs. It's my nose, she thought, and pinched it hard, but the blood leaked out anyway. She let go and began to wipe the blood from her legs, but it smeared on her skin and mingled with the dirt from her hands. The bad light made it hard to see, but she knew the blood was coming fast and hard. When she looked down for the shoes, she saw she had bled on them, too—a large red spot on one heel and three drops on the tip of the other. Lily grabbed her canvas bag and began to rub the shoes with the material. She spat on the cloth and rubbed, but as she leaned close to the shoes to clean them, she saw more blood drop onto her legs. Still, she didn't give up, but held her nose with one hand and tried to clean with the other hand, but she could feel herself beginning to panic. The shoes were getting ruined. The white leather had turned rust-red and filthy with her attempts to clean it, and suddenly she wanted to cry. I can't leave them here now, she thought. She watched as more blood dropped onto the toes, and covered the laces with her hands. Lily looked up and out through the slats of the crate toward the smoking can and saw that Dick had disappeared. Now, she thought, and carrying the shoes in one hand she made her way to the garage doors and stuck her head cautiously into the light. Without examining her hands very closely, she saw that the blood on them appeared much redder now that she was outside. She looked toward the house and saw nobody. Then she looked in the other direction, but neither Dick nor Frank was anywhere in sight.

Lily looked at the smoke rising from the can and thought, I'll burn them. There'll be nothing left of them. It was the perfect solution. She sprinted toward the fire, dropped the shoes into the ashes and then, feeling a surge of relief, fled toward the ditch and threw herself headlong into the grass. For several seconds she didn't move. Then she turned around to look at the smoking bin. She saw no flames. They're not burning, she thought. They'll come out in the morning and find them, and they'll see that they're covered in blood. What if they're hers? What if they took the suitcase inside for safekeeping because it belonged to her? Lily jumped to her feet, ran back to the fire and looked into it. Sure enough, the shoes had been charred and scorched, but not burnt up, and when she bent toward them to pick them up out of the ashes, she smelled something sweet and putrid that made her stand back for a moment. Then she plucked the shoes out of the fire. The hot leather burnt her fingertips, but she held on to the shoes and took off toward the ditch, where she threw herself into the grass for a second time and let the shoes fall to the ground. Then she looked at them and laughed—one short, miserable laugh at her own stupidity. When she picked up the two charred things to put them into her bag, they weren't hot anymore, just warm. As warm as somebody with a high fever, she thought, and then she pushed her bicycle up the ditch into the road. Her nose had stopped bleeding, but her thumbs and index fingers throbbed as she gripped the handlebars. When she looked up,

Lily saw that the sun had disappeared entirely under thick, gray clouds, an ordinary shift in weather that nevertheless caused her some amazement. She pedaled hard with her head down against the traffic and hoped the increasing gloom would hide her.

Halfway home, Lily saw a turquoise-and-white Pontiac come speeding toward her, and when the car was only yards away, she noticed Dolores at the wheel. She was driving with the windows open, a Loretta Lynn song blaring from the radio as the car's headlights shone on Lily for a second or two. In that brief moment Lily saw Dolores look directly at her, but the woman's face gave no sign of recognition. Maybe it's her night with the twins, Lily thought. Rehearsal must have started without me. And thinking of the Arts Guild, Lily understood all of a sudden that she missed Hermia, as if Hermia were a close friend of hers. She felt a drop of rain on her neck as she drove past the Webster city limits sign. Then she felt another, and another.

When Lily opened the back door and looked up the stairway to the landing, she saw Mabel step out into the hall and look down at her. The bare bulb shone down on Mabel's gray hair and whitened it. "I'm glad it's you, Lily," she said, and then, focusing her eyes, she said with a little cry in her voice, "You've had an accident!"

After that, Mabel was all business. Her anxiety of only hours before had vanished, and Lily saw that she moved like a different person. Efficient and brusque, she ordered Lily to come to her apartment to get cleaned up and fed, and after Lily threw the bloody bag with the burnt shoes into her closet and called Mrs. Wright at the Arts Guild, who accepted her lie about falling off her bike, she obeyed.

Lily sat down on Mabel's sofa and listened to the sound of water running in the bathroom. While she waited for Mabel, she looked for the Japanese couple but didn't find them. Then Mabel was standing in front of her with a basin of water and a washcloth. She drew a chair close to the sofa, set the bowl on the floor and without another word began to wash Lily's face. Mabel patted the cut on her forehead gently, lifted Lily's hair and moved the warm cloth along her neck. Then she wiped Lily's legs and dried them just as they were beginning to itch from the wetness. Even as it happened, Lily knew the washing marked a change between her and Mabel that could never be undone, and yet she didn't resist it. The woman's touch, the way her hand moved with the cloth, was so tender that Lily felt her throat tighten with emotion. When Mabel lowered Lily's hands into the basin, the warm water aggravated her burns and she gasped. Mabel took both Lily's hands in her own and turned them over—both thumbs and two of the fingers on each hand had blistered at their tips. Mabel looked up at Lily, her eyes steady, but she said nothing. She left the room and a few moments later returned with a fresh basin of water.

Then Mabel started to talk. She didn't preface her remarks, didn't give any reason for her sudden desire to tell Lily what she had never told her before. She just jumped in and said, "My father loved me, but he had no gift for affection. He rarely touched me, and when he did, his body was wood. I pity him now. It was my mother who held me and rocked me, me and my brother, and she had hands, Lily, that when they touched you, you felt the calm of every calm thing in the world, and when she died—I was younger than you, seventeen—it was as if all that was good and light had been snuffed out of my life. I left my father and my brother one day in the spring, after a year of plotting and planning. I ran off with Owen Hartwig, a freethinker from the *Aberdeen Weekly*, to get married."

"But I thought your husband's name was Evan," Lily said.

"It was. I left Owen Hartwig at the altar, or rather at the courthouse." Mabel paused. "I couldn't stand the way he looked close-up, you know, nose to nose. It sounds ridiculous but I don't believe it was, really. Something about his body repelled me."

"But you thought you loved him?"

"I liked the idea of him—hard hitting newspaperman with a radical streak. I forgot I'd have to live with those thighs."

"What did you do then?"

"I became a chambermaid in the Grand Hotel, established residency and eventually went to the university at night."

"And your father and brother?"

"They stayed on the farm. My brother farmed that place until he died, ten years ago."

"The farm?" Lily looked at her.

"Outside Aberdeen, South Dakota."

"South Dakota? I thought you came from out east somewhere."

"No."

"But you've never even mentioned it. You're like a city person through and through." Lily dried her hands on the towel Mabel handed her.

"Books."

"Books?"

"Yes, I wanted to live a great and passionate life, a life of risk, beauty and pain." Mabel laughed. "The last part seemed to come naturally."

"Have you?" Lily looked into Mabel's eyes. "Has it been like that?"

Mabel smiled. "I think that it's not what happens in life so much as how you imagine what happens, how you color events. It's rather like the idea of the changeling when I think about it. Substitution is involved. When I worked in that hotel and made people's beds and cleaned their toilets and straightened their perfumes and their soaps and emptied their ashtrays into a tub, I felt humiliated every single second because I imagined that I was destined for something else, but the truth is, I had no reason to believe that. I was a poor girl from the South Dakota sticks. But I had read a lot of books, and those stories wrote mine, if you see. You know who gave them to me?"

Lily shook her head.

"My mother."

"Is that why you're always giving me books to read?"

Mabel narrowed her eyes at Lily. "Maybe," she said and stood up abruptly and left the room. She returned with a long, black shirt and tossed it at Lily. "Here put this on. You'll look good in it, and we'll put that dirty thing in bleach." She nodded at Lily's T-shirt.

"Why did you take this apartment, Mabel?" Lily said and looked at her hard.

Mabel shook her head. Her small face looked suddenly tired. "It reminded me of a place where I once lived—these little rooms." She took a deep breath. "I wanted to return to it. I suppose . . . " Mabel shook her head.

Lily stared at the black shirt in her lap. As she pulled off her T-shirt, her blistered fingers throbbed, but she pushed her arms into the sleeves of the new shirt, and when it hung open around her, Lily looked down at the long row of buttons, then back up at Mabel.

Mabel buttoned the shirt. She held the material away from Lily's breasts so she didn't brush them with her moving hands, and her fingers left a scent of perfume behind them. When she finished, she looked into Lily's eyes and said, "Secrecy isn't always a bad thing, you know."

"Isn't it?" Lily thought about the shoes.

"Confession is a problem," Mabel said. "In friendship, anyway. The listener can't always bear the weight of it. That's why I've always thought a priest in a box is a beautiful thing— the guilty person whispering through a hole into an ear that can hear anything. Freud understood that, too, with the couch. You didn't have to look at the analyst. It's all lost now. People stare straight into the eyes of their psychiatrists."

Lily watched Mabel's face. The woman turned her head away from Lily toward the window. "I wonder if he's on vigil again tonight. Whoever he is, he's up to something." Mabel smiled a small thin smile that disturbed Lily. It looked out of place. Then she walked to the window and pulled back the curtain. Her motion was both dramatic and self-conscious, but Lily couldn't quite tell whether Mabel was making fun of herself or not. "I am that merry wanderer of the night," she said as she peered out the window. Lily recognized Puck's line. "No," Mabel said. "Maybe it's too early." She turned around. "He'll be back though."

"How can you be sure?"

"I heard it in his footsteps: unfinished business."

Mabel fed Lily a sandwich and insisted that she keep the

shirt, which was silk and probably expensive. Lily protested but then gave in.

Before Lily left for Ed's, she stood on the landing with Mabel to say good-bye. The woman leaned forward and put her lips to Lily's cheek. She barely grazed the skin, but the feeling of the kiss lingered as Lily walked down the stairs, out the door and into the street. When she opened the door of the Stuart Hotel, she could still feel it, as though Mabel's lips had left an impression on her face.

The story Lily told Ed to explain her cut and burns not only rang true, it sounded more plausible than the truth. She had slipped in the kitchen at work, grabbed the stove to block her fall, but rather than catch her balance, she had burned her fingers and smashed her head on the oven door. As she told it, she saw it happening like a real memory, and to some degree it supplanted the actual story. Dull fiction took the place of ridiculous fact, for the simple reason that it seemed more real than reality. Ed believed Lily, and Lily almost believed herself.

As he lay beside her in the narrow bed that night, he talked to her. It wasn't a conversation, but a monologue. Ed stared at the ceiling and began to describe her body part by part. He began with her hair, moved to her forehead and included the cut. He described her eyebrows, her eyes, her nose and mouth and chin. Slowly, meticulously, he moved down her body without ever looking at her, providing such detail that she felt her body no longer belonged to her, and even though she wanted him to touch her, she didn't ask him to because the sound of his voice in the darkened room filled her with such intense pleasure and expectation that she didn't want it to stop. But when his description reached her toes, he kissed them. Lily wondered how many women he had made desperate with this kind of talk, and yet when he kissed the burns on her fingertips so softly that the slight pain his lips brought only made her happy, she forgot all about the other women. They had no faces and no names, after all, except Elizabeth—and that was only a name.

Lily woke in the night to pee, stood up in the room, and before she opened the door to the bathroom, walked to the window and looked out across the street at her own building. A single light burned in Mabel's living room. Lily guessed it was the desk lamp and that Mabel was still working on her book far into the night. Then Lily searched the street for signs of the man Mabel said kept watch there, but saw nobody. The instant she turned her head to walk away, however, she heard a noise beneath her, maybe from the steps of the hotel. She pushed open the screen and hung her head over the edge to see who it was, but again she saw no one, only heard him running down the alley beside the hotel. She listened for more, but whoever it was had either stopped moving or had gone too far to be heard.

Sunday afternoon, Mabel accepted Ed and Lily's invitation to visit them at the Stuart Hotel, and within half an hour of her arrival, she fainted. The moment Mabel tripped through the door wearing a pale purple shirt, narrow black pants and a cloud of perfume, Lily could feel the woman's nervous excitement. She talked a blue streak, careening from one subject to another in a high tremulous voice while she gestured with her hands to make her points. The weather had turned hot and humid, and the rain, which hadn't amounted to more than a drizzle the day before, still threatened. Ed turned the painting of Dolores around to show it to Mabel, then the painting of Stanley. She looked at each one very closely but didn't stop talking. She was especially attracted to the narrative boxes along the top of the canvases and launched into a discussion of memory that had something to do with walking through a house, room by room. Ed seemed to understand perfectly, but Lily found it hard to follow. Mabel said that she used the "device" herself to remember speeches or texts and that for her the most important thing was "walls." Ed turned around the portrait of Tex, and Lily watched Mabel look at the painting of Tex and then collapse. She fell so fast that if Ed hadn't been only inches away, she would have landed on the floor. Ed carried Mabel to his bed, laid her down on it and felt her pulse.

"You don't think it was the painting, do you?" he said in a whisper. "Maybe the nudity came as a shock. Her pulse is okay."

"She's not that kind of old lady, Ed. Anyway, it's only men who think seeing a penis is some big deal. Women couldn't care less."

He smiled at her comment, then turned to Mabel. Only seconds later the woman opened her eyes, but during that intervening moment Ed looked at Mabel with an expression of such intensity that Lily was taken aback. Mabel moved, woke, and her waxen face regained its color quickly.

"I'm so embarrassed," she groaned.

"It's hot," Lily said. "Your nerves."

Mabel sat up and stared at Ed. "I don't understand it," she said slowly. "It's the painting, of course. It happened once before many years ago when I was a student, with a reproduction, if you can imagine that. The professor passed around that famous Grünewald painting of the dead Christ. I took one look at it and keeled over. At the time, I didn't know what an impression that same painting had made on poor Dostoyevsky, but it did comfort me a bit when I read about his response." Mabel looked wildly around the room for a moment, then back at Ed. "Maybe they'll drop like flies when you exhibit it. Wouldn't that be exciting?"

"Don't get too worked up," Lily said and patted Mabel's hands.

Ed looked at Mabel closely. "I want to paint you," he said. He moved his head to the side and stared at Mabel's neck, then her legs. Lily didn't like seeing him look at Mabel in this way, but the woman herself seemed pleased. She straightened herself and lifted her chin.

"You do?" she said.

"Yes, very much. It's a commitment, you understand. I would start drawing right away, and you would have to talk to me for hours and hours. It's a bit like going into a hole with someone for a week, which, frankly, can be unpleasant, and then there's the problem of finding a story for the boxes. Sometimes, that's hard for people. I pay by the hour, of course, not a lot, but—"

Mabel interrupted him. "I agree."

Ed grabbed both Mabel's hands and said, "We'll start tomorrow."

Lily watched them. She had introduced them to each other, and now within forty minutes of their meeting, they were talking about going into a hole together. If Mabel hadn't fainted, Lily realized that it probably wouldn't have happened. She couldn't explain why she believed this, but she did, and she watched the two of them with a new wariness. She had wanted them to like each other, but not this much, and she resisted their sudden rapport by saying very little. Mabel seemed calmer after fainting, but she talked nevertheless, mostly about the portrait of Tex and what was in it that she hadn't wanted to see. "It'll go straight into my book tonight," she announced. She seemed happy, almost proud of having keeled over after looking at a picture. When Lily said she thought it was the heat, not the painting, both Ed and Mabel turned skeptical eyes in her direction, so she gave up that line of argument. Despite her willingness to discuss the painting, Mabel wouldn't look at it again. Ed turned it to the wall, hiding the big man and his ugly fantasies. Lily looked at the back of the canvas and, wanting to leave Mabel behind as the main subject of the afternoon, asked Ed what Tex was really like.

"Really like?" he said. "I don't know. He has a thing about outlaws—Wild West characters. He brought a gun to one of the sittings—a forty-five—big thing, scared the shit out of me, if you want to know the truth. But I had a strong feeling that if he saw my fear, it would go badly, and I did my best to stay cool. As it turned out, the gun wasn't loaded. He was kind enough to show me the empty chamber, and then he settled down to work. The gun was an ornament really, didn't need bullets." Ed paused. "He said they banned him from the reenactment of the Jesse James robbery, and it broke his heart."

"No," Lily said. "They said he couldn't be Jesse James, and that's the only part he would take."

Ed nodded. "Jesse James keeps coming up. Just the other day Dolores told me she'd seen him."

"Dolores of the painting?" Mabel said.

Ed nodded. His eyes looked distant. "She'd been drinking and wasn't too clear on the details, but she said she'd seen

him in the woods, or rather his ghost, coming out of a cave."
He paused. "It's gruesome, actually, now that I say it.
According to Dolores, he was carrying a woman's head."

Lily looked at Mabel, who had turned to Ed. "What?"

"That's what she said. Pink elephants, I guess."

Mabel wrinkled her forehead.

The absurd story rattled Lily more than she would have
liked to admit, and she didn't say anything. It reminded her of
some other story she couldn't place. She rubbed the blister on
her index finger against the blister on her thumb and felt the
liquid inside them move back and forth.

Ed looked at Mabel. Lily wished he would look at her.
"The fact is, Dolores is an unusual woman. She has a kind of
instinctive intelligence."

"Not everyone would use that adjective in front of that
noun," Mabel said, "but I do understand you."

Lily cleared her throat. Ed and Mabel looked at her. "I
guess the head was a ghost, too, huh?"

"She didn't say," Ed smiled.

Lily smiled back at him. She stretched in her chair. "I'm
hot," she said and continued to look into his eyes. She undid
three buttons of her shirt, untucked it and tied it under her
breasts. She felt both of them watching her, and knowing they
were looking made her happy. "There, that's better," she said.
Lily stretched again slowly, rolling her shoulders backward
and then raising her arms above her head so the gap of bare
skin beneath her shirt widened. Then she looked at Ed and bit
her lip.

He gave her a suspicious look, and as he smiled, he shook
his head in gentle reprimand. The expression launched a
sudden fantasy—Lily imagined pushing Ed to the floor and
climbing on top of him. She smiled, crossed her legs and

turned to Mabel, whose face made it clear she hadn't missed a second of the exchange between Lily and Ed.

Mabel squinted at Lily. She made no attempt to hide her irony. "Lily Dahl," she said, as though she liked listening to the sound of the name. "Let's show Mr. Shapiro Hermia." She paused. "The fight. I know Helena's lines."

"Now?" Lily said.

Mabel nodded. "I think this is a very good time. It will be our rehearsal. When we're done, I'm going to leave. You start: 'You juggler.' "

Lily and Mabel performed the scene three times for Ed. Mabel was a far better Helena than Denise. The third time Mabel lifted her face to Lily's and said, "Good Hermia, do not be so bitter with me. / I evermore did love you, Hermia, / Did ever keep your counsels, never wrong'd you." Lily listened to the words and blushed.

At ten o'clock the following morning, Bert told Lily that she had just seen Mabel Wasley walk through the door of the Stuart Hotel. Lily turned immediately toward the street, but Mabel had already disappeared inside. She wished she had seen her, if only to catch a glimpse of the woman's clothes. How had Mabel decided to dress for the "hole"? Then she tried to imagine the conversation between Ed and Mabel. She saw Mabel gesturing dramatically as Ed leaned toward her with that engrossed expression he had had when Mabel fainted. I wonder why he doesn't want to do a portrait of me, Lily said to herself. It was the first time she had thought about herself as someone Ed could paint, but as soon as she did, she felt bad. Why had he wanted to paint Mabel, but not her? Lily remembered the paintings, saw each person on the canvas:

Dolores, Tex, Stanley. They're all so private, Lily thought. In fact, when she thought about the pictures, she had the feeling that Ed was painting privacy itself—people who looked straight out at you, but who were alone at the same time. He chose people for a reason, didn't he? Suddenly Lily felt that he would never choose her and that he saved a special kind of intimacy for the people he painted. She tried to see herself as one of them. What would she have to tell in the boxes if he asked her? Lily saw the ground where her grandparents' house had been. The new owners had razed it to the ground. And now it's like nothing was ever there. But that's not *my* story, she thought. And thinking of Mabel and Ed across the street, Lily felt annoyed that they were together. She imagined Mabel in some drooping silk number and felt a pang of regret about her own clothes. She could almost hear Mabel talking—a stream of sentences filled with the names of people Lily had never heard of. When she left the cafe, she was inventing Ed's painting of Mabel for herself. She imagined the woman the way she had seen her the day before—a small body on the narrow bed, drained of color and nearly of life: the portrait of a corpse. Lily found the image comforting.

Standing outside Ed's door, she heard them talking. Ed's voice was low, confidential, a little hesitant. She couldn't hear what he said, but she thought he sounded exactly the way she had imagined him. Lily's neck and jaw hardened at the sound. Then she heard Mabel answer, her voice pitched much higher. "She had one blue eye and one brown. A rare trait, and once you noticed it, utterly arresting. I didn't see it at first, but when I did, I couldn't stop looking at those mismatched eyes. I honestly think that if her eyes had been the same color, I wouldn't have responded in the way I did. She was very beautiful and very quiet. If she had talked, it might all have been different, too. I suppose I fell in love with her without ever saying it to myself or to her or to anyone until twenty years later when I allowed myself to think it. She was like a cat, really, or maybe a cat bewitched. She had no goodness in her, but she wasn't bad either. She was empty of all moral sense. I used to rub her back for her and her feet, and I remember that touching her troubled me. It wasn't only a sense of the forbidden. That vacuum in her frightened me. But she knew more about me than I did myself. She teased me like a lover, luxuriated in my devotion the way she did in everyone else's, just because she had an appetite for it. And then she was gone, ran off. I never saw her again . . . "

Lily turned around and walked down the hall. She went quietly but quickly, her pulse drumming in her ears, and she ran all the way home to her room. She went straight to her closet, snatched the canvas bag from the floor and threw the filthy thing on her bed. She took out the shoes and looked at them. She turned them over in her hands and picked at the frayed leather with her fingers. The fire had colored them— black, brown, ocher, yellow. Spotted and speckled with burns near the heels, the toes of both shoes had been scorched through. She brought them close to her face and smelled them, breathing in the odor of ashes and then the stink she remembered from the fire. I have to get rid of them, she said to herself, but she couldn't bring herself to toss them into the garbage. She laid them side by side on the floor and stared at them for a minute. They're the sorriest excuse for shoes I've ever seen, she thought, and then with slow, deliberate motions, she removed her sandals and slipped her feet into them. One tore. The other flapped around her instep. Without understanding why, Lily felt cruel wearing those charred, dilapidated shoes, and right then she decided it was a feeling she wanted.

Without taking them off, she set her alarm to wake her for rehearsal, lay down on her bed and closed her eyes. Lily was dreaming when the alarm woke her, but whatever it was, it died with the clock's ringing, and she remembered nothing of it.

Lily suspected it was her mood, but the play changed for her that night. In the first scene when Mr. Pumper made Egeus's speech exactly the same way he always did, Lily heard the threat in it for the first time: "I beg the ancient privilege of Athens; / As she is mine, I may dispose of her, / Which shall be either to this gentlemen, / Or to her death according to our law." And she heard the violence in what Theseus said, too. "To whom you are but as a form in wax, / By him imprinted and within his power / To leave the figure or disfigure it." The metaphor, lost on her before, jumped to life, and Lily saw the image of a young woman, her face and body smashed by a man's fist. Lily remembered Mabel in front of the window when they had practiced the lines together. "Just one turn," she had said, moving her fingers as if she held a screw, "and comedy is tragedy."

All through the play she heard words and phrases she hadn't remembered hearing before, and behind the familiar people, behind their T-shirts and shorts and clumsy performances and forgotten lines and Mrs. Wright's instructions to be "airy" and to "step lightly," and behind the noise of hammering and sawing from the set builders downstairs, and even behind the muggy weather that hung in the room like a weight, she felt the presence of another play that was almost real, or as real as memory is. Even though she couldn't really smell the trees, the thistles and the honeysuckle, she remembered that she had smelled them, and she remembered the bloodroot blooming in early spring in the shade of the woods, and the buttercups coming up in the meadow, and the tall grass alive with grasshoppers, jumping and quivering as she waded through it, and she remembered stepping out of the creek to find black leeches all over her legs and running home without looking down, and Lily imagined she understood Martin's map then of the two places, and she longed to go home, back to her house where she had lived with her parents before she grew up, before her father's cancer, before the Ideal Cafe and before Ed and Mabel, back to what she remembered, to milkweed and cow pies and the creek.

Music accompanied the actors for the first time that night, a string quartet that played well. Without the music, Lily knew that she probably wouldn't have felt what she did. The music was emotion for her then, not a reflection of feeling so much as feeling itself, and listening to it after her bad day, she fell into a state that resembled a low fever. A little light in her head and achy in her joints, she played the part of Hermia in a sort of trance.

When rehearsal ended and the music stopped, Lily tried to shake herself to full consciousness but found it hard and didn't listen to anyone or notice the other actors until Ruth Baker walked up to her carrying a large bolt of white fabric in her arms and said, "This is the material for you and Denise. Do you like it?"

Lily stared at the whiteness and blinked.

"I'll meet you in the costume room and get you measured."

"Okay," Lily said.

"Didn't you hear Barbara's announcement?"

Lily looked into Mrs. Baker's round face and down at the

woman's belly which bulged under khaki pants. "I'm sorry. I must have been daydreaming."

When Lily walked through the door into the wardrobe room, she saw Denise standing on a low stool. Mrs. Baker stood on the floor beside her with a measuring tape, and Martin Petersen was sitting on the floor Indian style with a long piece of fabric draped over his knees. He held a small notebook in one hand and a pencil in the other. The naked lightbulb on the ceiling enhanced Martin's whiteness, but Lily nevertheless had the impression that his skin color was fading with each passing day. I'm sure he's paler than he was a week ago, she thought. What is he doing here, anyway?

"Martin's helping me out," Mrs. Baker said as though Lily had asked the question aloud.

Lily nodded and watched Denise step off the stool. It was normal that Martin should help out, wasn't it? He was a handyman, after all. Then why did she feel his presence was calculated, that it had something to do with her?

Lily stepped up on the stool and watched Denise leave the room. Denise's walk annoyed Lily. It was stiff and self-conscious. Her roots are getting dark, Lily thought, and felt Mrs. Baker move the tape measure along the length of her leg. She called out the numbers and Martin scribbled them into the notebook. Lily looked down at him for a moment and saw three needles stuck into the fabric of his shirt. He bent toward the page, and the needles shone for an instant in the light.

Mrs. Baker clicked her tongue as she worked. "You girls," she said. "Such teeny-weeny sizes. Of course fifteen years and four children ago, I had a twenty-six-inch waist myself, hard to believe now, but I've got the wedding gown to prove it." As she felt Mrs. Baker loop the tape around her waist and tighten it, Lily heard Martin breathing, and the sound made her blush. His pencil scratched the pad. She closed her eyes for an instant and then felt dizzy. She swayed on the chair. Mrs. Baker caught her elbow.

"Lily, are you all right?"

She looked into Mrs. Baker's concerned face. "Yes," Lily said. "I just lost my balance."

"We're done, dear."

Lily stepped off the stool, and Mrs. Baker left the room, muttering something to herself about Titania and sequins.

Lily looked down at Martin. The cloth lay beside him now, and she saw that the zipper of his jeans was half open. For a moment she imagined his penis, testicles and pubic hair underneath the denim, and his sex seemed real to her for the first time. After rocking back and forth a couple of times before he spoke, he said, "W-why don't you come to my house now. We can talk for a while. I-I-I have something to show you." He paused, and when he spoke again, Lily detected barely audible music in his voice. "I think you want to come now. The woods are just behind the house."

She stared at Martin and then at a purple velvet cape that lay in a heap behind him and said, her eyes still on the velvet, "Why did you say that about the woods?"

Martin quoted Oberon's lines to Puck when the fairy king sends his squire to find the herb that will enchant Titania. Every time she heard it, she imagined it the same way: Cupid's arrow flying in a great arc until it hit its mark in an open field. Martin didn't stutter at all. "It fell upon a little western flower, / Before milk-white, now purple with love's wound: / And maidens call it 'love-in-idleness.' " He looked at her steadily and boldly. He didn't sound like Martin Petersen at all. The quote was a dare.

"Why not?" she said to him. She shook her hair on her back and looked directly into his eyes.

If he was surprised, Martin didn't show it. He stood up, stuttered something about his truck, and Lily followed him outside. Walking behind him, she knew she was making a mistake, but it was a mistake she wanted to make. If it weren't for Ed, she wouldn't be going home with Martin. If she was at Martin's, she couldn't be with Ed, but if she was home, she might not be able to keep herself away from the Stuart Hotel. At the same time, she felt drawn to Martin and curious about the house she had been forbidden to visit.

Sitting beside him in his pickup, Lily watched the road ahead of them as Martin drove in silence past the Dilly Home and Courtland Hill and onto the highway. The seats had a vaguely chemical smell. Lily put her elbow out the window and moved close to the door to be as far away from Martin as possible. She let the wind blow onto her face and looked into the night. For a few seconds she didn't know Martin was starting to speak, but then she turned to him and heard him sputter, "Do you know what the 'little western flower' is?"

"No," Lily said.

Martin paused.

Lily didn't look at him, but she felt the effort he was making to say the next word.

"A p-p-pansy."

"Really?" Lily said, and then she remembered her mother's pansies lined up in trays before she put them into the ground, some had white petals with deep violet or blue splotches at their centers. "It makes sense," she said. "I can see it."

Martin nodded. Lily looked at his profile in the light from the dashboard. He moved the clutch into second. Lily leaned back against the seat and thought that sometimes experience was good for its own sake, that Martin Petersen was at the very least an interesting character, and that this too might be an adventure.

He drove fast, not crazy fast, just fast, and Lily sensed urgency in him. They passed the Bodlers', and Lily saw a single light burning in the house upstairs, and she looked at the tall junk heaps, black against the wood behind them, and felt a sudden pang of anticipation. Martin turned onto the gravel road that passed beneath an arch of trees and stopped in front of the tiny house. It was completely dark.

When the motor stilled, Lily heard crickets in the grass. She opened her door, and Martin cried, "W-w-wait!" Lily was so startled she waited, watched Martin run around the front of the truck, appear at her door and hold out his hand to help her down. Lily played along.

"Thank you, kind sir," she said.

Once she was standing on the ground beside him, Martin bowed and made a flourish with his hand.

He flicked on the porch light when they reached the house. Lily looked around her and noticed a dying plant on a small table—its leaves so withered it was unrecognizable. Martin opened the front door, and Lily stopped behind him. The odor she had smelled in the truck was stronger in the house, glue or some chemical. They walked straight into what must have been the main room. Martin turned on the light. A worn sofa, a couple of straight-backed chairs and a table were the only furniture. Martin was telling her to sit down, and Lily walked toward the sofa, asking herself why the room made her feel bad. She remembered that Martin's father had had lips with almost no flesh to them, and for some reason she had a sudden image of him with a rifle trudging across a field, although she couldn't remember where it came from. The room had no bookshelves, but there were books in piles everywhere, and after she sat down Lily read some of their titles: *Gray's Anatomy; Stalin: A Biography; The Many Uses of Molds; Drawing the Human Figure; The Third Reich; The Future Eve; The Numberless Planet.* She also saw a pile of science fiction and detective paperbacks and at least one romance called *Baxter Manor.* In the nearest corner she noticed a heap of two-by-fours and a toolbox sitting on the floor beside a pile of old clothes or material, a large pair of scissors, bits and pieces of foam rubber, spools of thread, tubes of paint and several knives laid neatly in a row. The overhead light didn't illuminate the corner fully, and in its obscurity Lily also saw the vague shapes of things she couldn't identify. The knives unsettled her, but she told herself that in daylight they would probably look innocent.

She turned away from them to the opposite corner of the room, where she noticed a rocking chair with a large black piece of material draped over its arm. Taped to the wall was some kind of collage pasted onto a world map. The map looked hand drawn and reminded Lily of the map Martin had given her. On and around it were newspaper clippings, color pictures from magazines; some of them looked torn, others neatly cut. Lily stood up from the sofa, walked toward it and heard Martin grunt behind her, but she pretended not to hear. Stopping in front of the collage, Lily noticed that the center of the collage was blank—no pictures, no drawings, nothing, but because it was surrounded by so much stuff, the emptiness seemed significant. Then she looked at a picture of a starving child, most likely taken from an advertisement for an aid organization like Save the Children or CARE. Beside it Martin had taped a photograph of a young model from a fashion magazine in an evening gown. The juxtaposition was obvious and awful, but as she looked more closely she saw that the simpering model and the miserable child had expressions on their faces that were weirdly similar. She looked from one article and picture to another—an old photograph from Vietnam, articles about John Wayne Gacy, Jack the Ripper, June Putkey, the Webster girl who stabbed her mother a couple of years ago, an article with the headline, "Thousands Visit Statue of the Virgin Alleged to Have Healing Powers," and a grainy photograph of death camp victims in open graves, more ads for clothes, beer, cigarettes, images of gardens with fountains, flowers and trees. She saw a number of clippings from tabloids including, "Man Has Head Transplant and Lives," "My Baby's Father Is an Alien" and "Satan's Burial Ground Discovered in Utah. Scientists Uncover Hundreds of Horned Skulls." Just beside a magazine ad for toothpaste that showed a young woman with snow-white teeth, Lily saw a star beside Bergen Belsen and beneath the star Martin had drawn a box that looked similar to the box Martin had drawn for her but narrower. Lily closed her eyes for an instant. The muscles in her shoulders tightened. She could feel Martin behind her and turned quickly toward him. "What is this, Martin?"

He regarded her evenly, his lips tightly shut. She saw his head shake slightly, saw his tongue, his teeth. He stuttered unintelligibly.

"How can you stand to have this up, to see these things all the time?" She rested her hand on the back of the rocking chair and felt it sway under her touch. The black material hanging over it brushed her leg. She stepped back.

Martin pointed to an ad for the telephone company that showed a mother embracing a child in a green backyard. "Th-there are nice pictures, too."

"I know, Martin, but beside the rest, they look like a joke, and all those pretty models and the flowers. I don't know."

Martin turned away from her. She heard him sputter through the first consonant and then his words came fluently but with that same lilt in his voice she had heard before. "It's a mix, this and that. What *is*. And it's all got a name. Everything's *called* something, even"—he paused and pointed to Auschwitz—"even places that shouldn't have one. I read about a lot of things. I see stuff on TV." He moved his head toward an old set with vinyl sides painted to look like wood grain. "Black and white. I don't want color."

They were silent for several seconds. Lily didn't like the smell of the house. She turned her head toward the bedroom door, which was standing open. She could see an unmade bed covered with loose papers, a desk and a few inches of a dresser. "What did you want to show me?" Lily said. "I have to go home soon."

Martin walked past Lily into the bedroom. She heard a drawer open and close. He returned with a piece of newspaper and asked her to sit down again, which she did. "It's this." He gave her the old, yellow piece of newsprint.

Lily looked down at a small photograph of a child, a girl no more than two or three years old with short dark hair. She was smiling broadly. "Who is it?"

"Becky Runevold."

"I don't think I know who that is," Lily said.

"Her father killed her sixteen years ago." Martin paused. "T-t-today. She would've been our age."

"Today?" Lily said. "Did you know her?"

"No."

"But it was a long time ago. Where did this picture come from?"

"The *Pioneer Press*. Mom cut it out."

"Your mom knew the family?"

Martin shook his head.

"So why do you have it?" Lily's voice sounded shrill.

Martin took the little square away from Lily and stared down at it. "You see it, don't you, Lily?"

"See what?"

"It, it looks like you when you were a little girl."

Lily pulled the picture away from Martin. "No, it doesn't."

Martin faced Lily. He nodded slowly. "Yes, it does."

"I should know better than you," Lily said.

Martin shook his head. "N-no, usually it's other people who see it, not the person." He stretched his lips, nodded and said, "It's like you grew up for her—in a way." Martin tugged at the picture in Lily's hand, and she let go of it.

Lily stared at Martin. "No, it's not," she said.

"Didn't happen in the Cities. Outside Farmington. Drowned her in the bath."

"Why?" Lily whispered the word.

Martin shrugged. His expression as he moved his shoulders was calm but fixed, his eyes absorbed in a distant thought. Then he said, "It hath no bottom."

"You really love the play, don't you?" Lily said.

Martin squinted at her as though she were yards away. "N-no," he said.

"You're always quoting from it."

Martin stumbled over the next words. "It's easier," he finally said, "than saying it myself."

"But you wanted to be in it," Lily insisted.

Martin nodded.

"And the map, Martin. Why did you want me to have that?" Lily wanted to ask about the box but stopped herself.

Martin turned away from Lily. He looked straight toward the window and chanted like a kid on a playground. "She's out there right now."

"Who?" Lily said.

"She's not alive."

Lily caught her breath. She had turned several corners since she had agreed to accompany Martin back to his house, and she decided this was the last. "I want to go home," she said.

Martin stood up immediately and began to walk to the door. For a second, Lily didn't understand what he was doing. He opened the screen door and moved quickly across the porch without turning off the light. Lily followed him, and when she stepped out onto the porch, she saw him standing beside his truck holding the passenger door open for her.

Without saying anything, Lily climbed in. Martin drove the whole way in silence. Lily couldn't tell whether his silence meant anger, sullenness or resignation. His face showed nothing. But Lily didn't want to talk. She sat close to the door and watched the road, paying attention to his every move. While he drove, she imagined sudden skids and collisions, the truck swerving into the wrong lane and speeding into oncoming headlights. When Martin stopped the truck on Division Street in front of the cafe, Lily turned to him. He looked very young to her at that moment, with his soft face and unfashionable short hair. Lily looked through the windshield and said, "Bye." Martin leaned toward her, but Lily pulled at the door handle and jumped down into the street. Martin moved to the passenger seat and stuck his head out the window. "You won't let him paint you, will you, Lily?"

She opened her mouth and stared at him. She knew what he was saying, understood he meant Ed, but she said, "What are you talking about?"

"I-i-it's important that he doesn't paint you. Not you." Martin paused. "F-for your sake, Lily."

She looked away from him. "Good-bye, Martin," she said. Lily walked up the alley toward the back door that led to her apartment and watched Martin's truck pull away. Then she looked across the street into Ed's window. She saw two figures in the light—Ed's and Mabel's. They were seated across from each other in the room's only chairs. Lily saw Mabel lift a hand and gesture toward the ceiling. Still talking, she said to herself. Lily watched the two of them for at least a minute before she closed her eyes and held her breath. Her longing to rush to Ed and throw her arms around him was so great, she shook from the tension of holding herself back. Then, after counting to one hundred to give herself enough time, she pulled on the back door, discovered somebody had locked it, dug out her keys, opened it and went upstairs to bed.

Before she fell asleep, Lily thought she smelled something burning—a distant fire, maybe, its smoke carried into town on a wind. It can't be the shoes, can it, still stinking from the fire? She remembered the map and the pictures on Martin's wall, and then the empty space in the middle. Was he going to fill that in? Somehow it was that blankness that stuck in her mind now, more than any of the images or words she had seen all around it. She's not alive, Lily thought. He must have meant that little girl—Becky. Lily put on a tape to forget about

Martin and the dead girl and Ed and Mabel. She listened to *The Best of Aretha Franklin* twice and while she listened, she imagined herself on stage in a green, sequined dress. She was singing out the words "You make me feel like a natural woman," and in the fantasy she had a voice like Aretha's, a voice that seemed to come straight from heaven.

The moment Lily put her hand on the doorknob to enter the cafe, she heard the jukebox click and a song begin: "Do You Believe in Magic?" Lily opened the door and saw Vince dancing and singing alone in the space between the booths and the counter. His back was to Lily, and she watched his hips sway as he jiggled his fingers like a flapper. She saw the bald spot on the back of his head orbit as he rolled his shoulders, and then he toe-heeled his way over to the coffee machine. Lily smiled. The fat man had grace, lightness. She watched him dip and sing, " . . . in a young girl's heart." He made a pivot, caught sight of Lily, and without missing a beat of the song, held out his hand and said, "Join me, doll." Lily took the outstretched hand, and they danced—bobbing, bumping butts and wailing out the refrain together.

When the song died, Lily said, "You're in a good mood this morning."

Vince was breathing hard and a vein stood out on his forehead. "You, too," he said. He shook his head. "You look beautiful, positively fresh and dewy. I guess that new guy is treating you right." Vince paused, wiped his forehead, hesitated, then blurted out, "Isn't he a little old for you, honey? As an old man myself, I feel I ought to warn you off." He smiled. "Age doesn't make you better."

Lily blushed. "You know, Vince, you don't really decide. It just kind of happens."

"Yeah, I know." Again he hesitated, scratching his upper arm vigorously. "Hank's been hanging around the cafe lately, and I figured you ought to know."

"I haven't seen him."

"He's been coming to see me in the afternoons, and early last night I bumped into him outside the Stuart."

"Hank?" Lily said.

"He's in a bad way."

"Hank?" Lily repeated.

Vince moved his head back in false surprise. "Yes, Hank. Remember him? Tall, good-looking guy. You dated him for about a year."

Lily clicked her tongue. "Vince." She groaned the name. "Last night?"

"That's right. I stayed late doing the books, and when I left, there he was sad-sacking around in the alley, mouth drooping to his shoes."

"That doesn't sound like Hank," Lily said.

"He knows about—" Vince moved his head in the direction of the Stuart Hotel. "I took him home with me, gave him the standard talk over a bottle of bourbon—the no-woman's-worth-it load of crap. He went to work snockered."

"That was nice of you, Vince."

"It's none of my business, Lily, but I think you should talk to him."

"It won't change anything."

Vince took Lily's right hand and patted it. "I know that, but Hank's problem is that he can't believe it. He just can't believe it."

Lily looked into the street and sighed. "The funny thing is, Vince, that anything can happen. I mean, breaking up with Hank is ordinary. All kinds of really crazy stuff is going on all the time. You've got to expect it."

"Hank hasn't learned that yet. He goes by the book. College, graduate school, good job, pretty wife, smart, happy kids." He looked closely at Lily. "I don't suppose he ever saw it."

"Saw what?"

"What I saw right away—the dissatisfied, hungry devil in you that jumps in front of trains and laughs it off."

"Where'd you hear about that?"

"It's legend, Lil'."

"I was just a kid."

"You were old enough to know better."

"I don't do that stuff now, Vince."

"No," he said and folded his arms. "You've graduated to bigger stuff."

"Cut it out."

Vince looked out the window and squinted. "I've got lead in my skull. It's going to rain. It's going to rain hard and it's going to blow."

Lily laughed. "You've been out of Philadelphia too long. You sound just like an old farmer."

"Old farmer, shit," Vince said. "I've had a barometer in my head since I was seven. My grandma used to call me 'the weather vane.' "

Vince was right. The weather changed. The dawn sky turned a pale green, and not long after that, Division Street was as still as a picture of itself. At six-thirty, Boomer waltzed in, and the three of them served a few early birds who ate fast and hurried home to beat the storm. Black clouds rolled in, a wind came up and it started to howl. At seven, they turned on the radio and listened to a man announce that a thunderstorm warning had been declared for Minneapolis and the surrounding areas, Webster included. Lily called Bert, told her to stay home, and they closed the cafe. Rain pummeled the street. The store awnings cracked in the wind, and it thundered close. For a minute or two it rained so hard they lost sight of the hotel. Boomer pressed his nose against the windowpane and muttered "Yeah" with a moronic regularity that began to annoy Lily.

The three of them sat in a booth and played seven-card stud while eating yesterday's pie and listening to the screen door rattle on its hook. The gutters flooded, and in the street the fragile new tree, planted only days ago by the Webster Beautification Committee, bent low in the wind. Lily hoped she hadn't left her window open, and then she thought of Mabel upstairs. For an instant she imagined the little old woman being swept out her window, her body sailing over the rooftops like a handkerchief.

"It's your turn, Lily," Boomer said.

She looked at the dishwasher. He never sat still. At that moment he was jiggling his shoulders and head. Lily eyed the Elvis T-shirt he was wearing, "The King" inscribed on it in huge letters. Then she lifted her eyes to Boomer's face and stared into his eyes behind the thick glasses that had been treated to further home repairs. Aside from the masking tape wrapped around the frames, there was a piece of wire, coiling upward from his right lens like a loose mattress spring. The mad eyewear above the face of the rock-and-roll icon made the boy look like an assimilated extraterrestrial. He whined at her, "You're holding up the game."

"Keep your shorts on," Lily said and studied her hand.

She took two cards, and when she saw the straight, she didn't blink.

Vince meditated for a couple of seconds and pushed a bottle cap into the center of the table. "Did you hear about Dolores?"

"No," Lily said.

"Arrested."

"For what?"

"I'll bet I know." Boomer grinned.

Lily looked at the boy's chipped tooth—a little white spike at the front of his mouth.

Vince ignored him and nodded at Lily. "They say she broke into one of the caves outside of town."

"You're kidding," Lily said, staring at her cards.

"Your boyfriend bailed her out," Boomer said.

Lily held her cards over her mouth and nose and watched Boomer over her hand. "Who told you that?"

Boomer leaned back in the booth and folded his arms. "I got connections in the department."

"You and everybody else," Lily said.

"Not anymore, you don't." Boomer sang the words in a high, jeering voice.

Lily looked at Boomer's smug expression. I'd feel sorry for him, she thought, if he weren't such a little creep.

Vince sighed noisily and scratched his neck.

"Stuff it, Boom," Lily said. "Are you in or not? I'm raising you three."

The storm started to quiet around eleven. It stopped raining, but gusts of wind rattled unseen objects in the street, and water continued to rush in the gutters. A thin yellow light leaked through isolated holes in the clouds, and the buildings, sidewalk and parking meters were cast in a shadowless glow that Lily couldn't remember having seen before. She stood by the window for a minute and looked out. She used to think God was in storms, but she didn't think that anymore. She stared up at the flat roof of the Stuart Hotel and into the clouds tinged with yellow and gray. She remembered the newsprint photo she had seen the night before, and suddenly the simple fact that people lived and died seemed strange to her, not terrible, just strange. She looked out and remembered her grandfather's body after he had died in the hospital from the last stroke. He had looked younger. Everybody had noticed it. And then Lily imagined Helen Bodler in her grave. She was clawing at the dirt above her and pushing, pushing up with all her might. And then in Lily's mind, she managed to dig herself out and sit up. She climbed out of the fresh grave, and Lily imagined her standing beside the long, shallow hole. Clumps of earth hung from her hair, soiled her mouth and nose, filled her lashes and brows. Helen brushed off what she could, turned her back to Lily and began to walk down the driveway and away from the Bodler farm. She didn't hurry. When miracles happen, nobody hurries. Lazarus couldn't have run. He stood up, Lily thought, and walked out of the tomb still wearing his shroud.

The telephone drove Lily out of her room that afternoon. She couldn't stand looking at the stupid thing any longer. Several times she had lifted the receiver, only to put it back down. "Let him call," she said to the phone aloud. "He can call me." Mabel's apartment was unusually silent—either she was out or had finally fallen asleep after a night of insomnia. When she looked into Ed's window, she couldn't see a thing, but she guessed Mabel was there with him, and the thought frustrated her. Lily called Bert instead.

"Let him call," Bert said.

"I was afraid you were going to say that," Lily said.

"Let me put it this way," Bert said. "You don't want him if he doesn't want you, right? It's better to find out now."

Lily listened. She didn't say it, but she thought, Of course I want him. Since when don't you want people just because they don't want you? Sometimes you want them more. She said, "Yeah, thanks, Bert." They talked about the storm for a couple of minutes, and, after a pause, Bert said, "I heard he went to Swenson's."

"What?" Lily said.

"Shapiro, he went to the funeral home." Bert took a breath. "Said he wanted to draw one of the corpses. Well, the only dead guy in there was old Oscar Hansen . . . "

"Who told you this?"

"Mr. Swenson himself. Said it took him by surprise, you know. Had to ask the family for permission, since Oscar couldn't say yes or no."

"Jeez, Bert," Lily said. "Did they let him?"

"Well, I guess Oscar's son said, 'Help yourself,' more or less, but the daughter isn't so sure." Lily heard Bert put down the phone. "If you take one more bite of that pie, Roger, I'll hog-tie you and send you back to your mother." Then to Lily she said, "I don't even know why I'm telling you this. I just thought you ought to know somehow."

Lily was silent.

"Lily?"

"I'm here. I'm thinking about it."

Bert laughed. "It's not a crime to draw stiffs, you know. I

mean, he's such a nice guy, and, well, you could see how it would be interesting. I've always had a hankering to go in there and have a look around myself."

Bert's defense of Ed eased Lily's mind. "Yeah," Lily said. She hesitated, then added in a soft voice, "You're a good friend, Bert."

"Ah, get out of here," came the voice on the other end of the line. Lily hung up. She wished that just once Bert would say it back.

Knowing it would be the last time, Lily slid her feet into the burnt shoes. She didn't wear them long, just long enough to mark the occasion. Then she wrapped them in the white cotton fabric she had used for curtains, put the bundle gently inside her canvas bag and left the room. She locked the door.

Lily pedaled her bicycle through the maze of fallen branches that had been ripped from trees during the storm, their leaves still unwilted. It made her feel good to be returning the shoes. They couldn't go back into the suitcase or even into the garage, but she would put them somewhere secret and quiet, where they could molder into nothingness undisturbed.

The sky showed new holes of clear blue, and the cool air invigorated her. She raced, pedaling so hard she panted. When she neared the Bodlers', she spotted their truck and stopped well short of the driveway. She wheeled her bicycle into the ditch, laid it on its side and walked up into the field. Then she turned to look toward the Klatschwetter farm. The sky was immense and clearing fast. She smelled cow manure, an odor she liked, mingled as it was with alfalfa and earth warmed by the sun. Her eyes moved across the road to the horizon past a copse of midget trees, a silo and a red barn, then back again to the Guernseys and Holsteins out to pasture.

Slow animals, Lily thought as she watched them—a head to the grass, a tail flicks a fly, and then that bovine adjustment of haunches near the fence. The barbed wire was electrified. She could see the silver ribbon along its lower edge. It may have been the familiarity of what she saw that moved Lily, or the bigness of that landscape that dwarfed her in a way she found comfortable, but she gazed out at the scene with no thoughts at all until she heard a sound behind her, and then she started and whirled around to see what it was.

Frank Bodler was standing about three yards away from her. His eyes were hidden under the brim of his cap, but she could see his grimly set mouth and jaw. Lily couldn't understand where the man had come from. Only seconds ago she had looked across the field and seen no one. He was carrying a large, half-rusted spade, and he tamped the ground with it twice. Lily watched him nod at her, then signal for her to come. For several seconds she didn't move. She hugged the bag against her side and waited.

Frank grunted the word "Come."

Lily went. She wasn't quite sure why she went, but she followed the man across the field and stared at the large oil stain on the back of his filthy trouser leg. He hunched a little as he trudged forward with the spade over his shoulder. They know, she thought. They're going to confront me, ask me where the shoes are. They must have seen me. Lily began planning her confession. I'll tell them the truth, she thought. But the truth sounded insane to her. I'll confess without mentioning their mother. But how can I explain burning them? I panicked out of guilt. I threw them in the fire. When they reached the kitchen door, Lily paused. She remembered falling, remembered the wet floor against her skin. She heard herself swallow and then crossed the threshold. Disoriented, she walked into a roll of flypaper. The sticky yellow substance encrusted with flies brushed her ear, and she gasped before she could squelch it. Frank paid no attention. He moved through the kitchen into the second room, which had a little more light from two small windows. It reeked of mildew. Frank pointed at a ripped sofa, waited for Lily to sit down on it, opened a door that led to a third room and disappeared, closing the door behind him.

Lily placed the bag between her and the arm of the sofa to conceal it with her body. In the rounded olive screen of a very old television set, she looked at her own distorted image and turned away from it toward the window. Through the cloudy pane, she saw the top of a blooming peony bush. She swallowed again loudly. The room was crammed with objects— two toasters near her feet, a box of rags or clothes at the end of the sofa, a heavy, black rubber cord dangling over the back of a wicker chair. To avoid looking at the cord, Lily eyed the ceiling and noted the elaborate water stains, which resembled the map of some imaginary country. She was still studying its ragged coastline when Frank returned to the room with Dick.

They stood together in the open doorway of the third room. Frank stepped forward, thrust his arm violently in her direction and said in a voice so loud that Lily jumped, "Was it her?"

Dick walked toward Lily. She hunched her shoulders and pushed herself tightly against the bag as she watched Dick coming toward her in a half-crouched position. Apparently he wanted to keep his head at the same height as hers. He stopped, rested his hands on his knees and stared at her closely. Lily could see dust in his eyebrows and dirt in the creases of his wrinkled face. She swallowed and felt sure Dick could hear it. The swallowing had become an irritation. Her saliva seemed to build up so fast in her mouth that she couldn't ignore it. How was it, she wondered, that she had ever swallowed without thinking about it? Dick continued to examine her. Then he moved his head back.

"Yup," he said. His voice was high. Lily realized she had never heard him speak and that the timbre of his voice had nothing in common with his brother's. I'm sunk, she thought. She considered her first line. The words "I'm sorry" began to form themselves in her mouth.

The men seated themselves in two of the several miserable chairs that lined the other side of the room.

"Yer Lars Dahl's girl," Frank said.

Lily nodded.

"Know yer dad," he said. "Good man, yer dad. Knew yer granddad, too." Then he turned to his brother and yelled, "Lars Dahl's girl!"

Dick was deaf. Lily hadn't known this. She looked from one man to the other. "I work at the Ideal Cafe," she said as loudly as she could without screaming.

Frank narrowed his eyes.

"I've waited on you lots of times." Her voice sounded childlike. Was it possible they didn't recognize her?

Frank scratched his hairline, and Lily saw gray flakes fall onto the front of his shirt. She looked toward the corner where he had left the spade and made a guess at how long it would take for her to leap over and grab it. Cautiously, she began to inch down the sofa, taking the bag with her. She felt a loose coil poke her thigh and stopped.

"Dick's the one seen you."

Lily waited for the accusation.

"Yesterday evenin' in the field."

Not last night, she thought. Last night I was at rehearsal and then at Martin's. . . . She looked at Dick.

"Guess it don't matter now," Frank said.

Dick leaned toward her again. He closed one eye as though that would improve his vision.

Frank was silent. The three of them sat without saying a word for at least a minute. Then, not able to take it anymore, she shouted, "I don't understand."

Neither man answered. They glanced at each other. Then, apparently responding to the look from his brother, Dick slowly rose from the chair and shuffled into the kitchen. Intermittent clatter sounded from that room for several minutes. Frank reached into his shirt pocket and retrieved a pouch of chewing tobacco, took a pinch of the tiny brown leaves between his thumb and index finger and lodged the tobacco inside his cheek. As far as Lily could tell, he had no consciousness of her presence. Maybe I can just stand up and leave, she thought. She eyed the spade again, considered getting up, then stayed put.

Eventually, Dick emerged from the kitchen carrying a brown plastic tray with a tin coffeepot, three cups and some oblong cookies smeared with white frosting arranged on a plate. His boots never left the floor. He pushed his feet forward like a child on skates for the first time, his eyes fixed on the cups, his hands trembling. The room had no table on which to lower the tray, but Dick clearly had his next move planned. He came to a full stop and began to bend his knees a little at a time. Once he had lowered himself about six inches, he held the position for a couple of seconds as if to confirm that he had gone that far, bent over and abruptly set the tray on the floor. Cups clinked, cookies slid, but the tray was stabilized in a spot beside one of the toasters. Without standing up, Dick started the business of pouring coffee. He handed her a cup, and Lily looked into the black liquid. Grease bubbles floated on its surface, but she brought the dirty cup to her lips and drank. It didn't taste bad—a little oily, but strong and good.

Dick watched her intently. "Egg," he said.

"Pardon me?" Lily shouted.

Frank shouted back at her. "There's an egg in the coffee!"

Dick nodded. He righted himself and poked the cookie plate under her nose. Lily took a cookie.

Once they had settled themselves with the coffee and cookies, Lily roared at Dick, "I don't understand. You couldn't have seen me here last night. I wasn't here."

Dick nodded, but Lily wasn't sure what the nod meant, whether he was signaling that he had heard her or that he agreed with her. He spoke in that odd voice of his. "I seen Marty carryin' you across the field and over the road."

"What?" Lily said, but not loudly enough. Then she corrected herself and yelled, "Marty?"

"Marty Petersen from down the road," Frank said.

"Yesterday?" Lily said.

Dick continued, his eyes on the window. Slowly he extended his arms in front of him, his elbows bent. Lily watched the coffee cup in his right hand tip dangerously. "I seen Marty carryin' you like you was fainted or ..." He didn't finish but lowered his arms without spilling and then rubbed the cup with both hands. "It was you," he said to the window. "I seen your eyes and face and hair. I called to him." Dick changed his voice. " 'Mar-ty!' I says. 'Who you got there? Come back, Marty,' but he din't answer me. He walks on 'cross the road and down by the creek and into the woods.

144

I ain't got the legs to run no more, so I goes into Frank and tells him what I seen." Dick glanced at Lily for an instant, then fixed his eyes on the window again. He nodded, squinted, turned back to her and said, "But here you are in the peak of health."

Lily leaned forward and stared at Dick. "What time was it?"

Dick looked at Frank, his face a question.

Frank said, "I'd say early evenin'. Wasn't dark yet."

Both men were silent. Lily looked from one to the other. It was crazy. The whole thing was nuts. She waited for them to speak.

Neither one said a word for at least half a minute. Then Frank took a breath and said, "Well, that's that."

Lily stared at Frank and swallowed. He gave a little push and raised himself from the chair, then started for the kitchen. This was her cue to leave, and she didn't feel she could ignore it. She set her cup carefully on the floor, nodded at Dick, who didn't respond, and then followed Frank to the door.

She tried again. "It must have been someone else," she said. "And if it was someone else, it could be, well . . . " She didn't finish that sentence but added another. "I don't think we can just let it drop like this." Lily hugged the bag with the shoes in it and looked down at the floor. Frank's boots had left prints on the linoleum, which was already thick with mud.

He didn't answer her. Instead, he opened the screen door and held it ajar for her.

Lily walked outside, turned on the stone step and looked at him. "Mr. Bodler," she said. "If you see anything else, will you promise to call me? I can leave you my number."

He let the screen door slam shut and eyed her through it. "Ain't got no phone."

Everybody has a phone, Lily thought. It doesn't matter how poor you are. Everybody's got a telephone.

Frank put his nose close to the screen. "It's Dick," he said in a confidential tone that surprised her. "Don't like 'em, don't like hearin' those faraway voices without no bodies. Even before he lost his hearin', he din't like it." Frank shook his head at Lily. "Said it was like talkin' to a spirit, and what's the sense of aggravatin' him with that? We had one. Sold it to Pete Lund. He collects them old phones, and we got a good price for it. Don't miss it neither. Folks come here or we go there, don't matter."

Lily nodded at him. "I see," she said. "Good-bye, then."

The man did not say good-bye. Neither brother seemed able to punctuate comings and goings in the usual way, and Lily found the absence of these words unnerving. She watched Frank turn, move across the kitchen floor and disappear. Then, instead of walking to her bicycle, she took a right and headed for the woods behind the house.

Lily chose a spot at the foot of a small cliff that followed the creek. The place was deeply familiar to her. As a child, she had roamed up and down Heath Creek, and the landscape had lived inside her ever since. Still, as she stood at the edge of the steep bank overlooking the water, she felt a change. It had been years since she had visited this spot, and it appeared to have shrunk. It took her several seconds before she realized it was she who had grown and that her new height had changed the proportions of everything else. The current of the swollen creek pushed at countless stalks of snake grass that bent over the water. The light through the trees glinted unevenly on the gray water. After she scrambled down the earth wall, she kneeled near the place she had picked out and dug with her hands. The soggy ground loosened easily, and when the hole was finished, she lifted the shoes from her bag, still wrapped in the cloth, and laid them gently inside it. After pressing them firmly into the hole, she pushed the wet dirt over them and fussed for a few minutes with the look of the surface, patting and smoothing until the spot was round and even. She examined her work, then leaned back on the wet ground and closed her eyes. She heard a woodpecker—a distant dull hammering, then a rustle of foliage from above. Lily looked sharply toward the noise, her ears straining to hear more. Leaves moved, a branch snapped. Would Frank have followed me? she thought. She stared at the cliff. It was one thing to get down, another to get up. If someone was there, by the time she crawled to the top, he would be long gone. She stood up, brushed her filthy hands on her shorts, stamped the mud off her sneakers and stared at the spot. Before she left, she found a smooth, oblong stone and put it there to mark the place.

Grabbing roots to steady herself as she dug her toes into the cliff, Lily scrambled to the top. She imagined Dick chasing Martin across the field on his short, stiff legs, and then Martin carrying a young woman in his arms, a woman with long dark hair like her own. There had to be a resemblance for Dick to make that mistake. Once she had scaled the cliff and was standing at the top, she looked beyond the house into the field and asked herself how it was possible that Dick, slow as he was, hadn't managed to catch up with Martin. Martin had been carrying somebody, hadn't he, so how fast could he run? Or maybe Dick had hallucinated the whole thing. Lily walked to her bike and pushed it up to the road. "She's not alive," Lily remembered Martin's words and looked up at the sky. The cool wind blew against her face and then she heard a sound in the grass to her right. A brown rabbit darted past her and she watched him until he disappeared behind a hillock.

Lily rode to Martin's house. She dreaded going, but she felt compelled to see the little house in daylight. Martin and his truck and his house and the map and the pictures all seemed worse in memory than they had when she was there, and now that Dick had told his strange story, she wanted to see the place again. She turned down the dirt road to Martin's house and pedaled up a shallow hill that she had barely noticed when Martin was driving and stopped at its crest. She could see Martin's truck in the driveway, and then Martin himself came running from behind the house, head down, and barreled through the door. Her bicycle bumped on the wet gravel and slid a couple of times as she coasted down the hill to the house.

What will he say when I tell him about Dick? she thought as she walked to the steps. Looking up at the door, Lily saw that it was open. Through the screen door she heard a squeaking noise and then the sound of somebody humming. She walked up the steps and looked into the living room straight at Martin. He was sitting in the rocking chair, which had been moved to the center of the room. The black fabric she had seen the night before was draped over his head as he rocked violently back and forth in the chair. And while he rocked, he hummed. Hectic, low and tuneless, the humming sounded more like an accelerated chant than real music. Lily didn't understand what she was seeing, but she had a powerful sense that Martin's rocking shouldn't be interrupted, that whatever he was doing, he was doing it alone. She saw him push his feet off the floor to make the rocker go fast, heard the excited murmur of his voice and looked at the black cloth swing with his motion. Then she turned around, walked down the steps to the driveway and climbed onto her bicycle. All the way into town, Lily saw Martin rocking in that chair. Why would he do that? Did it mean something? He had run like crazy into the house to rock and hum with his head covered. By the time Lily crossed the city limits, she wished she could keep on riding her bicycle all the way to Florida.

That night Lily watched Mabel and Ed from her window. They were sitting in chairs across from each other in Ed's room and didn't budge from their seats for over an hour. Mabel waved her hands as she talked and Ed sketched. Lily saw his arm move in long, broad strokes, and then she saw him change the motion and shake his wrist. When he finished one drawing, he would rip it out of the large book, throw it to the floor and begin again. While he drew he leaned toward Mabel at the edge of his seat. Once he pushed back a lock of Mabel's hair with his left hand, but Lily wasn't able to see the woman's expression because she was too far away. Several minutes later she watched Mabel cock her head to one side and hold her palms up. The gesture sent a small shock through Lily. She recognized it. They had practiced it together for Hermia when she speaks to Lysander early in the play: "Then let us teach our trial patience, / Because it is our customary cross, / As due to love as thoughts, and dreams, and sighs, / Wishes and Tears, poor Fancy's followers."

After work the next day, Lily found herself standing outside Ed's door. She couldn't keep herself away any longer. She heard Mabel talking, but she shut her ears to the words, knocked and opened the door before either of them answered it. It looked as though neither of them had moved since the night before. It couldn't have been true, but they were sitting where they had been sitting, heads together, with sheets of paper scattered on the floor around them. Lily shut the door behind her.

Ed turned to her. "Lily?" he said. "Where have you been?"

Mabel looked at her, too. Her sincere expression irritated Lily.

Where have I been? she said to herself and answered, "Around."

"We've called you several times," Mabel said.

So it's "we" now, Lily thought, but the fact that they had phoned comforted her.

"I guess I was out." She took several steps toward them. "How's it going?"

"Well," Ed said. "I've been listening to Mabel for two days." He paused, reached out his hand for hers, and Lily gave it to him. He held it tightly in both of his, and looked up at her. "I'm glad you're here," he said.

"Are you?" she asked. Her voice had no irony. She wanted to know.

"Of course I am," he said. The man stroked her hand, and Lily looked into his eyes. She saw nothing guarded in them, but at the same time she didn't know what to look for. She thought about Oscar Hansen on a gurney in Swensen's Funeral Home.

Mabel had turned her eyes away from them, and when Lily looked at her, she saw the woman's shoulders shake for an instant. Then she moved her hand out of Ed's grip and looked down at the drawings. In all of them, Mabel was sitting in the canvas chair, her position only slightly different in each one. Her expression, however, was never the same. One fiercely animated face after another looked up at Lily from the floor. Mabel glared in one, squinted and frowned in another, her lips were parted, her lips were closed, her hands were raised from her elbows or splayed at either side of her face. These were images of the intense, shivering Mabel she knew, and despite the fact that they were still, Lily could almost feel them move.

Lily looked at Mabel. "Don't you get tired of talking? Isn't it hard?"

Mabel laughed. "I'm exhausted. But I've remembered moments in my life I haven't thought about for years." She paused. "It's almost terrifying."

"And fun, I'll bet," Lily said.

Mabel's face changed, and she stared at Lily. She lifted her hands and went suddenly pale. Lily was afraid the woman would faint again and reached out for her, but Mabel waved her off. "Sometimes," she said, "when I look in the mirror, I'm shocked that I don't see that young face anymore, that person I used to be. I know I'm old, near the end of my life, but I'm still surprised."

Lily closed her eyes. She saw Martin rocking with the black cloth over his head and opened her eyes.

"Did you say something?" Mabel said loudly to Ed.

"No . . . " His answer came slowly.

With Ed's "No" still in her ears, Lily heard the door hit the wall and when she looked up, she saw Dolores Wachobski standing in the doorway scowling. She was wearing the same dress she had worn in the portrait—the white one with black polka dots. When nobody spoke, Dolores seemed to grasp the advantage of a surprise entrance, and she waltzed into the room. "Hi, Eddie," she said. "Long time, no see."

Ed stood up and walked toward Dolores. "Not that long," he said.

She's tanked, Lily thought, but Ed didn't look angry or nervous. He reached for his pocket, removed a tin of cigars, opened it and stuck one in his mouth. Lily watched the match burn for a second near the cigar. "How are you?" he said to Dolores.

The woman looked from Mabel to Lily with bleary eyes. She lit a cigarette herself and said, "Anybody want a cigarette? Let's all smoke." She didn't offer her cigarettes, however, or wait for a response. She blew the smoke straight at Ed and smiled. He smiled back, but without hostility. Dolores had been in the room only seconds, and already Lily wanted to smack her. Who the hell does she think she is? Lily said to herself, and stood up. Mabel didn't move.

"I've come to get my last pay," Dolores said and flicked an ash on the floor.

Lily glanced down at the ash and then up at Dolores. She made a face, hoping the woman would see it.

But Dolores was looking at Ed.

"I paid you, remember?" he said.

"I don't think so, sweetie." Dolores stretched her neck, then turned suddenly to Lily and barked, "What you laughin' at, girly?"

Lily knew she hadn't laughed. "He says he paid you."

"You his accountant now?" Dolores let one hip loose and laid her hand on it. Ed moved closer to Dolores, but the woman wobbled toward Lily, placing one high-heeled shoe carefully in front of the other. "I've got some advice for you, honey. I'd stay away from him. He ain't what he seems, all nice and sweet." She shook her head back and forth. One of her ankles buckled for a second, then she straightened it. A flicker of pain passed over her mouth—the first sign of emotion that had shown through the swagger. "Hear?"

Lily smelled the liquor on her breath and moved her head back an inch.

"He ain't for little girls. He's got a rough side, you hear me?"

Lily looked at Ed. His forehead was wrinkling, and she saw him put a hand on the woman's shoulder. "Dolores," he said in a quiet voice. "Go easy."

She whirled around at him and nodded. "Me?"

Lily heard Mabel behind her, but she didn't turn around. Mabel slipped her hand into Lily's, and Lily took it.

"Would you like a loan?" Ed said quietly.

Lily stared at him and then at Dolores. She tried to guess the woman's age. Was she forty yet? The dress showed a lot of cleavage, and the material was thin enough to reveal the roll of flesh around her middle. The skin on her naked arms was white, smooth and only slightly freckled. Dolores adjusted her hip, and the unconscious motion stirred in Lily an awareness of the woman's body as distinct from her voice or clothes. Lily saw Dolores turn toward Ed and put her arms around his neck. Ed's hands moved to the woman's waist, and Lily imagined him pulling the dress down over Dolores's shoulders. Why isn't he embarrassed in front of me? She looked at Ed's face above the back of Dolores's head, but the man didn't meet her eyes.

Dolores was whispering now. "Remember, Eddie, I told you about Jesse James. I seen it again."

Mabel squeezed Lily's hand, and Lily looked at her. Mabel's face looked drawn and tired, but her eyes were sharp.

Lily felt she would have given anything to listen to Mabel's thoughts.

Dolores stood on tiptoe and leaned heavily against Ed, whispering uselessly. Lily could hear every word. "I seen Jesse's ghost with me, Eddie, only it couldn't be me because I was watching, but there was two of me." She took a breath. "And when I saw it I hadn't had a drop. You hear me? I was as clear as a bell and I saw him sitting in the grass outside the cave with the spitting image of me beside him. And Jesse, he was a living ghost, but the ghost of me was dead as a doornail, and I'm telling you now so you don't forget that I've had a sign. My life's coming to an end."

She pulled away from Ed, straightened the front of her dress and narrowed her eyes in an expression that seemed both shrewd and distant. "And then," she said, "I heard music playing right out of the sky." Dolores moved her head to one side. "What d'ya think of that, Eddie boy?" She took in Mabel and Lily at a glance and spat out the words "Music from heaven!"

She paused a moment, as though waiting for her words to sink in, then swivelled on her heels and walked to the open door, her big black purse swinging from her hand. Ed followed her, and the two of them stopped in the hallway. Lily watched Ed reach into his back pocket, take out his wallet and hand Dolores several bills. Lily couldn't tell how much money he gave her, but Dolores took it with a smile and brought the purse close to her face. After fumbling with the clasp, she opened the bag and dropped the crumpled paper money inside.

Lily had heard Ed's offer of a loan to Dolores as proof of his kindness, but when the actual bills appeared, they sickened her. More than seeing the man's hands around the woman's waist, the sight of those bills gave Lily a feeling that not only was there intimacy between them, there was some kind of arrangement. He could easily have walked Dolores down the hall. Giving her money would have been a secret then, but he chose not to hide it, and Lily found his openness inscrutable.

She listened to the clatter of Dolores's high heels in the hallway, heard the sound recede and then vanish. The carpet on the stairs must have muffled their noise.

Mabel excused herself, saying she was "worn to the bone," and left them. Before Lily could say a single word, Ed lunged at her, lifted her off the ground, carried her to the little kitchen table and laid her down on it. Then he bent over her and started kissing her neck. She had a hundred questions for Ed about Dolores, but she didn't ask them, not then. I've been taken by storm, she thought to herself as she looked up at him. She liked the sound of it: "by storm." It seemed to suggest that Ed was her own violent weather.

By the time Lily walked into the Arts Guild, the place was both crowded and noisy. She stared at the cardboard trees with tissue paper foliage strung along their branches and at Debbie Larsen and Genevieve Knecht, whose arms were flapping as they pretended to fly across the stage. She heard the quartet tuning and the cast chattering and suddenly wanted to close her eyes and press her hands to her ears to shut it out. How can anybody get into character with all this racket? she said to herself and sat down on a folding chair to wait for Mrs. Wright to call the cast to order. Lily looked down at her hands. Her blisters had turned into tough bits of red skin. She rubbed them, and then, out of the corner of her eye, saw Bottom's Ass head emerge from behind the curtain—now painted, with tufts of hair for a forelock and scruffy mane. She looked up and saw Martin holding the head in front of him, his face quiet, a white bandage wrapped around his left hand. Loud "hee-haws" came from the stage, and Lily watched Ronald Lovold dart from behind Martin and grin at the head.

That evening the play showed improvement, and Lily began to think it might not be an embarrassment after all. Even Denise was less flat. The new sets and props excited the cast to better performances, and Lily, too, was glad for the painted backdrops, fake trees and artificial moonlight, but when she moved and spoke, she forgot the scenery. She didn't hear or see Mabel anymore when she played Hermia. Mabel's coaching had moved inside Lily, and with each rehearsal Hermia changed, her character gained tightness and shape. In the end, the Athenian girl was a tough little broad, and that's how Lily played her.

It might have been neater if what was outside the Arts Guild would stay out and what was inside would stay in, but that's not how it worked. When Lily spoke to Lysander, she looked into Jim's face and gave him the feeling she had for Ed, and Jim responded with an expressiveness she hadn't seen in him before. And when she watched Cobweb tiptoe around Bottom, she perceived an ominous presence in Martin's fairy that made him better than the others. He never abandoned character. Even when the little fairies snickered at the ridiculous head on Oren's shoulders, Cobweb's white face never faltered from its distant, nearly unconscious expression. Several times during rehearsal, Lily felt Martin staring at her, felt his eyes on her neck or back, and when she turned around he was always there to meet her glance, and Lily wondered if scientists had discovered how it is that you can actually feel someone's eyes on your body. She worried about his hand. How had he hurt it? She wished she could remember what his hands had looked like in the rocking chair, but she didn't have any memory of them.

After rehearsal she put her hand on his shoulder and said, "Martin." She spoke in a low voice she instantly regretted because it sounded confidential, but he turned, looked at her and smiled. His eager expression felt like a trap. "I have to talk to you," she said and corrected her tone.

Martin didn't speak, but he took Lily's hand. She let him do it, but she found the bandage rubbing against her palm unpleasant. As they walked through the door, Martin gripped her harder. She couldn't understand why he would do this with an injury. She moved her fingers to signal that she wanted him to release her, but Martin only squeezed more tightly. "Your hand," Lily said. "It's hurting me."

Martin let go, but he didn't say anything. They seated themselves on the steps, and Lily spoke to the street rather than to Martin, explaining to him what Dick had told her. "You don't think," Lily said finally, "that Dick made it up, do you?"

"Dick doesn't lie," Martin said.

"Well, I mean that he imagined it?"

"No."

Lily turned to him. "You mean you were really carrying somebody across their field the day before yesterday?"

Martin's mouth twitched once. "Y-yes."

Lily hadn't expected this response. She hesitated, then said, "Who was it?"

Martin turned his face toward hers. He didn't stutter. "You," he said. "It was you."

Lily studied his face to see if he was joking. She opened

157

her mouth, closed it, and then said, "That's not funny, Martin."

He looked at her with blank eyes.

"I wasn't there. You know that. Who was it? Dick was, well." Lily sighed. "I think he was scared that, that the girl, was hurt, or . . . " Lily finally said it, "dead."

Martin shook his head. "Th-there are lots of things w-we don't understand, Lily."

Lily gestured with her hands. "That's bonkers, Martin. I sure as hell know where I am from one minute to the next. I sure as hell know I wasn't with you in some alfalfa field outside the Bodlers'."

Martin stared at her without blinking.

"Why are you doing this?" Lily asked him in an urgent whisper. "What good will this do?"

Martin shook his head violently, then looked down at his knees.

Lily grabbed Martin's shoulder. "Martin, if Dick saw you, then he didn't see me."

Martin didn't answer. His face looked stony.

Martin turned his head away from Lily. He stuttered something Lily couldn't hear.

"What?" she asked loudly. Then she heard people behind her talking near the door.

Martin's shoulders were shaking. He gasped. "Ma-mama," he stuttered.

Lily reached out for him. "Jesus, Martin," she said in a whisper. "What is it?"

"Everything okay?" Mrs. Wright said from the door.

Lily didn't answer.

Martin stood up with his back to Lily. His head was lowered and his back rounded as though someone had hit him in the stomach. He grunted and Lily thought she saw saliva hit the sidewalk. Someone ran down the steps behind her. It was Mrs. Baker. She put her arm around Martin, and Lily watched him quake under the steadying arm. "Ma-ma-ma-ma," he sputtered.

Mrs. Baker held Martin but turned to Lily. "What happened?"

"I don't know. We, we were just talking," Lily said. She stood up. She rubbed her face hard and shook her head. "God," she said and walked over to Martin, who was leaning on Mrs. Baker now, his head still down. "Do you want me to go, Martin?" she said and then looked up at the doorway. A dozen people stared down at her. She turned back to Mrs. Baker.

"Maybe that's best," the woman said.

Lily took a last look at Martin, who remained hunched but had stopped trying to speak. He was puffing hard and then Lily saw him bring his hands to his face and cover it. The streetlamp illuminated Martin's left hand, and she saw clearly the wrinkled Band-Aids and piece of gauze that had been wrapped around his palm. But these only partially concealed numerous long, sharp cuts that ran in all directions between his knuckles and the top of his hand.

Lily hurried away from the Arts Guild, across the railroad tracks. She paused once to turn around and look at the group of people gathered around Martin under the streetlamp and wondered what he was saying, if anything. Her knees shook as she walked. Lily looked up at the moon and thought, How the hell did all this happen? It's like I'm involved with him now, like we're in something together. "It was you." A mysterious leaden guilt settled in Lily's chest. What have I done? she thought and watched her white sneakers move forward on the pavement. She heard someone walking toward her and looked up.

A tall man wearing a cowboy hat and a gun belt came striding toward her, and for a moment Lily thought she was seeing things. Like a gunslinger in an old Western, the dark figure approached, his hands held inches from the guns on his hips, and Lily guessed it was Dolores's ghost, or maybe Tex. The man came closer and Lily recognized Hank. He said her name.

"Hank, what are you doing in that getup?"

"I'm Charlie Younger in the reenactment, remember? Rolf gave me the costume at the meeting. There's more to it, but I'm on my way to the station, and I thought the guys would get a kick out of my six-shooters."

Lily looked at the pavement. "You didn't tell me about it."

"They thought Allan Fisk was going to do it, but he punked out."

"Oh." She looked at his hips. "Are the guns real?"

"Of course not."

"They look real," she said.

A train whistle sounded loudly behind them, and Lily heard the guardrail fall across the tracks. Hank's black sneakers were only inches from her own.

"I miss you," Hank said.

Lily studied the loose rubber at the front of her shoe. Why don't I miss him? she thought.

"Don't you have anything to say?" he said.

"Not really." Lily rubbed a mosquito bite on the back of her leg with her sneaker. She could feel Hank's anger, but she didn't know what to do about it. Martin's fit had exhausted her. She hung her head and looked down. The fact is, she thought, I'm really stupid with Hank. I'm not so stupid with other people.

Hank waved the back of his hands at her in frustration. "If you think," he said loudly, "that that guy's going to stick around here for you, you're dead wrong."

"Oh, Hank," Lily said.

"You know I'm right. What is he, fifteen years older than you? For Christ's sake, Lily, you're making a fool of yourself. He's not even divorced. Everybody in town knows he's going to leave you high and dry. He's got women coming out of his ears, for Christ's sake. He's a fucking Don Juan. You're no different from all the others." Hank rubbed his forehead hard. "Not to him."

Lily raised her eyes. "I don't care." Her intonation was even, stubborn.

"You don't care!"

"No."

Hank moved toward her. He bent down and looked in her face. "Who are you?" he shouted. "What are you?"

Lily clenched her jaw shut. She kept her chin down and her mouth shut. Behind Hank she could see the grain elevator in the moonlight.

"Answer me!" His voice broke.

Lily bit her lip. "How can I answer that?" she said. She felt tears in her eyes all of a sudden, and she lifted her face to keep them from running down her cheeks.

Hank held out his arms. "Oh, Lil'," he said and leaned toward her.

She put her arms around him tentatively. She remembered

his smell and his shirt—the one that said "Minnesota Twins" on the back. She stood on tiptoe and whispered to him, "I'm sorry, Hank. I can't. I just can't."

Lily pulled away from him and ran across the bridge and then past the Red Owl Grocery. She was still running when she reached Division Street. She slowed to a walk when she saw Rick's and glanced at two men standing a few feet away outside the Corner Bar. One of them was wearing gray coveralls from Olaf's Garage, and as she approached them she read the name tag sewn on his pocket: "Steve." Lily noticed that his arms were too long for his short body, that he needed a shave and that he had clearly noticed her. When she walked past them, "Steve" started making panting noises, and in her peripheral vision she saw him throwing his hips back and forth. He smirked. For once Lily decided not to ignore the insult. She whirled around and started screaming, "What is it? I'd really like to know. What the hell is it that makes a shrunken little weasel like you think he's some big stud, huh?"

Steve glared at Lily. She could see he was searching for a retort while making an effort to hold on to his leer. Then his friend started laughing, and Lily saw Steve's expression change to uncertainty. Laughter followed her down the block, and she heard Steve say, "What's her problem?" She walked slowly, conscious that their eyes were following her, and she made certain her posture was erect, her gait dignified. When she reached the alley beside the Ideal Cafe, Lily turned, seated herself on the ground beside one of the large garbage cans and cried.

It took her a long time to fall asleep that night. Mabel was typing in the next room. There was no light in Ed's window, and although she knew he might be lying on his bed at that very minute, exhausted from hours of work, she also knew he might have gone out, and Lily wished she could wave her hand or mutter an incantation and look in on him wherever he was. Instead, she played her tape of *Don Giovanni* softly so Mabel wouldn't hear. She remembered Dolores's ankle buckling in Ed's room, and it made her think of Mabel's shaking hands and of Martin's stutter, that word he had started but never finished outside the Arts Guild. She felt unsteady herself. Everybody's quivering, she thought. Everybody except Ed. She remembered his hand on Dolores's hip. And as Lily pictured his quiet face and deliberate movements in her mind, she realized that the calm in him was also something hard and stubborn, that Ed was like a man who, finding himself in a terrible storm on the road, refuses to turn back and instead plants his feet on the ground, leans into the wind and keeps on walking.

Noises from the street, Mabel's typing, and half-conscious thoughts accompanied her first two hours in bed when she was neither really awake nor really asleep. Moonlight shone too brightly on her eyelids through her thin curtains, and lilliputian voices chattered lines from the play. Her pillow was too hot. She fluffed and patted and turned it over again and again. Just before she felt herself finally dropping into sleep, she heard Howie Bickle's voice in her head. Howie was Starveling in the play and Moonshine in the play within the play. A slow talker from a farm west of town, he dragged out every vowel: "This lantern doth the horned moon present." Then, after what seemed to be only minutes of sleep, she heard the alarm ring and sat up in bed. Moonlight was still shining through the window, which didn't make sense, but Lily stood up, walked toward two rectangles of light that illuminated the floor and saw a young woman lying there with her eyes closed. Lily bent over to examine her. "So you're here," she said. The woman didn't answer, but Lily didn't expect an answer. She looked down at the body and noticed a long piece of white fabric wrapped tightly around her hips, her shoulders and breasts. The fabric puzzled Lily. Why was her stomach bare? Lily looked at the girl's navel with interest, and while she looked, a word suddenly came to her that solved the problem of the young woman: "bellclose." The word elated her. I know, she said to herself. I know. But then as quickly as it had come, the feeling left her, and she thought, She can't be here. I've got to get her out. Lily bent down to lift the young woman off the floor, but the body that looked as soft and white as dough wouldn't budge, and after tugging hard, she discovered that the young woman's hands had been attached to the floor with screws. Lily panicked, and in her panic she began to suspect she was dreaming and tried to fight her way out of the dream and away from the moonlight shining on those bloodless palms screwed to the floor, but telling herself to wake up had no immediate effect. She was drowning in the dream and struggled toward its surface, flailing and kicking her way up and out as she told herself to wake up. With her hands above her head, she pressed against something soft and wet, bursting through it to find herself awake and lying in her bed. The moonlight had disappeared. Nobody was on the floor. Had the nightmare taken place outside her room, Lily might have found comfort in waking to those four walls, but the distance between dreaming and waking had been too close. She sat up in bed and tried to recover the word in the dream that had made her so happy. She felt herself reaching back for it, finding it not in her head, but in her mouth. She had said it in the dream: "bellclose." It's nonsense, she said to herself. Mabel wasn't typing anymore, and in the silence of her room, Lily tried to stay awake, but couldn't. She slept again, dreamed again, and found the young woman on the floor again. I'm dreaming, she said to herself. I have to wake up, and Lily woke in her room and looked out and saw the moonlight shining down on the young woman's body. And so it went all night. Time after time, she told herself to wake up, and she did, but sometimes she woke from a dream inside the dream and found the body again. After a while the police came into the dream and Hank with them. They broke through the floor, poked their feet through the ceiling and crawled in from the window. They pounded at her door in a rhythm as steady and relentless as a drum machine.

At work the next day, Lily's arms and legs felt weak. The caffeine from the five cups of coffee she had drunk to clear her head raced through her body, and she felt suddenly aware of her nerves, which seemed to be vibrating just beneath her skin. Vince was unusually quiet that day, but Boomer yattered on about Graceland and Elvis sightings every time she came into the kitchen. At about nine o'clock she was standing across from Vince, staring at two sunny-side-up eggs for Russell Malecha, when Boomer started waving the doughnut he was holding in her face and said to her in a falsetto voice, "Earth to Lily, Earth to Lily."

"What is it, Boom?"

"Heard you're already two-timin' yer new boyfriend."

Lily picked up the plate of eggs and started for the door. "Where'd you hear that rot?"

Boomer shoved the doughnut into his mouth. Powdered sugar stuck to his lips as he widened his eyes behind his lenses.

"Heard it from a kid who don't lie. Said he saw you at the quarry, stark naked." Boomer chewed. "With some cowboy."

Lily's back was pressed against the swinging door and she stopped. "Cowboy? What the hell are you talking about?"

"Said you was lyin' on his lap, sleepin' or sunbathin' or somethin'." Boomer opened his mouth and grinned, revealing half-chewed doughnut coated with saliva bubbles.

"Shut your mouth, Boom." Lily heard her voice rise. "Whoever you talked to is cracked. You hear me? Cracked. I haven't even been to the quarry this year, and as for cowboys—what the hell is a cowboy? This town doesn't have cowboys, not real ones, anyway. This is complete shit."

Vince stared at Lily, his eyes small, and Boomer went on chewing the doughnut with a surprised look on his face.

Jiggling a frying pan of sausages, Vince said, "You feeling all right? Wrong time of month?"

"No, Vince, it's not the wrong time of the month. How'd you like it if people were talking that kind of crap about you?"

"Are you kidding? I'd love to be known as the guy hanging around the quarry with naked broads."

"It's not the same," Lily said, and pushed her shoulder into the door behind her. She looked again at the two perfect yellow yolks on the plate and felt suddenly light-headed. "It was you." That's what he had said. The cafe looked new to her when she turned around, and for a moment the red booth where Martin usually sat undulated in the sunshine that came through the window, and Lily thought, I'm dizzy again. I have to sit down. She moved the plate into her right hand and reached for the counter with her left. I'm so tired, she thought as an explanation. She took a couple of breaths, delivered the eggs, and when she turned away from Russell, a fragment of the dream came back to her—the white material that bound the woman's breasts and marked her flesh with a deep red line like a cut.

A week earlier Boomer's story wouldn't have touched Lily, and she knew it. It was listening to Boomer after she had listened to Dick, Dolores and Martin that had unnerved her. The stories didn't match, but they overlapped, and the similarities among them were making her skittish. Either there was a virus on the march in Webster that caused hallucinations or everybody was seeing the same thing and thinking it was something else. When Lily stood in the cafe and watched Bert making lively conversation with Emily Legvold, who had recently left the Moonies and looked like herself again, Lily decided the visions weren't imaginary. There were too many. Then through the window she saw Mrs. Pointer walking with a group of kids from the Elizabeth Barker School. The children shuffled along in twos and held hands. A chubby boy, who looked about sixteen, broke away from his partner. Turning to the cafe window, he scrunched up his face and then did a little dance for the people inside. He had the distinctive features of Down's syndrome—small eyes and a flat nose. The silly joy in his face as he wiggled his hips and threw his head back jolted Lily from her meditation, and she laughed. He saw her and bowed. Lily watched the kids laugh and clap. Mrs. Pointer walked calmly through the line and stopped beside him. She took him by both shoulders and started to rub the boy. His face looked frenzied now, and his tongue darted in and out of his mouth. Mrs. Pointer continued to rub his shoulders with strong strokes, and the boy's expression grew calmer. Then, taking his hand in hers, she drew it toward his partner's—a girl with two short braids that stuck out on either side of her head—and folded their hands together with a little shake that seemed to mean they shouldn't let go. She walked back to the head of her class and signaled for them to continue walking, which they did, and soon every child had passed out of view.

Lily saw Bert move away from the cash register holding a copy of the *Webster Chronicle*. "Have you read the police log, Lil'?"

Lily shook her head. She surveyed the tables to check on her customers. Everybody looked okay. Bert stuck the paper under Lily's nose and she took it.

"Get a load of the headline," Bert said.

Lily looked down at the police log on the Records page of the paper. The wits at the *Chronicle* had given that week's log the headline "Squealer Apprehended on Division Street."

"Down here." Bert's finger pointed to the entry for Tuesday, June 11.

Lily looked down at the paper. The print seemed out of focus. She had to concentrate on the letters to read.

"Police made a traffic stop.... A fight was reported in Viking Terrace.... A black bag containing insulin equipment was found on Bridge Square.... A man on Albers Avenue reported noises in his basement. Officers discovered a gopher in a window well.... A woman on Dundas Street heard people talking outside her window. Police were unable to locate conversationalists.... A complaint of loud music at the Violetta Trailer Park was received. Officers asked residents to turn it down.... A pig was reported loose on South Division Street. Officers rounded up the critter and returned it to its owner.... A man carrying an injured woman was reported on Highway 19 at the city limits. Police checked the area but found no one."

Lily stared at the last entry. Then she looked up at Bert.

Bert looked puzzled. "All right, it's not that funny, I admit it."

Lily stared at the log again.

"Lil', hon, you okay?"

Lily looked into Bert's brown eyes. "Something's going on, Bert." She turned to the window. "I don't know exactly what, but I think somebody's hurt or even dead. She has dark hair. That's all I know." Lily walked toward the window and looked at the inverted neon letters that read "IDEAL CAFE" from the outside, and she felt Bert's fingers brush her shoulder behind her. At her friend's touch, Lily felt suddenly pained.

"What are you talking about? Did you see something?" Bert said.

Lily moved her neck and looked at Bert. "I haven't seen anything," she said.

"It's Shapiro," Bert said. "He's not good for you."

Lily made a face. "What does he have to do with it? It's not him."

Bert stared at her, her lips slightly parted. Then she said, "What's going on?"

Lily rustled the newspaper in her right hand. She waved it at Bert. "I'm not sure."

When Lily wandered into the street after her shift and looked up at the Stuart Hotel for some sign of Ed, she regretted not explaining more carefully what she had meant to Bert. So many strange things happened in the world. All her life she had heard the most unlikely stories that were true. Hadn't Mrs. Knutsen and Mr. Walacek dropped dead on the same day in houses right next door to each other on Elm Street? How often did that happen? Hadn't Ernie

Applebaum disappeared four years ago without a trace until he turned up last year with the carny people running the Shake 'Em Up ride for Jesse James Days, tattooed from head to toe? And hadn't June Putkey attacked her mother with a knife in their kitchen on a Sunday afternoon? Had a single person in town known that June (who was known to Lily chiefly for the stickers she plastered all over her purse) had it in her to do such a thing? She snapped, Lily thought. But what had made her snap? Had she really hated her mother, or had she just hated her then? Lily imagined a knife in the girl's hand and blood in a sink with dirty dishes. And then, Lily thought, there are people who don't feel anything, people who can do anything, anything at all, like that man in Chicago. Martin had an article about him on his wall. Lily remembered that Gasey had been a clown at children's birthday parties. Nobody had been able to see what was inside him. But Martin, Lily thought, Martin isn't like that. And yet when she remembered Martin rocking in that chair as hard and fast as it would go, she wasn't so sure anymore. Through the glass door of the hotel, she noticed Stanley walking up the stairs with a mop and pail. Just after his feet disappeared, she thought, Martin's up to something. I can feel it.

When Lily walked through Ed's door the next day, Mabel was sitting in front of the window only a few feet away from Ed's canvas. The figure in the painting was the same size as Mabel herself. Lily looked at the splotches of color and the soft contours of the woman's body, which were still unfinished. Ed hadn't flattered Mabel, hadn't turned her into some- one younger or prettier. The woman in the painting was Mabel as Lily knew her, and yet this two-dimensional Mabel had a quality about her that Lily didn't understand. Standing in front of the picture, Lily felt that Mabel was talking directly to her. The woman leaned forward, holding her thin white hands at either side of her face. Her eyes were narrowed as if to focus better and her mouth was open. He got her, Lily thought—that hot-wired look. But still something in the picture bothered her. She could feel it, and she must have been seeing it, but she couldn't say what it was. Lily moved very close to the portrait. She sensed that both Ed and Mabel were waiting for her response and that she should have one ready, but she didn't want to speak before she knew what she was going to say. Then she stepped back three or four feet to examine the painting again. The painting was making her uneasy. It's her face, Lily thought. She looks wild, almost batty, and then Lily realized that she was looking at someone who was desperately happy, so happy that her expression could easily be mistaken for something else: craziness, pain, even fear. She's so happy, Lily said to herself, because she's talking to him. And although Lily had always understood that Mabel was lonely, she had never seen it so naked. "What do you think?" Ed said.

Lily nodded. "It's the best one," she said in a flat voice.

She glanced at Mabel, who looked very calm next to the canvas. "But," she said, "it's a little scary, too, because," she stammered, "it's so personal." Lily wiped sweat from her upper lip. Her stomach gurgled. Maybe I'm coming down with something, she thought. Looking from Ed to Mabel, she sensed that between them they had made something she couldn't touch. Not the painting. The painting had come out of it, but that wasn't what she meant. Lily stepped away from the canvas and turned to Mabel.

"There are lots of things I don't know about," she said.

"Like painting, but I can tell that Ed painted you as you really are, and I know that takes a lot of talent. You must have told him all about yourself for it to work." She paused and lowered her voice. "Maybe you even told him things you never told anybody before." She looked at Ed. "But I wonder if he told you about him. I mean the stuff that really matters." Lily took a deep breath. "All day long you sit here and listen to people telling you their most private thoughts—Tex and Dolores and Stanley and now Mabel. They're telling you about their parents and their sweethearts, and even about their secret fantasies, and you take it all in like a big sponge—in the name of art." Lily heard her voice go shrill on the last word. She tried to calm herself. "You've told me about yourself, but it's nothing compared to what these people have been telling you. I don't even know who your mother was." Lily pointed toward the open door. "Right through there, I saw you giving Dolores money like she's your oldest friend in the world, but you don't tell me beans about it. And everybody in town's jabbering about all the girls you've had, a goddamned assembly line of tits and ass, and from you, nothing." Lily's jaw shook. She hadn't known she was this upset. Her own words were egging her on. "And then I hear you were over at Swensen's digging up corpses to draw. Did you mention that to me? No sirree! And"—she stopped and looked at them— "just for the record, I'd like to know where the hell I fit in? The two of you are so tight these days, there's no goddamned room for anybody else!" Lily looked at the two surprised faces. She waited, but neither one of them said anything.

Lily nodded at Ed. Mabel looked white.

After several seconds, Ed started talking. His voice didn't sound agitated, but his forehead wrinkled, and Lily was glad to see some sign of distress in his face. "I know that I'm stubborn about my work," he said, "and I know that while I'm doing it, it's sometimes hard for me to think about anything else. I feel responsible for the people I paint, because the portraits are not just about borrowing somebody's body for a while. That's why I gave Dolores money. I'm not done with her, just because I'm finished painting her. Do you understand?"

Lily saw that Ed was looking for words.

"And I don't pry," he said. "Whatever people tell me, they tell me freely. I'm not picking at people's souls for ugly secrets . . . " He sighed and rubbed his face. "And as for this red-hot lover business, I honestly don't know what it's all about. It's been overblown to such a degree that I don't even recognize myself." He paused and examined Lily as if he were trying to remember something. He smiled. "I guess I was stupid to think that I could slide in and out of the funeral home without causing a stir. For years, I've been thinking of doing a series of paintings called 'The Dead.' I've always had something very quiet in mind, not sensational or ghoulish— no murder victims or anything like that." He took a breath. "As for Mr. Hansen, the funeral's tomorrow, and I missed my chance. I did a sketch from memory, but it's not enough. It's too bad because I liked his face."

Mabel was watching Ed very closely, and Lily could see signs of strain around her mouth.

Ed continued to look at Lily. "As for you, I can't see that my painting interferes in any way with my feelings for you." He looked down at his hands, turned them over and flexed his fingers. "Being with you has made me very happy."

Lily knew Ed wasn't lying, knew that he believed every-thing he had said, and yet she felt cheated by his answers. It all made sense, and yet there was something wrong with it. She didn't know why his painting of Mabel changed what was between him and her, but it did. She just couldn't explain it. She didn't know whether Ed's logic was false or whether logic didn't work in trying to answer what she had said. It was like pointing at a squashed gopher on the road and having it explained to her with an algebraic formula.

After that, the three of them hardly talked for about an hour. Mabel sat in her chair, and Lily found a place on the floor. Ed went back to the portrait, and Lily watched him. Sometimes he closed his eyes as though he were looking at a picture of Mabel inside himself. He paced, and Lily listened to his steps, back and forth, back and forth. Mabel watched Ed intently, and Lily felt sorry for her. She's so happy to be near him, Lily thought. He painted her happiness, but he doesn't see it. With the real person, he's blind.

When Ed asked Mabel to talk to him again, he didn't ask Lily to leave, and neither did Mabel. Their conspicuous inclusion of her didn't comfort her much, however. She might be allowed to overhear Mabel's monologue, but her speech was meant for Ed and nobody else.

"I met Evan only days after my twenty-sixth birthday in a bookstore. I loved him right away. After three days we were married, and we stayed together until he died—fifteen years. And that was short. We had no children. The doctors couldn't find anything wrong with me. Of course that was a long time ago. It might have been Evan. We never knew." Mabel paused. "But it's funny what you think about later, what you remember . . . " Mabel wasn't looking at Ed or at Lily, but out into the room. "I remember how he changed with the seasons, his body, I mean, how he looked in different lights—summer and winter. You know, there's a time when you feel the seasons moving—when fall becomes winter or winter becomes spring—that ambiguous threshold. He was lit differently, and he smelled different, and I"—Mabel rubbed her hands and looked at the ceiling—"I loved that change, but I also loved remembering that he had been like that before—last winter or last spring. . . . I've often thought about my marriage in terms of seasonal light." Mabel cocked her head near her shoulder and smiled shyly. Like a girl, Lily thought.

After a silence, Mabel said, "The grief was terrible, but it was ordinary, if I can use that word. It wasn't anybody's fault that Evan died. People die. They die suddenly like Evan or slowly like my father, and I wasn't so stupid as to ask, 'Why Evan? Why the person I loved most in the world?' Why not, after all? It's when you've made your own grief, when you're guilty, that it can't be borne."

Lily stared at Mabel's rigid posture. What Mabel had said about guilt aggravated Lily's own dread, not of Martin, she realized, but of herself. She heard Ed speak and Mabel answer him, but she didn't listen to the content of their conversation. Ed moved toward the canvas. He looked at it, his eyes half closed, and spoke to Mabel. "It's yours as much as mine. In about a week, I'll want to know what the story is."

Mabel nodded. Her head seemed very small and her lips pale.

The rest of the afternoon passed slowly. Lily lay on the floor with a pillow while Ed painted, and Mabel sat quietly in her chair. Lily took out a copy of the *Star* that was in her bag and began to leaf through it. She had bought it because it had a picture of Marilyn on the cover. But when she turned to the article inside, she saw it wasn't about Marilyn at all, but a housewife in Normal, Illinois, who was gradually turning into Marilyn Monroe. Although it was written in the third person, the article was called "The Spirit of Marilyn Monroe Is Taking Over My Body." A series of six photographs accompanied the article, showing the slow transformation of Angela Hokenburg, a brown-haired, long-nosed person, into the radiant, platinum Marilyn. Lily studied the pictures. The story was trash, but it made Lily think of the photos she had seen of Norma Jean on a beach somewhere with her brown hair and unplucked eyebrows. They turned her into Marilyn Monroe, too, Lily thought.

She didn't know she had slept until she woke to the feeling of fingers moving across her forehead. Half awake, she thought it was her mother, and she began to say "Mom," but didn't finish the word. She heard Ed's voice saying, "Don't do anything crazy. Just stay where you are."

Lily opened her eyes and saw Mabel withdraw her hand quickly. She was lying on Ed's bed, and outside it was night. Lily looked at Mabel. "What's going on?"

Mabel looked tired, and her disheveled hair fell around her face. "You didn't have rehearsal, so we let you sleep. Ed carried you to the bed. You didn't stir."

Lily sat up. "Who's on the phone?"

"Dolores Wachobski, I believe," Mabel said, raising her eyebrows and twisting her mouth to one side. "She seems to be having some kind of emergency."

Lily looked at Ed. He had hung up the telephone and was standing. He rubbed his mouth.

Lily said, "What does she want?"

"She's had a bad scare, more ghosts and *mishegoss*."

Lily puzzled over his last word but didn't ask him about it. "You're going over there?"

Ed walked toward her. "There's no one else, Lily." He reached into his pocket, feeling for car keys, and she heard them jingle.

"I'm going with you," Lily said.

Ed looked at her. "I honestly don't know what to expect. She's plastered and raving."

"I don't care," Lily said.

"I don't care either," Mabel said.

Ed drove to the trailer park, which lay on the riverbank across from the Dairy Queen with its huge illuminated ice-cream cone. Through her open window, Lily smelled the water and felt the station wagon rock on uneven ground. A turquoise trailer shone for a moment in the headlights before it disappeared with the dying sound of the motor.

Ed pounded on the door of Dolores's trailer, and when no one answered, he walked inside. The long room Lily saw from behind Ed wasn't at all what she had expected. In the first place, it was very clean. In the second place, it was fussy. There were knicknacks everywhere: carefully arranged porcelain children, angels, dogs, cats and horses, a large blue-and-white Madonna with child, a big bowl of cat's-eye marbles, and a number of objects with little sayings or slogans on them: a small stuffed Cupid held up a sign with the word "LUV" on it. "B.S. ARTIST" was written on a miniature license plate that hung over the sink. "Woman of Power" had been stitched into a needlepoint pillow that lay on Dolores's carefully made bed, and as Ed headed toward the bathroom to check it, Lily noticed yet another sign—a wooden heart with the words "Little Girl's Room" carved into it.

Just before they left the trailer to search outside, Lily

noticed a photograph propped on the dresser. She could feel Ed's anxiety and saw that Mabel had already gone outside, so she glanced at it for only a moment, but the little girl in the picture, dressed in a fluffy white confirmation dress, was obviously Dolores, and the slender woman beside her had to be her mother. As she headed for the door behind Ed, Lily understood that she had not deduced the identity of Dolores's mother, but had recognized her, not from life, but from Ed's cartoon figure in the narrative boxes above Dolores's painted head.

They each took a different direction. Lily walked toward the river, trudging between rows of trailers as she listened to a disc jockey drawl out the name of a song. Lily felt the gravel road end, heard the music stop abruptly and waded into the tall grass near the riverbank. Ed was calling Dolores's name, but Lily couldn't bring herself to open her mouth. A mosquito whined in her ear and she swatted it blindly. The trees and the water ahead darkened suddenly and, looking up, she saw a cloud drift across the moon. The grass made her legs itch, and she bent down to give them a good scratch before she tromped forward and felt a hard object roll under her sneaker. Lily squatted in the grass, reached out for the thing and felt the cool, round glass of a bottle in her hand. Liquid sloshed inside it, and when she raised it to her nose, it smelled of whiskey. As she crouched in the grass holding the half-empty bottle, the moon came out from behind the cloud and lit the tops of the trees along the river. Through them she could see the shine of river water, and then, only feet away to her right, a white hand was curled in a loose fist. She crawled toward it. Dolores was lying sprawled out on the flattened grass, face up. She's breathing, Lily thought, looking at the woman's huge breasts move up and down. "Vomit, piss and booze," Lily thought and held her breath against the stench. The woman's skirt was hiked up around her waist, and her pale flesh glowed through a big rip in her stocking. Lily leaned over Dolores and whispered, "Get up!" But Dolores didn't move. Taking the woman by the shoulders, Lily started to shake her. She shook gently at first, waiting for a response, but the woman's head seemed as heavy as a bowling ball. Lily shook harder. "Wake up!" she whispered. Nothing happened, and looking down at Dolores's unconscious face, Lily felt a surge of irritation. She shook Dolores violently. The woman's head thumped against the ground as Lily threw here entire strength into shaking her, and that was when she realized she was enjoying it, that this shaking had an energy, a life all its own, and that it felt so good she didn't want to stop, and she shook more. Dolores opened one eye, and Lily saw a glimmer of liquid white. The woman's mouth parted and her lower lip drooped. Lily let go of Dolores's shoulders, but the flabby, stupid expression on the woman's face hadn't gone away. She looked at the hole in the black stocking and slapped it. When Lily withdrew her hand, her palm was stinging, but she lifted her arm to do it again. At the same moment she heard Dolores groan, and the sound startled her. She hadn't expected her to wake up at all. But that's what was happening. Dolores had raised herself up on one elbow and was staring at Lily through eyes that looked like illuminated slits in the night.

Lily started to shout for Ed and Mabel. She called out their names until her voice was hoarse, and even after they answered her, she kept yelling their names over and over again, as if she was the one who needed to be saved. Tears ran down her cheeks, but she wiped them away when she saw Ed racing toward her. He puffed hard as he knelt over Dolores, who raised herself to a sitting position, threw her arms around him and began blubbering words Lily couldn't understand.

Not until Dolores was lying on her bed did Lily see how sick she looked. Her skin was flat white, her eyes red, and the flesh around them a curious shade of violet. Running makeup had turned her cheeks black and green, and partly digested food littered her naked chest and the front of her blouse.

Mabel was the one who wiped Dolores's face with wet paper towels, who cleaned her chest and arms, who removed her filthy clothes and ruined stockings and managed to get her under the sheets. Throughout her cleanup, Dolores moaned the word "No." She tossed back and forth on the bed, her movements so meaningless that it took Lily a while to understand that the woman wanted to sit up. Finally, she managed to raise her body by herself and yelled at them, "Look at me! Am I cut?" Her head flopped forward. "Am I cut?" Then she started to cry, and Lily found the crying much worse than the moaning or shouting.

Mabel crawled onto the bed and grabbed hold of Dolores's shoulders. She looked very small and thin beside Dolores, but her decisive movements compensated for her weakness. She pushed Dolores back down on the bed, grasped the woman's flailing hands and held them tightly. "You're not cut," she said. "Do you hear me? You're not cut."

Dolores stopped fighting and lay quietly on the bed. "I saw it," she said, her voice between a whisper and a groan. "I saw him with a knife."

"No," Mabel said. "You're not cut. You'll feel better tomorrow."

Lily turned away. She saw Ed standing in front of an open

cupboard with a bottle in his hand. "We'll let her sleep now," he said.

Lily walked over to him and put her cheek on his chest. His shirt smelled vaguely of turpentine, and that smell combined with the arms that came around her and the touch of the whiskey bottle against her back made her want to cry for no reason she could think of anymore. From behind them, Dolores said in a slurred voice either "I'm finished" or "It's finished," and Lily heard Mabel say, "No, no, no. Go to sleep."

The three of them were silent in the car. Ed drove slowly now, and Lily remembered Dolores in the trailer, her belly speckled with moles and the ragged mark left by the elastic around her middle as she lay naked on the bed. Lily cried without making any sound. Shame was choking her. Her lungs were so tight with it, she couldn't sit still. She wriggled in the seat, looking out one window, then the other. Dolores knows, Lily thought. She knows what I did.

Lily saw Ed glance at her in the rearview mirror. Mabel's head was motionless. Ed started singing. Lily couldn't understand it. It seemed so sudden, so silly, but he was singing. In a low, raspy voice, he sang, "Row, row, row your boat." He sang the whole song and then started over. Mabel joined him and made a round of it, her high, thin voice quavering over the words. Lily listened and wiped her cheeks with her hands, and then she sang, too. They all sang, and they were still singing when Ed parked the station wagon in front of the Stuart Hotel.

Even before Lily opened her eyes Sunday morning, she knew the sun had been up for hours. The bedsheet and pillowcase smelled of heat and dust, and she felt the moisture under her arms and between her legs as she turned over on the mattress and understood she was in the bed alone. She heard Ed, smelled paint and coffee, and felt the sunlight on her eyelids. For a moment she let them open and saw the fringe of her lashes as a moving shadow. She decided not to open her eyes, not yet. Her mind was empty. There was nothing but the light and the warmth of the day, but as she sank toward sleep again, she remembered a long row of tall windows with sills painted pale green. It must have been the sunlight that brought them back to her. Through one of those windows she saw the orange school bus in the parking lot under enormous elms. Late spring, she thought, the field trip to the state hospital. I was in the fifth grade. She remembered standing in the large, narrow room lined with beds on either side. The boy had been lying in one of them, his image as clear now as when she had first seen him. He must have been twelve or thirteen. He lay in a bed that had sides like a crib and wore nothing but diapers and plastic pants. He didn't move and he didn't see her, but his long limbs had a whiteness and softness that fascinated her—the skin of an infant. She remembered a man's voice saying, "profoundly retarded children," and that word "profound" had stayed with her. For years afterward it had meant that motionless boy with vacant eyes.

Then Lily remembered last night and her shame returned, an ache of regret coupled with a fear of being found out. What if Dolores confronted her, or worse, told Ed and Mabel? Could she deny it and say Dolores had invented the whole thing? Could it even be mentioned without Lily going to pieces? She could hardly contain it now. Her whole body was racked with shame. She sat up and stared at Ed's naked back in front of the canvas of Mabel. He held a cup of coffee in one hand, and she could see in his neck and shoulders that he was thinking about the picture, so she didn't speak to him. She remembered Dolores saying "No!" over and over again and looked past Ed's head through the window, as though the air outside might relieve her agitation, but it didn't. She looked down at the tan line below her breasts, at her brown stomach and the pale skin just above her pubic hair. Then she put her feet on the floor, stood up, walked over to Ed and stood beside him. Without putting down his brush, he drew her into him and she laid her head on his chest. She could feel drops of his sweat on her forehead and couldn't resist moving her cheek against the hairs.

"Good morning," he said. "Poor, tired girl."

His kind voice made her feel worse. "Do you think Dolores is okay?" Lily said.

"I called her about an hour ago. She's alive."

"Is that all?"

"I think she needs a few more hours to recover complete consciousness." He smiled.

Lily looked up at him. "Remember when she talked about being cut?"

Ed touched Lily's cheek. "Dolores told me this morning that she thought she saw herself being murdered."

Lily pulled away from Ed. "What do you mean? How can anybody see that?"

"She must have been delirious," Ed said.

"Jesse James?"

He nodded.

Lily looked into his face, and he looked back at her with

his still wide eyes. He was looking at her, and he seemed to be paying attention to her, but she had the feeling he really wasn't. There was something missing in those eyes. She had felt it before and she felt it now, that Ed was both there with her and not there. He acted like he cared about Dolores, but Lily suddenly wondered if he did. Behind him she could see the painting of Tex and the box where the man was strangling the woman. Jesse James, she thought and grabbed Ed's elbow. "What if it was real?" she said. "What if she saw a real murder? Did you ever think of that? People have been seeing things, Ed, not just Dolores." Lily started jabbering. She heard herself doing it, but she couldn't stop. Her voice rose and cracked as she told him about the police log, Boomer's cowboy, Martin's cuts, and Becky Runevold. She wanted to make him listen, to startle him. "Her father killed her," Lily said under her breath. "People will do anything, Ed." She caught her breath. "Do you hear me?"

"Take it easy," he said. He looked down at his elbow, and Lily saw she was digging her fingers into his skin. She let go.

Ed rubbed his hands together. "I don't know about what other people have seen or not seen. But I think that Dolores is unstable and, well, not completely trustworthy."

"You mean she's a liar?"

Ed rubbed the flats of his palms together in and up-and-down motion as if this gesture helped him think. "Maybe not an out-and-out liar, but manipulative and prone to exaggeration. She's melodramatic—the star of her own show. When she called last night, what frightened me wasn't what she thought she had seen, but that she would kill herself, to, to get back at me."

"For what?"

Ed's eyes turned cloudy. He looked past Lily. "For finishing the painting, I suppose."

"That's weird," Lily said, looking straight at him. "And I'm not sure I believe it. I'll tell you another thing. I don't think Dolores was going to kill herself. Her house is much too clean."

Ed returned her look and smiled. "Cleanliness and a desire for death don't mix, is that it?"

"That's right," Lily said. "That house was cleaned for company, and I'll bet that company was you. But that doesn't mean she didn't see something. Maybe it's Tex! Couldn't Dolores have seen Tex? How would you feel if somebody's been killed? Wouldn't you feel guilty for painting him doing that?" She pointed at the canvas.

Ed lifted his hands toward her. Lily knew she was being unreasonable, but she shouted anyway. She liked it. It was as good as screaming or crying onstage. She was inside the emotion and also outside it. She felt anger, and at the same time she was watching herself feel it. "Well, won't you feel responsible if he's hurt some woman out there?"

Ed was saying "Enough." He grabbed her by the wrists and held them firmly. Lily flapped her arms against him, but she didn't resist with much force. She loved him holding her wrists like that. His secure grip aroused her, and she fell toward him and started kissing his naked shoulder.

"What am I going to do with you?" he said.

Lily kissed his ear. She didn't know why, but he had said the right thing. It excited her more. Her face felt damp against his neck. Then she let her head fall backward. "Whatever you want," she said.

He kissed her upper arm and bit it, not hard, but she

could feel his teeth and wondered if they would leave a small red mark.

Monday was quiet. The day brought no more rumors about Lily or anybody else. The *Chronicle* came out, but there was nothing of interest in the log. Lily waited on Stanley Blom at about six o'clock that morning, and when she told him she liked his portrait, the old man smiled and said, "It ain't a pretty sight, but then a fella like myself can't hope for that." Lily had avoided looking at Stanley's hunchback then and mumbled something about the picture having "character." "That's just a nice word for ugly," he said. And when Lily blushed, the man laughed so hard that he started coughing. In the afternoon, Ed painted Mabel, and Lily watched. The weather was hot, but not too hot, and when Lily recalled that the storm had roared through town only last Tuesday, it seemed impossible. It feels like months ago, she thought. That was the day I buried the shoes. When she thought about slapping Dolores now, she suffered acute discomfort, but it wasn't quite as bad as it had been, and she was beginning to think that she was the only one who knew about it anyway. Dolores had been dead drunk. At rehearsal that night, Lily kept her distance from Martin, and he didn't speak to her. He had rebandaged his hand, so the cuts were invisible. Jim said he'd heard that Martin cut himself at the Grastvedt farm fixing the fence, and Lily believed it. In fact, during those hours of practice, her suspicions waned. What were they made of anyway? Hearsay, rumor, the stories of drunks and crazy people, and the wacko speeches of Martin Petersen himself.

At nine-thirty on Tuesday morning, it all changed again.

Lily heard Professor Vegan's voice rising above the hum of conversation in the cafe and turned her head to listen. He came in once a month with three other retired professors. The four men called themselves "The Over-the-Hill Gang." They ate big breakfasts, and once their stomachs were full, they would launch into Kierkegaard. Lily had been told that they'd been chipping away at the philosopher for three years, word by word, sentence by sentence, paragraph by paragraph, as patient and relentless as the day is long. This year there had been only two books, and they had the grimmest titles Lily had ever seen: *Fear and Trembling* and *The Sickness unto Death*. But the men joked and ribbed each other, and every once in a while Professor Schwandt laughed until he cried. It was true that weather, sports and politics got mixed in with Kierkegaard from time to time, but the men's doggedness impressed Lily— and they tipped well. "The creature had wings," Professor Vegan was saying, and Lily moved toward the table of professors with the coffeepot.

"If Gladys had been alone, I probably wouldn't have paid much attention. Gladys, as far as I can tell, is very nearly a Holy Roller—evangelical in the extreme. I can't remember the name of the sect she belongs to, but they do their fair share of trembling and moaning. Marit, on the other hand, is a hard-headed woman if there ever was one, and I would never doubt her powers of observation. She saw the darn thing, too, in broad daylight, only yards from the house."

Lily poured Professor Hong coffee even though his cup was nearly full and watched Professor Vegan. He had an ironic smile on his face and lowered his voice for effect. "It came walking along the creek bed from the north very quietly—a translucent being in white with a gigantic pair of wings." He gulped his coffee and watched the faces of his three colleagues. "And"—he paused—"there's the matter of the suitcase. After all, who would invent that detail? A supernatural being trudging along with its belongings in a bag."

Lily looked intently into the coffee and clenched her teeth.

"Send a memo to the religion department," said Professor Nichols.

"A seraph," said Professor Hong, "on the loose in Webster."

The men laughed.

Professor Schwandt shook his head. "It's the suitcase that bothers me. An angel with luggage. Smells of heresy, doesn't it?"

Professor Nichols smiled. "Yes, I've always assumed that divine messengers travel light."

"I wonder what it was, really." Lily interrupted them. "Who it was."

Professor Vegan shook his head and looked at Lily. "Beats me, but when I came home, both Marit and Gladys were pretty shaken. Whatever they saw, it must have looked not just improbable, but impossible."

Lily poured more coffee all around and left the table. She watched Frances Herda pat Lynn Strom's shoulder and say loudly, "Keith Ellingboe just isn't worth it. If you want my opinion, he's been acting like a horse's ass for three weeks." Lynn picked up her orange juice glass and sniffed into it. Wings, Lily thought, and a suitcase. Frances turned her head, and the tiny gold earring in her right ear gleamed for a second in the light from the window. She moved again, and the glint disappeared. Lily carried the coffeepot toward the door. She wanted to go back and ask Professor Vegan whether his wife had mentioned the size or weight of the suitcase and whether she had thought the "thing" was a man or a woman. Lily had met Marit Vegan. Her oldest daughter, Iris, used to baby-sit for her, and the whole family had always struck Lily as indomitably sane. The Vegan house lay on the land above the creek, only a quarter of a mile from the Bodlers' on the other side of the highway, and it was close to the caves. Suddenly, she wondered what she had done with Martin's map. She walked past Bert and stood near the door. The light outside was so bright she couldn't look into it. She squinted toward the street. They saw something, all right, she thought. The suitcase Lily had found in the garage had disappeared into thin air. A man carrying an injured woman, she said to herself, near the city limits. Warm liquid ran onto Lily's foot. She opened her eyes and saw that the coffeepot had tipped in her slack wrist and that coffee was running onto her white sneaker.

Behind her she heard Vince yelling, "Watch the pot!" She turned around to look at him and set the coffee near the cash register. "You okay?" he said. Lily didn't answer him. She was thinking. I can't just let this go. Somebody has got to do something. I can't stay here and pretend nothing's happening. Lily wiped her shoe with a napkin and faced Division Street again. The bright sunshine was hard to look at. Lily reached for the screen door and opened it. I'm going now, she thought. It can't wait. She walked out into the street, turned right and then right again up the alley to her bicycle.

Lily rode past the Ideal Cafe and saw Vince standing in the doorway in his white apron. He waved a spatula at her and roared, "Where do you think you're going! Get back here! If you don't get your ass back here in two seconds, you're fired!"

She didn't pay any attention to him. Vince was standing in another dimension, like a person in a movie she could watch without him affecting her directly. He had fired her twice before, but both times he had rehired her within twenty minutes, and both times it had been his fault for being such a hothead. Now she was the one who had walked out on him, and it seemed only fair that he should fire her. There was something oddly pleasant about the uproar she had created: the fat man screaming in the doorway, the startled faces in the cafe. It had been so easy, had taken only a couple of seconds to turn the Ideal Cafe upside down. Lily knew where she was going. She was looking for someone—a nameless girl hidden at Martin's or at the Bodlers', in the woods or in the caves. Whoever she was, she must look something like both Lily and Dolores. Whoever she was, Lily felt she had to find her. Just beyond the Webster city limits, Lily imagined the suitcase lying abandoned in the woods, and she imagined her fingers on the lid pulling it open a couple of inches, and then in the fantasy she slammed down the lid to shut out the horrible contents.

Standing outside Martin's house, Lily felt excited. Her excitement outweighed her dread, maybe because Martin's truck was gone and the house looked unoccupied. She walked onto the porch, opened the door and peered into the room. The rocking chair had been moved back to the corner, and she could see the black cloth, the collage of crimes and advertisements with its blank center. She walked inside. This, too, was easy. You put one foot in front of the other, she said to herself, and you're in. She touched the black cloth for an instant, but dropped it quickly. The chemical smell remained strong in the house, and again she wondered what it was. When she looked for the knives, she saw that they had disappeared. Lily remembered Dolores yelling about being cut, remembered Martin's hand, and, as she walked through the open door into Martin's bedroom, she thought that cuts like the ones she had seen on Martin's hand couldn't have come from fixing a fence. Stacks of books lay on the floor, and on a table she saw the copy of *Gray's Anatomy* that had been in the other room before, a book of photographs called *The Nude,* and a fat white book entitled *Prosthetics*. A fly buzzed past her cheek, and Lily listened for cars on the road, but there were none, only highway traffic in the distance. Lily moved to Martin's desk, pushed away the chair and opened the desk drawer: bank receipts, several index cards, paper clips, a copy of *Playboy*. Then, looking down, she noticed a dark heap on the floor, bent over and reached for it. Clothes, she thought, just clothes, but when she pulled out a blue T-shirt and looked at it, she noticed it had a tiny bow at the neck and a tag inside that said "Lady Susan, size 7." Lily stared at the tag, took a deep breath and threw the shirt back under the desk. From somewhere outside she heard a dog barking, and she ran out of the house. Pedaling up the gravel road toward the highway, she suddenly remembered she had forgotten to shut the desk drawer.

Two cars were parked in the Bodlers' driveway: the twins' truck and a Pontiac that Lily thought looked familiar. Lily jumped off her bicycle and ran to the door. She rattled the screen and called inside, "Hello! It's me, Lily. I have to talk to you!" Yelling into that house, Lily felt that she had temporarily given herself permission to act wildly, but could withdraw that permission at any second if she had to.

She yelled again. "Let me in! It's important!" Heavy footsteps came from the next room. Frank appeared in the kitchen.

"Hold yer horses," he muttered. As he trudged across the

kitchen floor, he pulled at his trousers, and stopped behind the screen. He raised his bloodshot eyes to her and grunted.

"I have to talk to you again, to you and Dick, about what he saw." Lily hesitated. She looked intently at him to show the urgency of what she was saying and then added, "It could be a matter of life and death."

She wasn't at all sure, but Lily thought she saw a hint of amusement in Frank's eyes. "Easy does it," he said and stared at her without blinking. He did not open the screen door.

"Mr. Bodler," Lily said, "let me in."

Frank scratched his neck. "Dick's restin'."

"This won't take long."

Frank rubbed his nose with the back of his hand. Then he lifted a finger slowly toward the ceiling like a person testing the wind and said, "Hold on."

Frank disappeared. Lily heard voices from inside the house while she waited. Listening, she thought she heard a woman's voice, but Dick's voice had the timbre of a woman's, and it could have been him.

Frank returned, motioned for her to follow him, but said nothing. He led Lily through the second room and then kicked open the door to the third. The kick gave her a start, and she braced herself as she followed him into the bedroom. The room was incredibly dark. She saw nothing but a bar of hazy light straight ahead of her. Two or three seconds later, she realized that the light came from a window, its opening obscured by a tall stack of boxes, and that the visible glass was coated with a thick, yellow film. A hulking dresser with a cloudy blackened mirror above it stood against the left wall, and when Lily turned to look at it, she saw the blurred reflection of two people lying on a bed. The mirror's distortion con-

fused her for a moment, but she turned to her right and saw
Dick Bodler and Dolores Wachobski together on a small bed
that sagged under their weight. Dolores was sitting, wedged
close to Dick, who was lying down, his head propped on an
uncovered pillow. Bolt upright near the end of the bed were
Dick's boots. Their long, creased tongues hung out from
between knotted laces, giving them a vaguely doglike appearance. Dolores was wearing a thin pink dress that buttoned up
the front, and because that dress was the only clear color in
that dark room of muddy browns and grays, her body looked
separate from everything else around her. The puking,
bloated, whiskey-logged woman of three days ago had been
replaced by a steady, sober person in pink. The transformation
was so complete, Lily found it almost supernatural. This
wasn't the Dolores she had shaken and slapped the other
night. Holding a neat fan of playing cards in two hands,
Dolores turned her head to Lily and said, "You look a little
mussed up, honey. Anything wrong?" Then she lowered her
eyes to her cards. Dick hadn't shown Lily any sign of greeting
or recognition. He lifted a hand that had been hidden behind
his thigh and brought several badly smudged cards up to his
nose. Then he narrowed his eyes. Lily shifted on the floor, felt
her foot knock something, heard a sloshing sound and looked
down at the floor. Her toe had knocked into a coffee can that
was serving as a spittoon. She smelled rancid tobacco juice
and felt thankful she hadn't spilled it.

Lily tried to focus her eyes. The vague light, the dust that
floated in the room made it hard to see, and she felt that the
momentum of the afternoon had suddenly been lost. The
world had slowed down and then collapsed into this funny,
filthy room. But she spoke anyway. "I want to ask you about

Martin Petersen." She took a step toward the bed. Nobody moved. Frank stood in front of the tower of boxes and surveyed the three of them with blank eyes. Dolores and Dick looked at their cards. "Martin Petersen," she said again.

After several seconds, Dolores patted the bed. "Join us for a game of gin?" Her voice was bright and clear.

I'm tired, Lily thought, really tired. "No," she said. "I just want to talk."

"Sit down then," Dolores cooed. She smiled and motioned with her head to a spot on the bed near the boots.

"I'll stand," Lily said.

Dolores threw back her head and hooted.

Dick continued to look at his cards. Then he raised his eyebrows as though he were surprised by what he saw.

Dolores laughed again.

The laugh seemed to remain in Lily's ear even after it was over. She looked straight at Dolores. "On second thought," she said, "move over." Lily crawled over Dick's legs and nudged Dolores forcefully with her elbow. "Make room, honey," she said, emphasizing the word "honey." The bed sank further under her weight, and for an instant Lily thought it might go crashing to the floor. She crossed her legs Indian style and beamed at Dolores. "This is comfy," she said.

"Well, how do you do!" Dolores said. It was not a question. "For a minute there, I thought you was just a teeny-weeny bit scared of me, or maybe Dickie here?" Dolores patted the man's trousers, and a small cloud of black dust rose from the cloth.

"No way," Lily said and wiggled her shoulders in an exaggerated gesture of getting comfortable. Dolores's sarcasm relieved Lily's guilt. She really is a bitch, Lily thought. "I want to know exactly what you saw that day in the field—when you said you saw Martin Petersen," she shouted at Dick. He didn't look at her. A bird whistled outside, three distinct notes, each one higher than the one before.

"Why?" Dolores said.

Lily's leg brushed Dolores's hip. The contact made her uncomfortable, and she felt her face getting hot. "Dick," Lily began and corrected herself, "Mr. Bodler says he saw Martin Petersen carrying"—Lily rubbed her face—"me"—she paused—"across the field out here last Thursday night, but I wasn't there."

"You?" Dolores squinted at Lily.

"Remind you of anything?" Lily said. "Like Jesse James?"

"No," Dolores said, but her lips were parted in an expression of confusion.

Dick sat up.

"Well, let's face it," Lily said, "it wasn't Jesse James."

Frank had turned to Lily, and he stepped forward.

Dolores looked at Lily and spoke between her teeth. "I saw Jesse, and I saw me. I know what I saw, and it scared the bejesus outa me. It wasn't Martin Petersen, and it sure as hell wasn't you."

Lily shouted at Dick. "How did you know it was Martin? Wasn't it getting dark? I'm not saying you didn't see anything, but how could you be so sure? In the police log last week there was a report about a man carrying an injured woman just outside of town. It's the same thing, don't you see? I've got it right here." Lily dug into her back pocket for the clipping and waved it in front of Dolores. "You didn't call the police, did you?"

"I never call them clowns," Dolores said. She took the clipping from Lily, stared at it and sucked the inside of her cheek.

Frank walked over to Dolores and held out his hand for the clipping. She gave it to him, and he read it for at least a minute. Kindergarten speed, Lily said to herself. "Wonder whose pig it was," he said finally.

"You're sayin' Marty Petersen's walkin' round town with a dead woman and that's what I've been seeing?" Dolores said, "Wearin' cowboy duds? That it ain't visions? Is that what you're sayin'?"

"Maybe," Lily said. "I'm not sure."

"What about the music?" she said. "I heard music."

Lily ignored her.

Still holding the bit of wrinkled newspaper, Frank sat down on a crate piled with magazines and spat into the coffee can. "That boy was born with thin blood," he said. "Runs in our family." He spoke slowly.

"Who's he talking about?" Lily asked Dolores.

"Must be Marty."

"You and Martin are related?" Lily said in a loud voice.

Frank nodded. "As I was sayin', he inherited it, thin blood, female-like, if you know my meaning, a little like Dick here." He lowered his voice when he mentioned his brother. "Only Dick ain't clever, and Marty's wicked clever—not just with his hands neither. He reads a lot a books, comes here and pages through every one we get in to see if he wants it, and takes whatever he likes. He's got big ideas 'bout things, an' when he ain't cursed by stutterin', he goes on and on till I can't take it no more, a regular chatterbox he is, once he gets goin'."

Lily interrupted him. "How are you related?"

Frank looked at her. "Our mother and Martin's grand-mother was sisters."

"I had no idea."

Frank nodded. "Norwegians," he said. "Those girls was born here, but their parents come from a little place in Sogn Valley, name of Underdahl. Took the name from there: Underdahl." Lily watched the back of Frank's head in the mirror and saw his bald spot wave in the reflection.

Dolores looked at Lily. "Like you."

"There are lots of Dahl names," Lily said, as if an explanation was called for. "It means 'valley' in Norwegian—Overdahl, Grondahl, Folkedahl—lots of them." She heard her voice drop. She knew it was silly, but the coincidental overlapping of her own name with Helen Bodler's maiden name unsettled her.

"Sure," Dolores said. "I went to school with a girl called Hallingdahl."

They were all silent. Helen Underdahl, Lily said to herself, and burped. It was a silent burp, but she tasted vomit in her mouth and swallowed to get rid of it. She looked at Frank and in a loud measured voice said, "Do you think Martin is capable of—" She stopped. "Would Martin hurt anybody?"

Frank leaned forward on the crate. "The truth is, Miss Dahl, you can't know nothin' about nobody now, can you? Seems to me you yourself could hurt somebody if the time and place was right. That's so, ain't it? Even them that's closest to you, you can't really know 'bout them. One day you wake up and find out. Folks say, 'It ain't possible, can't happen.' You live a little longer, and it happens." Frank nodded his head. "People are full of surprises. I seen a lot a things that weren't supposed to happen, Miss Dahl, and it ain't so easy to say who's to blame. That's the nature of things. The day comes when you wake up in the mornin' and look out the window and you can't see nothin' but grasshoppers so thick they black out the sky. And then before you know it, a drought sets in, and your fields burn as sure as if you'd taken a torch to your own crops. That's just the way of nature, but then the price of eggs goes so low, it ain't worth sellin' em. Costs more to raise the chickens. An' whose fault is that, Miss Dahl? Was it them politicians in Washington, don't know a heifer from a steer?" Frank shook his head and stuck a pinch of tobacco into his cheek. He narrowed his eyes. "And the day comes when a god-damned inspector from the goddamned Twin Cities drives up in his fat car and tells you you gotta slaughter your animals, every last one of 'em. Hoof-and-mouth, he says. But it turns out, Miss Dahl, they wasn't sick. Them cows wasn't sick." He raised a fist at Lily. "And the day comes when you don't know your own people, don't know what they are or what they're thinkin', and that's gotta be the worst. They turn their backs on you and leave you high and dry. It don't matter that it ain't you done nothin'. You're mixed up in it somehow, and that's all that matters. Pity's cheap, Miss Dahl, and those that pity don't like to come too close. They stand at a good distance cluckin' their tongues and shakin' their heads, but they won't get their hands dirty, and that ain't much when all you've got left is a patch of land with the devil's mark on it." He nodded. "Folks surprise you. That's all there is to it. You're askin' me if that boy could do somethin' bad. I'm tellin' you, you bet he could, but that don't make him much different from nobody else."

Lily looked at Frank. The length of his speech had aston-ished her. In a low voice she said, "Martin's got pictures and articles of dead people on his wall—murdered people—did you know that?"

"You think that's different from havin' the pictures in here?" Frank tapped his temple with a finger.

Lily's mouth was dry. "I, I don't know," she said.

Dick was stirring on the bed, and when Lily turned to look at him, she saw that he was sitting up. He let go of the cards and watched them scatter onto his lap and the bed. Until then, she had felt the man had been absent, absorbed only in the numbers and the faces on the cards in his hand. Lily didn't know what he had heard or not heard, but his face took on a sudden expression of joy. He threw back his head, opened his mouth and laughed without making any sound, his chin bobbing. He hugged himself and began to rock back and forth on the bed, bumping both women with his shoulders. Lily moved out of his way and knocked Dolores in the shin with her knee.

"He don't mean nothin' by it," Dolores said to Lily. "It's one of his peculiars." She smiled. "Peculiarities. Every once in a while it comes over him—just like that." She snapped her fingers. "I think we oughta leave him alone. Frank's the only one who can get him out of it, if it don't stop by itself."

Lily looked at Dick and shouted at him, "I have to go now, Mr. Bodler."

The man stopped his motion instantly, looked her straight in the face and said, "You're leavin'?" He looked at his brother. "Miss Underdahl is leavin'?"

"Dahl," Frank said. "Just Dahl." He didn't speak loudly enough for Dick to hear. Lily knew he had made the correction not for his brother, but for her.

She crawled over Dick's legs and got off the bed. The

moment her feet touched the ground, he returned to his rocking and noiseless laughter. Lily saw her image wave in the dark mirror ahead of her, and she turned her head to avoid it. When she looked around, she saw Dolores giving Dick's leg a friendly pat as she moved to the edge of the bed. Dolores's dress caught the mattress, slid up her thigh and revealed the top of her stocking and garter. Lily remembered then that Dolores hadn't been wearing a garter the other night.

Lily shook hands with Frank and resisted a momentary impulse to wipe her palm on her jeans. Then she noticed Dick waving at her, and she understood that he, too, wanted to shake hands. She reached out to him. He took her hand, and Lily felt his warm, oily palm against hers, and when she looked at him, she saw recognition in his eyes. He must be mistaking me for someone else, she thought.

Drained of curiosity and somehow wounded, Lily stared at the Folgers label on the coffee can near her feet. Seeing the brothers and listening to Frank had picked at some old sore inside her, and although she felt the pain of it clearly enough, she didn't know what had caused it. She left the room behind Dolores, and walking through the second room, she noticed the peonies through the window. One fat, fading blossom was pressing against the dirty glass.

On the stone step outside the door, Lily blinked in the sunlight and noticed a dragonfly hover near her knee, then fly to her right toward a junk heap. When she turned to Dolores, she saw that the woman looked different outside. The wind blew the pink dress against her thighs, and the fine wrinkles in her face were plainly visible.

"You got a car?" Dolores said.

"No, my bike," Lily said, pointing at it.

"Go and get it. I'll give you a ride. We'll stick the bike in the trunk."

Lily didn't answer. She felt immobile and stared at a wheel in a pile of junk. Then she lifted her eyes toward the telephone wires strung along the highway and looked at a line of sparrows sitting on the wire: a row of small dark bodies. One turned its head abruptly to the left, alert to some invisible sound or motion, and then, an instant later, every bird spread its wings and flew up into the sky.

"Go on," Dolores said. "Get the damned bike."

Dolores drove fast, and Lily heard her bicycle bump in the trunk behind them. She stared out the window and thought about the girl's shirt under Martin's desk. It's hers, she thought. She smelled skunk from the road and turned to Dolores. Every time I lay eyes on her, she's different. It could be the booze, but you can't pour personality out of a whiskey bottle, can you? Lily studied the woman's lap, looking closely at her thigh under the dress. She tested her feelings, but she felt nothing, nothing at all.

"You're spooked," Dolores said suddenly. "I can see it."

"What do you mean?"

"Just what I say. You're spooked."

"I wouldn't say that," Lily lied to the road.

"I would," Dolores said. "Only Dickie ain't quite in his right mind. You can see that, can't you?"

"He's a strange person," Lily said. "But then so are you."

Dolores opened her mouth and after a moment, she laughed. "Me?"

"Ed said you were unusual or extraordinary or something like that. He doesn't know quite what to make of you."

Dolores smiled at the road. "That ain't the same as strange, honey. He's an odd duck himself, don't you think?"

"Ed?"

"Yes, Ed." Dolores mimicked Lily's intonation of the man's name, and this little cruelty put Lily on guard. "Most of the time, that man ain't here, if you know what I mean."

"No, I don't," Lily said. But she was lying.

"He lives in them pictures of his. You must've figured that out by now. Then, once in a while, his pecker drags him away."

Lily stiffened. "So that's what you think, is it?"

"I do. Nothing wrong with that."

"He was pretty worried about you the other night, and I don't think it had much to do with sex. If it hadn't been for him, you'd have woken up in your own puke down by the river." Lily's voice shook as she spoke.

"I'm on the wagon, case you hadn't noticed."

"I noticed. I was there, too."

"I know." Dolores said. She smiled at Lily. "All I'm saying is, if I wasn't in paint, I don't think he'd give a damn."

"I'm not 'in paint' and he cares about me," Lily said.

Dolores smiled. "How old are you, honey, eighteen?"

"Nineteen," Lily said.

Dolores nodded. "And our painter friend, he's 'bout thirty-five, wouldn't you say?"

"Thirty-four."

"That man's got tricks up his sleeves you ain't even dreamed of yet."

Lily sat on her hands and looked out the window. She spoke slowly. "That day in Ed's room when you said he 'plays rough,' what did you mean?"

"If you don't know, I sure as hell won't tell you. That's not my job, for Christ's sake."

They drove in silence for a minute or two. Lily studied the fields under the big sky through her window, and then she said, "Why did you hide from your mother when you were a little girl?"

"Guess he told you that," she said.

Lily nodded. "Was it a kind of game?"

Dolores's foot pressed the gas pedal and the car moved faster. "Told you 'bout that, too, did he? Guess it was fool-hardy of me to think he'd keep that to himself. Game? We played the game, all right. I'd lose myself, and he'd find me. I'd hear him stomping around and get real hot—"

Lily cut her off. "He didn't say that. He wouldn't say that." The pain in her voice was obvious, and Lily regretted it.

Neither of them spoke for about thirty seconds.

"Don't take it too hard," Dolores said finally. "There's a whole lot worse in this world than that kind of game playin'. There's a lot of men right here in town who've got a game no one'll play with them. I oughta know. It don't do nobody no harm, an' it's a comfort to them. I ain't ashamed of it." She paused. "The funny thing 'bout it is even weirdos run in types. There ain't nothin' new under the sun. Kinda makes you wonder." Dolores lifted a hand from the wheel and flapped it.

"But hiding's your game, Dolores, not Ed's."

Dolores slowed the car. "It takes two to play, honey."

But Lily saw the woman's face go slack with emotion. She's better-looking when she's mean, Lily thought. Dolores drove across the railroad tracks slowly, and Lily pressed her nose to the window. When she turned back to Dolores, the woman's face looked pink and moist with what may have been tears, although Lily couldn't see any drops in her eyes.

When they turned onto Division Street, Dolores said, "I didn't take money, you know. Only for the modeling."

"Right," Lily said. The car stopped in front of the Ideal

Cafe, and Lily remembered she didn't have a job. I'd better try to make it up with Vince, she thought, opened the door and slammed it shut. "Thanks," she said to Dolores, who was slumped over the wheel in a posture as dramatic as it was irritating. "What's the matter with you?" Lily spoke in a sharp voice.

Dolores lifted her head and looked at Lily with large, sincere eyes. "Tell the old lady thanks for the food and stuff."

"What?" Lily said.

"The stuff she brought over to me Sunday morning. It was real neighborly of her. I was pretty low at the time, so I didn't say much, but she's a good woman, and I'd like you to tell her so. Tell her I'm glad she told me what she did. She'll know what I mean." Dolores smiled sweetly. Then she tossed her long hair over one shoulder and said, "See you around," her voice lilting with false femininity. She tugged her dress down to her knees, wiggled her buttocks into the seat and turned the key. Lily moved back from the window and would have let Dolores drive off with her bicycle if she hadn't seen it in the partly opened trunk. "Stop!"

Lily's screaming at Dolores and the subsequent ordeal of untying the rope and lifting the bicycle out of the trunk didn't go unnoticed. It wasn't clear whether Dolores felt the customers in the Ideal Cafe staring at them or whether she saw Beulah Bjornson stop dead in her tracks outside Tiny's Smoke Shop to watch them. If she did, she didn't show it, and Lily couldn't help admiring her obliviousness even if it was just an act. She took her bicycle by the handlebars and said, "Thanks, Dolores." Then she added, "I mean it," because for some reason she did.

Wheeling her bicycle toward the cafe window, Lily looked inside. Two middle-aged women in Martin's booth stared back at her, and before Lily had time to squelch the impulse, she had dropped the kickstand on her bike and was making goggle eyes at them. She stuck her thumbs in her ears and wiggled her fingers. It was a silly, childish thing to do, but looking at those two astonished faces through the glass, Lily couldn't help feeling it was worth it.

3

Walking up the stairs, Lily heard scraping noises from Mabel's apartment. She should be at Ed's now, Lily thought. Something's gone wrong. Mabel was sweating when she came to the door, and Lily realized that she had never seen the woman perspire even in the worst heat, but now drops of sweat stood out on her upper lip, and her forehead shone with moisture. She was wearing a big white shirt rolled to the elbows, and her thin white arms were trembling.

"Mabel," Lily said. "What's going on?"

"I moved it back." She gestured at the room with a limp hand and sighed. "The whole room. . . . I didn't know where I was anymore. It was so stupid of me. I thought it was time for a revolution, you know, a new order, but I found it awful, just awful. . . . I was so unhappy with the sofa over there." She pointed. "It was like trying to learn Russian at fifty-seven. I did try that. My brain had calcified by then, and I simply couldn't do the cases, much less those sounds. It should have been a lesson to me, but oh, no, I had to be clever and bold and disrupt it all. My nerves simply couldn't take it, and pushing all that heavy furniture around . . ."

"You moved the furniture? When did you move the furniture? Are you crazy? You should have asked me to help you." Lily looked at Mabel's hands. The knuckles were red and swollen. She studied Mabel's face. "Dolores says thank you for the food, and she said that I was supposed to tell you she's glad you told her what you did, that you'd know what she meant."

"You've been to see her, too, have you?" Mabel looked closely at Lily.

"No. I ran into her at Frank and Dick Bodler's."

Mabel looked puzzled. "You don't mean those men with the bags who look like they just crawled out of a mine?"

"Yup," Lily said and folded her arms. Then she said softly, "Why did you go to see Dolores?"

"I wanted to ask her about Ed and, and the portrait."

"Why didn't you ask him?"

"I wanted the other side. And I wanted to know about the ghosts." Mabel wiped her upper lip. "I have to sit down." She sank into the sofa and sighed, her legs straight out on the floor in front of her.

Lily sat down beside her. "What did she say?"

"Not a thing. I talked. I guess she heard me. I wasn't sure."

"She's fresh as a daisy now," Lily said.

"The portrait's bothering me, Lily." Mabel rubbed her cheek gently, as if it were another person's skin. "I don't know what to do. You should see it now. We worked today. It's, it's, oh, I don't know, when I look at it, I feel upset. I'm well aware that no one's going to care one way or the other about the identity of the old lady in Edward Shapiro's painting, and yet I feel that I'm being pulled into a crisis a part of me willed and another part resists. I'm not sure Ed fully understands it. I'm not sure he even knows what he's doing, but there's something in him that's aggressive, not his manner, you understand, but the work—he strikes the heart." Mabel swallowed. "He painted his wife. Did you know that?"

Lily shook her head.

"It ended the marriage."

Lily didn't say anything.

"I guess it started out all right, and then something went wrong. He didn't go into it in detail, but you know what he said?"

"No."

"He said he *saw* her, really saw her." Mabel looked into Lily's eyes.

Lily moved her eyes away from Mabel to the window. She wondered what Ed had seen, and why she found it upsetting, but she said, "It's just a painting, Mabel. You're all worked up over nothing."

Lily stared into Mabel's white face and she spoke to her softly. "Is it the story in the boxes?"

Mabel turned away. She didn't nod or speak.

"Partly," she said in a soft voice.

Then a suspicion took sudden hold of Lily. "I'd be careful what you tell Dolores. You shouldn't trust her, Mabel. She could easily blab anything you say to the girl who does her nails down at Miriam's, to Willy at the shoe repair, to anybody!"

"I'm not sure that's who she is, Lily." Mabel smiled with her mouth closed. Her eyes looked shiny as she pushed away a wisp of hair from her forehead.

The two women sat on the sofa beside each other without talking for a long time. Lily thought about being fired and about rehearsal and that Martin would be at the Arts Guild, and then she told Mabel about Martin. It was a partial confession because she omitted details that had become part of the story, even though they weren't really a part of it—Helen Underdahl Bodler and the shoes she had stolen and burned and buried, Dolores in the grass, and Dick and Frank in that house. But Lily told her about Martin's note and the map, about Becky Runevold and the rocking chair. She told her about leaving work and snooping in Martin's house and finding the T-shirt. Mabel listened intently. She listened so hard her small body tensed all over, and when Lily finished, Mabel lifted her chin, stared at a blue wooden egg that lay in a bowl on the coffee table and said, "There are any number of explanations for that shirt," she said. "You do understand that, don't you?"

Mabel's words echoed in Lily's head after she had said them. She remembered touching the blue fabric, remembered feeling it was tainted, the sign of an unspeakable thing. Why had she been so sure that it had belonged to the girl people were seeing? Why hadn't it entered her mind that it might belong to somebody else: Martin's sister or a friend? Lily looked into Mabel's face. "Yes," she said. "But I feel there's something . . ."

The woman folded her hands in her lap and said, "Yes, there is something. A mind burning holes in the world."

Lily didn't answer this, and yet she didn't deny that the enigmatic sentence made a kind of sense to her.

"Would it be okay if I sat in on rehearsal tonight?" Mabel said. "I would like to watch anyway, but perhaps if I saw him . . ." She didn't finish.

"I think that's a good idea." Lily needed an ally, and she didn't want to face Martin alone. "He acts like he's got something on me," she continued, "like a blackmailer or something." Lily stopped talking. It was you, she said to herself and stared at the floor. The possibility, mad as it was, that she might have lost time and consciousness, that she might have remembered wrong or forgotten a crucial event played like a little tune in the back of her mind. It wasn't that she accepted what Martin had said as the truth, but she acknowledged uncertainty for the first time, and she felt it as an annoying melody of doubt, like a stupid chorus from a television commercial or pop song that you hum almost without knowing it, and every time you try to get it out of your head, you can't.

Martin's cuts must have been healing well, because he used the hand freely both onstage and off-. Mabel sat in a folding chair in the second row throughout, and Lily worried that there was nothing for the woman to see—in Martin, at least. Watching him herself, Lily saw an unobtrusive, cooperative young man who made a good Cobweb. He stared a little too much and blinked too little, but so what? Everybody was used to that. Lily began to wish he would do or say something to reveal himself. She hoped he would send her another note she could show to Mabel or that he would make a scene in front of the cast. While she was pretending to sleep at the rear of the stage and had opened her right eye just enough to see Martin patting Bottom's Ass head, Lily heard Mabel laugh loudly, and she daydreamed that Martin suddenly broke out of his role as Cobweb, turned to the audience and confessed. She didn't invent the exact content of the confession, but in the fantasy he shocked the audience. She saw him red-faced and stuttering, his arms flailing. By the time the fairies left the stage, the story had progressed to a point where the cast had jumped him and was hauling him off to the police station. After that, Lily decided to push her luck.

She took her chance once rehearsal ended and Martin walked past her carrying three costumes over his arm. He was headed for the stairs, and despite the fact that they were not alone—Jim, Denise and Oren were talking just beyond the doors—Lily moved close to Martin and said in a strained but quiet voice, "I know what you've done."

Martin stopped and faced her. He stared, but his face didn't move.

"I'm telling you I know," she repeated.

Martin nodded at her but didn't speak.

Behind Martin, she saw Mabel. Her eyes met Lily's, and in that instant Lily understood what she had done. She wasn't only lying. She was pretending to know what she didn't know, and it occurred to her that this ruse could put her in jeopardy. Martin appeared to be looking through her as he prepared to speak. His mouth moved, and his bandaged hand clutched at the blue material of the costumes. He motioned with his head for her to step aside with him and began to talk, stuttering badly over the first syllable, but the words were clear enough, and after hearing them Lily felt as if she had been kicked hard in the stomach: "So you've been to the cave and seen her." He paused. "I mean, *it*." Martin moved his head to one side. "D-d-did you expect me to deny it?" Then he looked down at his shoes. "You didn't move her, did you?"

Lily shook her head, but not in response to Martin's question. She couldn't accept what she had heard. Has he said what I think he's said? Martin's words had come and gone so quickly, and nobody else seemed to have heard them. Denise was giggling into Jim's face, and Lily saw Martin turn and walk down the stairs with the costumes as Mrs. Wright announced dress rehearsal for Thursday. "We're close, people, very close. You have two days of rest, so rest well and get ready for a big weekend. There'll be no stopping Thursday. If you make mistakes, it's like a real performance, just make the best of it."

Mrs. Wright's voice sounded remote. Lily didn't move. She heard chatter and footsteps and then someone hitting the triangle that was used when the fairies came onstage.

It was Mabel who decided to follow Martin. Lily reported the conversation in a voice she barely recognized as her own. She didn't know how she managed to repeat those words at all, but she did, and then she wondered if she fully believed them. The two women sat together in Mabel's old Saab and waited for Martin to walk through the doors, which he did in a matter of minutes. They watched him say good-bye to Mrs. Baker and saw the woman pat his shoulder affectionately. He walked slowly to his truck with his head down, his wrapped hand looking very pale in the darkness. He climbed into the cab of his truck and drove away. Mabel allowed the truck to move ahead of them for a block and then pulled the Saab onto the avenue and began to follow Martin out of town.

"He never touched Bottom or anyone else onstage," Mabel said.

Lily couldn't understand how Mabel could talk about the play now, but she didn't stop her.

"Have you noticed that?" Mabel's voice was a little hoarse. "He clearly made a conscious decision to play it that way, and it's very clever, because his gestures look like magic. He would get close, but there was never any real contact. His movements made me think of a mime." Mabel paused. "It was as if he were tracing the lines of things in his own invisible world, as if he had forgotten the boundaries of real people and real things. I suppose the actor who plays Bottom doesn't even know, because he's wearing that head."

Lily folded her hands and pressed them into her lap. She was thinking of the kiss she gave Martin when he left the stage the first day he rehearsed and the way his face had looked. The moon was almost full, and it seemed to sail along with them as they drove two cars behind Martin's truck. Lily remembered the latch on the box that Martin had drawn on his map. It was a handle, wasn't it? Too large for a chest. It wasn't a chest. Martin's left-turn signal blinked red ahead of them, and the truck veered onto Old Dutch Road. Mabel slowed the car and waited for the pickup to disappear behind the hill about a hundred yards ahead and turned. When the Saab arrived at the crest of the hill, Lily looked down and saw no lights and no truck.

"Where did he go?" Lily could smell the creek through her open window and manure and hay from the farm across the road. "There it is." The truck was parked on a slant— two wheels in the grass, two on the narrow shoulder. "We'll park on the other side," Lily said. "The old Dundas Road is straight ahead. It's all grown over now, or mostly, but you can park there. My house, my old house is right up the road, see, around that bend and past the fire-call sign." Lily took a breath. "I know every rock, bush and stump around here."

Mabel followed Lily's instructions and parked the car on

the old Dundas Road. When the motor stilled and Mabel had turned off the headlights, Lily said, "What are we doing?"

Resting her hands on the wheel, Mabel said, "I don't know. Are we near the caves?"

Lily nodded. "It must be where he's gone. But it's dark, Mabel. We don't have a flashlight, and even if we did, the caves aren't easy to get into."

"You're right. Let's go home. Let the police take care of it. If there's something to find in that cave, they'll find it."

"I want to look in the truck, anyway."

Mabel was muttering to herself or to Lily, "It's not uncommon for people who stutter to lose it when, well, when they're not themselves." She opened the car door and stepped into the grass. Lily followed, and standing in the night air, she looked across the field lit by the moon.

In Martin's truck, they found a coil of nylon rope, a wrench, a hammer and a large tarp. Lily knew these discoveries meant nothing. A handyman was bound to haul tools around with him, and yet when she reached for the tarp, her fingers touched something cold and wet, and she withdrew her hand as if it had been bitten.

Mabel was standing with her back to Lily, staring down the embankment that led to the creek. Under the road was a culvert, and Lily listened to the water resounding inside its metal walls. A train whistled in the distance, and cars hummed on the highway, but there was no sound of a person moving in the brush. Had Martin been close, Lily felt sure they would have heard him. Every cough, every stick that broke underfoot would sound in the relative stillness. Lily stood beside Mabel and looked down at the creek, where moonlight shone in hundreds of broken pieces on the moving water. It was light enough to see the fallen tree that crossed the creek like a bridge. That was where the water curved, and the bank was steep enough to make climbing difficult. The entrance to the caves lay a hundred feet beyond the fallen tree, and if you walked along the bank another quarter of a mile, you would wind your way to the Bodlers', to where Lily had buried the shoes. It all seems so remote now, like I dreamed the whole thing, Lily said to herself, and looked down at Mabel whose sober face was lifted to the sky. "Orion," she said and pointed.

Lily nodded and turned her head in the direction of her old house. She hadn't been to look at it since the new people moved in. The man worked at 3M and the wife was a secretary at Grundhoffer and Lundqvist. They had three kids.

"Lily." Mabel's voice had an awed inflection. "What's that?" She was pointing toward the creek bank, and when Lily looked, she saw that about a hundred yards away, not far from the fallen tree, a white form was floating slowly toward them. Exactly where it began and ended was hard to tell, because it trailed gauzy appendages that made no human sense. "What is it?" Mabel whispered.

Lily stared and shook her head. "It's too far away." But the impossible thing continued to come toward them, and in the seconds that followed, Lily shuttled between belief and disbelief. She saw an angel, and she saw a ghost, and she saw some mad version of the Holy Spirit floating in the woods, but as soon as she had named each one, she dismissed it and told herself it must be something else. She wanted to look at it, and she wanted to run from it, but when the thing emerged from the black shadows of the trees and stopped beside the creek in a place where the moon shone down on it, and Lily saw wings, huge transparent wings like an insect's, she grabbed Mabel's hand and pulled her across the road and down the bank to the other side of the culvert. She felt she would be safe inside the big metal tube and still be able to look at the creature. Lily dropped Mabel's hand, grabbed the metal ribs of the culvert and sought a toehold with her boots on the large metal screws just above the waterline.

"I'm going in. You stay here," Lily said to Mabel. Inside the culvert, the noise of the moving water echoed terribly. Her cowboy boots slipped twice and Lily could feel water seeping through the leather soles.

Mabel spoke behind her, and her voice bounced off the walls. "It's Martin, Lily. He's carrying something." The echo came as a series of three repetitions, each fainter than the one before—but Lily knew even without seeing it clearly for herself that Mabel had to be right. Leaning forward to peer through the round opening of the culvert, Lily identified Martin's pale hair and oval face in a cloud of white netting. Because he was much closer now, Lily could see that the four wings must have been part of Cobweb's costume. They were so thin that they shook slightly in the wind. Then Lily understood that what had looked like an interruption in his body was a long, dark bundle he was carrying in his arms. She heard Mabel breathing behind her and turned her head. The woman had slid into the culvert herself and was half standing, half sitting against its curved wall. She held herself there with shaking arms and legs, and because she didn't dare to let go, she motioned violently with her head toward the outside bank where they had come in. But Lily ignored the signal and turned back to Martin. He stepped into the water, and as he crossed the creek with his burden, his features took on an eerie definition in the light—his eyes stood out and his lips seemed unnaturally red. And then through the tarp or blanket Lily recognized the limp form of a person, the shape of knees over

Martin's arm, sagging buttocks and a covered head falling backward over his other arm. She choked back a cry and heard herself grunt instead, and that gagging sound echoed. Martin stopped. He looked straight into the culvert. He sees us, Lily thought. He must see us. Her hands slipped then, but she caught herself and saw Martin wiggle his shoulders to adjust the body in his arms, and the blanket slipped. In that second, no more than a second, Lily saw the girl's head uncovered, her small, beautiful face and her long, dark hair falling over Martin's arm. The stillness of that body was absolute, and Lily screamed. The echo was terrible, and while it was still reverberating off the walls, Mabel fell. When she heard the splash, Lily lost her footing and slid down the ribbed wall of the culvert into the cold creek water. She stood up, slipped again on the wet metal bottom and screamed again. The sound bouncing inside the walls was like a third person in there with her, a shrieking lunatic, and then Mabel was shrieking, too. Lily lunged toward her. She could see Mabel's head above water moving downstream. Lily planted her feet on the culvert floor and braced herself. The water was only thigh deep, but the current pushed her forward, and she struggled to keep her balance. There was no question of swimming. Mabel had been dragged outside the culvert now, and Lily was forced to walk toward her at a maddenly slow pace, but once she found herself out of that tunnel, she threw herself toward Mabel. Her knee hit a stone on the creek bed and she cried out as she grabbed what must have been Mabel's elbow, reached for the woman under her arms and pulled her up. "Lily," Mabel said. Lily pulled the woman onto the bank, and with Mabel's small, heavy head against her chest, Lily listened to the sound of Martin driving away in his truck.

Lily gasped for air. The wind felt cold on her wet clothes and the tall grass made her arms itch. She heard the high noise of mosquitoes in the grass.

"My ankle," Mabel said. She bent over and pulled up her pant's leg. Lily noticed that Mabel was wearing little ballet flats with no socks. The sky had darkened, and even when she bent close to Mabel's leg, she couldn't see enough to figure out what had happened to it.

Every movement Lily made after that seemed to occur in another kind of time. Seconds, minutes, hours went haywire. She couldn't begin to guess how long it took to get from one place to another. But she helped Mabel to the car, settled her into the passenger seat and examined the ankle with the door open for light. A bloody gash ran from the ankle bone up the shin, and the joint had already begun to swell and discolor. Mabel's face had turned gray-white, and her lips were tinged with blue. Lily had never seen Mabel with wet hair plastered against her head, and the absence of the familiar light wisps of hair that softened the old face gave her the appearance of another person. Shivering uncontrollably, Mabel said, "There's a blanket in the trunk." Her teeth chattered audibly. Then she said, "This is ridiculous," and laughed. "Absolutely ridiculous." When Lily looked at the woman's glassy green eyes, she wondered if Mabel was about to go into shock.

Lily helped Mabel take off her wet clothes. They stuck to her skin, and after Lily had pulled off the shirt and brassiere, she removed a couple of dead leaves from her friend's white abdomen, which had a long ragged scar across it. It was strange to see Mabel naked—to look at her thinning wet pubic hair and her shrunken breasts on either side of a bony rib cage—but the little old body touched her, and when she wrapped the blanket securely around her, Mabel said nothing. Then Lily moved the palm of her hand along the woman's cheek, and while she was doing it, she recognized the gesture as her mother's.

Lily stared at the road ahead of her and drove slowly.

"Something isn't right," Mabel said. She was leaning her head against the window, and Lily heard that her teeth were now quiet.

"What are you saying?" Lily let a car pass her.

"Did you notice the way he carried her?"

Lily remembered the form in Martin's arms, the face and hair.

"She was so light, Lily. Not even a child . . ." Mabel croaked with hoarseness. "And why did he cross the creek? He was on the opposite bank. He could have gone up that way to get to his truck. Why get wet? Why wade through that water, unless . . ."

"Unless what?"

"He knew we were there, and he wanted us to see him from the beginning."

Lily found it hard to speak, to say what she had seen without sobbing. "I saw her face."

"Yes," Mabel said. She cleared her throat as if she were going to speak again, but stopped. Then she said, "Lily, there was a resemblance." She paused. "A strong resemblance, didn't you think?"

Lily watched the white line on the road, appearing and disappearing under the right car wheel. "A resemblance?"

"To you."

Lily didn't speak. No, she thought. No.

"You didn't see it?" Mabel said.

Lily shook her head, but her stomach seemed to rise inside her, and the chill she felt under her wet sleeves had gone into her bones.

Lily held the phone with her shoulder as she tied Mabel's terry cloth robe around her body. She dialed the police station and glanced at Mabel, who sat with her leg up in a pair of navy blue pajamas holding a little makeup mirror in one hand and a towel in the other. She fluffed her hair and Lily marveled at the woman's vanity. It's one o'clock in the morning, she just saw a dead body, and now she's fixing herself up. The next thing I know she'll get out her lipstick. No lipstick appeared, but when Hank answered the phone at the police station, Mabel was pinching her cheeks to restore some color to her ashen complexion. He recognized her voice and said, "Lily!" The happiness in his tone bruised her.

"It's not about us, Hank. I wouldn't call you at work to talk about us. I have to report something."

Hank didn't answer this. He listened to Lily tell her story about Martin at the creek. She mentioned Dick and Dolores and the photo of the dead girl. He was so silent, she asked him once if he was still on the line. He said, "Yes," but that was all.

When she had finished, Hank said, "Is that it?"

"Isn't that enough?"

Hank took a breath. "Martin Petersen's running around town in his fairy costume or his cowboy suit, depending on who's doing the looking, with a dead girl—well, for at least a week now, maybe more. Must be a smelly corpse. And nobody's missing, Lily, no men, women, girls or boys. A couple of dogs and a load of cats, but no *person* in the whole county."

"Well, Dakota County isn't the world, Hank."

"That's right, it's not the world, is it? Maybe Martin's knocked off one of your boyfriend's whores come all the way from New York City. Nobody keeps track of who's missing there."

"Mabel saw it, too, Hank."

"Well, she's off her rocker, too."

"That's not fair, Hank, and you know it. You're mad at me, so whatever I say now is bullshit."

Hank didn't reply to this.

"Tell me one thing," Lily said. "Who called about a man carrying a woman near the city limits? I read it in the log."

"Don't fuck with me, Lily." Hank sounded terribly angry.

"I'm not."

"You called. You made that call."

"What?" Lily looked out the window. In a small voice she said. "No, Hank, I didn't. I swear to you I didn't. Did you take the call?"

"No. Pete did."

"But where were you? It was your shift, wasn't it?"

"I was taking a piss. That all right with you?"

"Hank," Lily said. "I didn't call. Why would someone call and pretend to me? And with you as dispatcher?"

"Maybe you forgot."

"Oh, Hank," Lily said. "Please . . . "

"Good-bye, Lily."

Hank hung up before she could say good-bye. Lily stared into the room. It was lit by a single lamp on a small table next to Mabel's chair, and the bulb glowed yellow through the old shade. Mabel clasped the mirror in her limp right hand, her eyelids partly closed.

"Are you asleep, Mabel?" Lily said in a whisper as she stood over the chair.

"No, Lily, just tired.

"It was Hank. He doesn't believe me."

Mabel nodded. "I can't get to the bottom of it myself, but they'll check it out, believe me, they will."

Lily washed Mabel's ankle, wrapped it and made an ice pack. She helped Mabel hobble to her bed and pulled the sheet over her. Mabel's face was pale as eggshell, and her hair had dried to its familiar whiteness. Lily pulled up a chair and sat beside the bed. Had the girl's face looked like her own? Wouldn't she have seen it? Dolores had been seeing herself all over the place.... Had Martin killed her? Maybe he had found her already dead after somebody else killed her—the cowboy, maybe Tex? Could Dolores, drunk on her ass, have seen the murder? No, it's all wrong, Lily thought. The timing is wrong. Dick's story. Professor Vegan's story. But for some reason the muddled theory of Martin's innocence gave Lily hope. She hoped Tex had done it, or some nameless stranger. Maybe Martin had tried to save that girl. Maybe he couldn't, and now, distraught and crazy, he had taken to carrying the body around in a tarp dressed as Cobweb.

She sat down beside Mabel on the bed and looked at her. Her placid, exhausted face was suddenly a burden, an annoyance. She didn't look upset. She looked at ease. She wasn't taking this seriously. Lily grit her teeth.

"Whatever has happened, Lily," Mabel said in a low wise voice, "you're not involved or to blame, except possibly in that boy's imagination." Mabel whispered this with her eyes half open.

"Imagination?" Lily repeated. "What does imagination have to do with it? Why are you so calm?" Lily stepped back from the bed. "What's wrong with you? You were there. You saw exactly what I saw, and yet you don't care very much, do you?"

Mabel studied Lily intently, but with a quiet in her eyes that Lily read as condescension.

"Well, I care!" she said in a loud voice.

"Lily, don't you see? He wanted us to look at him. It was a, a performance of some kind, something staged. We called the police. What more can we do now?"

Lily narrowed her eyes. Tears were streaming down her cheeks. "I don't even know who you are ... " She didn't finish. Mabel's face turned whiter. Lily ran out of Mabel's apartment and slammed the door. She heard Mabel calling her name, but she ignored the voice and fled to her own room.

Through the wall Lily thought she heard Mabel crying. She wasn't sure, but there were low noises coming from next door. Nevertheless, she did not go back to Mabel that night. She listened to the last of the sniffling sounds and walked to her mirror. There she removed the robe she had borrowed from Mabel and looked at her naked reflection. She examined her body sharply and coldly and then, lifting her right hand, she slapped herself hard in the face. After the slap, she moved closer to the mirror to study the mark on her cheek. And then, before she crawled into bed, she slapped herself again—for good measure.

Lily slept more soundly than she would have thought possible and woke at her usual hour for work. Her head ached and her limbs felt heavy, but her mind was empty. She walked to the window first thing, without turning on any lights, and knelt beside the curtain, the way she used to before she knew Ed. Then she pulled it back to see if he was awake and painting.

Through his window, she saw him in his underwear holding a brush near the hidden canvas. She was glad she couldn't see the picture. It was only then that she remembered Martin in his costume with the girl in his arms. Looking at Ed, she thought, it's already gone, now, this moment. There isn't really a "now" at all. Even saying the word "now" is too slow for it. Now slips into then so fast, it's nothing at all. And as ordinary as this observation was, Lily felt she was living it, and its truth hit her hard. Time was inexpressible. She turned away from Ed, headed for the shower and remembered that she had been fired. There was no Ideal Cafe for her, no job, but Lily decided to go and beg Vince to take her back. She had never begged for anything in her life, and because Vince knew her, she figured a display of humility might overwhelm him. But what if he had already hired somebody else?

When Lily opened the back door to the cafe and peered cautiously through it, she saw no new girl. She saw Bert shaking her head at her. "If you knew the trouble you've caused around here, you'd regret it," she said. "Ever since you left, Vince has been on the warpath, and you know what that does to Boom—he gets all shaky and whiny. What were you thinking of, girl?" Bert leaned close to Lily and turned her head to one side. "You don't look good, you know that? For once in your life, you look like a wreck."

Lily looked at Bert, and as she looked, she realized her eyes felt very dry, as though there weren't enough liquid in them. She grabbed Bert's arm and said, "I saw her last night."

"Saw who?"

"The dead girl. I told you, remember? Martin was dressed up in his costume for the play, and he, he was carrying her body—at the creek. Mabel saw it, too, only I don't think she believed her own eyes."

Bert took Lily by the shoulders with both hands. "I've seen it coming. You haven't been yourself. You haven't called me for days. That's not normal, and I've been calling you, but you're never home. She's in love, I said, out of her mind in love, but it's not just that. There's something in your eyes, too." Bert withdrew her hands. "Like you're not right. Like you're possessed with this, this idea."

"What?" Lily said. "You don't believe me? You think I would make this up? Somebody's dead, murdered, and you think I'm kidding? Possessed? What are you talking about? You think I'm lying?"

"I didn't say that."

"Yes, you did."

Vince walked through the door. "You!" he bellowed at her, pointing a fat index finger in her direction. "Get out! I fired you!"

Lily shuddered at the big voice, but she didn't move. "I came to apologize," she said. "I'm sorry. I wasn't thinking." Her voice broke, and she tried desperately to recover an even tone. "Lately . . . " she said.

Vince strode toward her. Lily could see real anger in his face. Sometimes Vince played at anger, roared for his own amusement to stir things up in the cafe, but now he meant it, and withstanding the pitch of his emotion was hard, terribly hard. Lily was shaking. "Lately, my life," she said, "has been . . . " She searched for a word. What was the word? Finally she said, "Going to pieces because, because . . . " Lily began to wave her hands at her sides, then near her face. When she felt the tears coming, she clutched either side of her face and started sobbing. "Oh, Vince!" she said. "Oh, Vince!"

The man's expression changed. He looked at Bert with his mouth open and said, "What the hell is this?"

Bert gave Vince a sour look and took Lily into her arms. When she felt Bert's embrace, Lily squeezed her friend hard. After several seconds she felt Vince's large, tentative hand touch her back.

"Hey, hey, hey," he said. "Where's that crusty, hard-assed cookie that I've come to know and love? I mean, holy shit, Lily, you've got more fiber in you than this."

Bert said, "Give the kid a break, Vince. Everybody's got their limits. I mean, you'd scare the living daylights out of a sumo wrestler with the look you gave her."

Vince removed his hand.

Lily felt her sobs subside, and she pulled away from Bert to look at Vince. "I'm sorry," she said. "I'll never walk out on you again. I'm not myself, it's true, but I'm going to be myself again, I promise." She sniffed loudly. She looked up at Vince.

"Hey there," he said. "Your mascara's running. Now get your butts back to work. I got Bert to cover for you," he said to Lily. "So I've got two waitresses from five to eight when I only need one, and I'm going to pay you both. So I never want to hear another word out of either of you about me being a cheapskate. You got that?"

Bert and Lily nodded.

Bert heard almost the whole story from Lily that morning during the shift—told in bits and pieces between tables and on runs to the kitchen. Lily could see that Bert was troubled by what she heard, but it wasn't clear what she actually thought of it. She shook her head and asked Lily about forty times if she was absolutely sure she'd seen a face in the tarp. "Couldn't it have been something else? A dog, maybe, or some animal Martin pulled out of the creek?" The other part of the story Bert couldn't get over was Lily's visits to the Bodlers. "Why would you go there? Don't you get enough of them here?"

Lily responded to these questions with shrugs. The shoes were inexplicable. To talk about them would only confirm Bert's worry that Lily was having some kind of breakdown. "They know Martin," she said. "They're his great-uncles or something like that."

Before Lily left, Bert said, "Maybe you should talk to someone, Lily."

"I've talked to you, Bert."

"No, I mean like a minister or counselor or something."

"You think I'm out of my gourd."

"Would you stop telling me what I think. I'm not saying that."

"You think Pastor Carlsen's going to fix this? Can't you just see him?" Lily lowered her voice and gave herself a sincere expression. She nodded gravely. "Let us turn to the Lord in his infinite wisdom."

"He'd be more practical than that," Bert said.

"The man wouldn't have a clue," Lily said.

"I'm calling you today," Bert said.

Lily nodded and walked through the back door and up to her apartment. She knew exactly what she was going to do. She had two stops that afternoon. The first was the Stuart Hotel. For the second, she needed her flashlight.

When Ed answered the door, he didn't look like himself. It wasn't only that he seemed worn out and the skin under his eyes had turned blue-black or that he hadn't shaved in days. Lily had seen him exhausted and unkempt before. She had a sense that some familiar quality in his appearance had disappeared overnight, and the man who began speaking to her was a stranger. Before she could say hello, he told her that Mabel had called and told him about last night.

Lily looked behind him at the portrait of Mabel with the blank boxes above her head. She didn't feel like crying anymore. She felt empty.

"Lily"—Ed leaned toward her and brushed her cheek gently with the backs of his fingers—"I have something to tell you. After I hung up with Mabel, I starting thinking, and I'm pretty sure that that kid was here, Martin Petersen. But he gave me another name, said his name was Hal Dilly."

"Hal Dilly," she repeated. "There's a Dilly family in Webster, but no Hal. They run the old people's home. Did he stutter?"

"No, but one morning around ten last week, Wednesday, I think, this kid knocked on my door and asked me if I would show him the paintings, said his name was Hal Dilly, that he wanted to study art."

"What did he say?"

"Not much, but he studied all the paintings very carefully, and then afterward, he kept looking around the room like he was expecting to find something else." Ed rubbed his forehead. "He asked me if there weren't more. I said no, and he left." Ed paused. "Mabel isn't sure about what she saw. She said it was so fast, just a couple of seconds, that she couldn't be sure . . . "

"I saw her," Lily whispered.

"I know." He frowned. "While he was here, I didn't think about it very much, but after he was gone, I had a funny feeling that something wasn't right, that he was making fun of me, laughing up his sleeve, but then I told myself I was being paranoid." Ed sat down and looked at his painting. His large eyes were wide open and still. "Don't go near him," Ed said, without looking at her. Then he looked up at her, reached out, clutched her arm and kissed it.

A few minutes later, Lily walked out the door and did exactly what Ed had warned her not to do. She headed out of town on her bicycle.

Heath Creek changed in daylight. As Lily walked along the bank through the brush where Martin had walked only hours before, she found it odd that she could see what was around her. Her eyes felt sore, and the steadily darkening sky caused a turbid gloom over the trees and water, muting their colors to grays and browns. Somewhere above her on the other side of the creek she heard children playing, and Lily wondered why children always sound the same when they play, that it didn't seem to matter who they were or where they lived. She walked on, stepping quickly through the underbrush along the curve in the creek. As she neared the cave, she stumbled over an old sign from the Sheriff's Department, its warning rusted into illegibility, and as she looked down at it, she heard the children above her chanting. She couldn't hear what they were saying, but their rhyming verses were ridiculing somebody, and she listened to their cruelty with a mysterious pang of guilt. Lily crouched in front of the boarded, nailed entrance to the cave.

She saw the little door right away. Someone had cut it out of the boards. It had real hinges and was standing ajar, as if the dwarf who lived inside was expecting visitors. She opened the door further and was met by the moist, cool air of the cave. Before she crawled inside, she shone her flashlight into the first low, wide room near the entrance. She remembered it.

There was no sign that anyone had been in here for a long time. From that first room, you could crawl through a passageway to another. Nobody she knew had ever ventured beyond the second one, but that room was larger—an adult could stand up in it. She shone her light toward it, then turned it off. Another light shone from the second room. After stuffing the flashlight into her back pocket, Lily began to crawl through the passage. She heard the steady trickle of water coming from somewhere nearby. The damp cave floor made her knees raw, and her shoulders grazed the sides of the tunnel. When she had almost reached the turn where the passage opened onto the second room, she heard someone begin to whistle the only song from the only opera Lily had ever been able to name, and that melody was so strongly identified with Ed, meant Ed and no one else, that for several seconds Lily didn't accept that she was hearing it. The cave walls distorted the sound. Its origin could have been anywhere. She froze and held her breath. The noise was like the door—sensual information she resisted. But Lily knew that she was going to lurch headlong into whatever was waiting for her, and an instant later she pushed herself around the turn in the passage and saw Martin sitting there beside a small kerosene lamp that was flickering in some inexplicable draft. The room was filled with objects, piles of material, cardboard boxes, spools of thread, paints, but Lily didn't examine them closely. Martin had stopped whistling, but he didn't seem to see her. He wasn't moving, but his huge shadow on the cave wall trembled and leapt. He kept his eyes on the ground for a couple of seconds, then looked up at her and said, "I knew you'd come, Lily."

"What have you done with her?" Lily whispered at him.

Martin narrowed his eyes and turned his head. Lily inched forward into the room to see what Martin was looking at.

Against the far wall of the cave, slumped in a wheelchair was the girl Lily had seen the night before.

Lily cried out and clapped her hands over her mouth. She started crawling for the passageway, but she felt Martin's hands on her shoulders. He pulled her toward him, his grip much stronger than she had expected. She fought him hard, but Martin dragged her across the floor of the cave toward the body. Lily closed her eyes. She hit and wept, and then she felt Martin stop suddenly. He was behind her, holding her arms tightly. She kicked him. "L-l-look," he said. "L-look."

"No!"

"Look!" Martin let go of Lily. She opened her eyes and looked at the girl in the wheelchair. She recognized the chair as the one Martin had bought from Frank and Dick. Martin had his hands on either side of the girl's face, and Lily saw that this was the face of a doll, a beautifully made life-size doll whose proportions, unlike most dolls, were accurately human. And that it was a girl, not a woman, with a small only half-developed body.

"It's a doll," Lily said.

Martin nodded. "B-but you knew."

"It's a doll." Lily stared at the modeled face with its painted eyes and parted lips, its long, dark hair that fell over its shoulders. My costume, she thought. It's wearing Hermia's dress. And while she looked, she saw—all at once—that the thing looked like her or maybe like her a few years ago. Nobody's dead, she thought. Nobody's dead, and she felt a vibration in her jaw and in her temples. She didn't speak. Neither did Martin. She looked at the doll. There was something wrong with it, but she couldn't say what it was. It's cold in here, she said to herself. My mouth is dry. She moved her tongue back and forth in her mouth and then she said, "Where did you get it?"

"I-I-I," he said, "m-m-made y-you. It t-t-took a long time—a y-y-ear."

"What?" Lily said. She looked at Martin. Why is he stuttering now? she wondered. I'm dizzy. She took a step backward. Then she tried to focus on Martin. "I thought you had killed somebody, Martin. You showed me that picture. You said she wasn't alive. Last night . . ." Lily felt confused. The moving light didn't help. There's something wrong with my eyes, she thought. "What have you done?" Lily looked at the doll again. "What is it?"

"H-her face, arms and legs are made from Sculpey—i-it's pretty new stuff . . . "

Lily hadn't meant for him to explain how he'd made it. "No," she said, but he continued his explanation.

"I-it's like clay, but you can f-fire it at home in the oven."

Lily imagined Martin removing the doll's head from his oven, then an arm. She put her hand to her forehead. "You didn't ask me. You, you've done this behind my back. You were whistling. . . . That's Ed's song." Lily shook her head and showed Martin her palms, as if they could ward him off. "You've been spying on me for, for a long time. I've, I've heard you sneaking around." She looked up at him. He seemed taller in the cave. "Why?" Lily stepped backward and heard plastic rustle under her feet. The air inside the cave was hurting her lungs.

But Martin did not answer the questions. He walked toward her and said, "You spy, too. You spied on him."

Lily watched Martin's face. He was the whitest of all white men, and he was everywhere at once, seeing, knowing. "Who are you?" she asked again. "What do you mean by this? What is it for?" She took a step toward the doll. The thought that it might have some purpose seemed terrible.

The doll was resting on the back of the chair, its face turned upward toward the cave's moist, dripping ceiling, and Lily looked down at the long hair that fell over the chair's cane back. The wig, she said to herself. The grotesque possibility that Frank and Dick had known all along raced through her. "Do the twins know about this?"

Martin shook his head. "O-only you. L-Lily, you must listen to me."

"Tell me, then," she whispered and lifted her face to his. "Tell me."

Martin seemed to find this command funny. He laughed—a short, bitter burst of humor, and then it vanished. He lifted the doll out of the chair and held it in his arms. Mabel had been right—the body was lighter than a child's. "Sit down," he said smoothly.

Lily shook her head. She didn't want to sit in the wheelchair, didn't want any part of it. "I'll stand."

Martin's face registered disappointment, but only for a second. He placed the doll gently back in the chair, arranged its hands in its lap and then let the head droop on its chest as though it were asleep. He talked to her in that rhythmical intonation she had become accustomed to, rubbing his hands and fixing his eyes on her as he spoke. He stepped toward her, but Lily backed away. "She's the one between, Lily."

"Between?" Lily said. She dug her feet into the cave floor.

"Between you and me, between Becky and you, between Dahl and Doll, between the word and the flesh, between you and you."

Lily looked at her fingers, which were oddly yellow in the kerosene glow. "What are you saying?"

Martin rubbed his mouth. He seemed disappointed and began to explain slowly as he stepped toward her.

"Stay back. Don't come near me."

Martin looked hurt, but he didn't approach her. "I, I," he stuttered and winced. "I made you, so she, you, is between us. And between you and Becky—older than Becky, younger than you, the way you were, the way Becky would've been." He rocked his shoulders to his own voice, turning his speech into an incantation. "She is the in-car-na-tion," he said, giving each syllable the same weight, "of your name into its thing . . . "

Lily shook her head. "That's the oldest joke in the world, Martin—a stupid pun. That's all I ever heard on the playground. It's stupid—"

He interrupted her. "N-n-n-no! It's very important." Martin worked to control himself. "The word becoming flesh, Lily—the in-between moment, before—"

"No. It's not flesh! It's not real! It's a doll!" The words came back to her, high, crazy. Lily felt a tear rolling heavily down her cheek.

Martin seemed to grow calm with her anger. "It's doll flesh," he said. Lily thought he looked smug.

"And, Lily, it's you before—"

"Before what?" She spat at him. She didn't mean to, but she saw saliva fly.

"Before you changed."

"Changed?" Lily took another step backward. "How do you mean changed?" She whispered the last sentence. I'm cramped in here, she thought. It's too small. I can't see.

Martin wrinkled his forehead and stared at her. "It's you in another form."

Lily didn't answer him.

"You're a woman now," he said softly. "But you didn't used to be," he said in a low, conspiratorial voice. "D-d-d-d," he sputtered. "D-A-H-L," he spelled. "I'm Dahl, too. Underdahl. Don't you see? It's all part of it."

"What are you talking about?"

"H-E," Martin spelled. "It's in Hermia; it's in Helen; it's in Underdahl." Martin motioned with his hands. He turned to the doll.

"The letters?" Lily said. "You think 'H' and 'E' mean something?"

"There are lots of 'H-E's'—they keep moving, from one to the other, depending—Hermia's father. Helen's husband . . . Becky's father . . . Hal Dilly." Martin smiled.

Lily breathed out several times. "That name," she said, "who does it belong to?"

"I went between you and me. You were my disguise."

"What?"

But Martin kept talking. "They would've killed him, you know."

"Who?"

"He's a Jew, Lily. The Nazis would've killed him."

"Ed wasn't even born yet." Martin hadn't moved, but Lily said, "Stay away from me."

"I-If he'd been there, they would have killed him." Martin was whispering at her now, his face gold in the lamplight.

"Don't say that, Martin." Lily felt like crying.

Martin held himself and rocked back and forth a couple of times. He chanted again to keep his stuttering in check, and he said, "She's the under-doll, Lily, you." The singsong intonation of his voice had become unbearable, and Lily shook her head back and forth at him.

Martin took a step toward Lily. "You never forgave me for the refrigerator."

"The refrigerator?" Lily said. She put a hand to her forehead.

"At the Overlands'. The refrigerator in the garage."

"What?" she said.

"Snow White." Martin said. He walked toward her.

"Get back," she said.

Martin stepped back.

But Lily stood very still. "The drawing," she said slowly, "is a refrigerator?" Did she remember a refrigerator? Had something happened at the Overlands'? Snow White, she thought. I was Snow White in the third-grade play. She remembered Andrew Wilkens only pretending to kiss her, because he didn't want to get girl cooties. But Martin?

"In the garage," he said. "I tied you up and shut you in the old refrigerator. It was lying on its back."

Lily stared at him. "Was it a game?" she said. She was trying to remember. She didn't speak or move. Do I remember playing with Martin? Snow White? Wasn't it my cousin George who I played that game with? Hadn't it been George who slobbered her face with kisses behind the grapevines? Lily remembered a pinched sensation between her legs as if she'd had to pee. Had she been in the darkness of a shut refrigerator, closed in, unable to breathe? Was that it? Or was she remembering George? She had played girl to his boy, and the funny thing about it was that there was as much pretending in playing that girl as if she hadn't really been a girl to begin with. There was something, though, some vague sensation of being shut in. Or was it her grandparents' outhouse? George had closed the door and left her there, and she'd heard him laughing about the poop and the stink. "It wasn't you," she said.

Martin didn't blink. "Y-you never forgave me. At first you wanted to get in. I dared you. I dared you, and I stuck you down and closed the door. I-it was s-so heavy."

Lily shook her head. "I don't remember," she whispered at him. "Why were you at the Overlands'?"

"To be with you, Lily."

Lily leaned toward him. "Have you made this up, Martin? Are you lying to me now?"

Martin started to shake his head back and forth quickly. "You, you died, Lily."

"What?" Lily turned her head and looked at the opening in the cave wall that would take her out.

"I-I-I suffocated you. Th-there wasn't air for you to breathe in the refrigerator. I sat on it."

"But I'm here, now, Martin. Don't be stupid. Even if it did happen, we were kids, right, playing a game?" Lily examined Martin's face. Stubborn, inward, his expression blocked her words and their meaning.

"I tied you up."

"No," Lily said. It made her uneasy. Had he tied her up? Had she ever been tied up in her life? Why did she feel as if she had? Why did she know the sensation of rope chafing her ankles and wrists? Had it happened?

Lily looked into Martin's eyes. They were wide open. "Th-th-then after a long t-time, I looked inside, and, and it was over."

"No, Martin," Lily said. "No."

"Y-you were d-d-dead. I killed you." He paused. "A-and then I kissed you, and y-you stood up in your white dress—"

"No," Lily said.

Martin nodded. He whispered, "Like Hermia."

"I didn't even own a white dress when I was a kid, Martin. My mother hated white. It got too dirty, and out there . . ." Lily shook her head.

"Y-y-you did," he said forcefully. "And so did Becky. She wore it in her coffin."

"Stop it, Martin," Lily said. "Stop it!"

Lily felt tears running down her cheeks. "It isn't true. You're saying it to"—she paused—"to . . . " She couldn't finish. Why would he say it?

Martin bent over the wheelchair and lifted the doll into his arms again. Lily could see that its body was stuffed with some kind of cotton fill. When she stared at the face, she saw that the color of its eyes was wrong. The kerosene lamp flickered in the draft and Lily took a deep breath. "The eyes are blue," she whispered at Martin. "They're blue."

"I-I gave her my color," he said. Martin held the doll up toward Lily. She moved backward and stopped. He was offering it to her, and for a moment Lily thought it looked like some poor princess being sacrificed to the giants. Martin's chin trembled and his white eyelashes fluttered. "I-I want you to have her."

Before she could stop him, Martin had rushed forward and thrust the doll at her. She grabbed it and felt its hair brush her arm. It's just a doll, she said as she looked down at it. It's a thing. Lily fought the dread that welled up inside her.

"I can't, Martin. Take it back." Lily tried to return the doll to Martin, but he lifted his hands in the air and stepped away from her, the white gauze of his bandaged hand waving before her.

"I, I want you to take her!" he said in a loud voice that reverberated inside the cave. "It won't work otherwise."

Lily stared at him. "What? What won't work?" The doll couldn't have weighed much more than fifteen pounds, but its arms and legs were awkward to hold and its head rested heavily on her right arm. She looked down at its placid face and noticed that its red lips were slightly parted and drawn together, and this expression, whatever it was, revolted her.

Lily dropped the doll.

Martin screamed. He screamed like a woman, and the noise broke something inside her. She turned around and was about to run, when she heard Martin scream again. He grabbed her ankle and tripped her. Lily clawed the cave floor, but Martin had thrown himself on top of her, and pulled her around by the shoulders. He still had the doll, and he pressed it into her while he held her down, its hard head between them, pressing against Lily's throat until she gasped for breath, but Martin didn't release her. "I c-c-can't breathe," she choked out. His embrace was powerful, and Lily could see the muscles in his arm bulging as he squeezed her. She fought him, jerking her head back hard and fast to free her throat, and once her head was away from his grip, she slapped at his hands and hit the doll several times. Then Martin started crying. In the shifting light of the lamp, she saw him shaking and heard his sobs.

Lily threw herself toward the passageway. She scraped her knee but didn't stop. She crawled through the tunnel across the first room and out the little door. She didn't shut it. The light astonished her. No noise came from the cave, and walking to her bicycle she had a sense that her legs wouldn't hold her, that they had gone bad all of a sudden, and she asked herself how she could ride home. She sobbed as she trudged up the embankment to the road, and that was when the dog appeared. A Border collie came trotting along the road toward her. She didn't know him, but she bent down to pet his neck, and as she looked into his face, she suddenly found it curious that he couldn't speak. The dog cocked his head to one side in a gesture of confusion or sympathy, and Lily pulled the animal toward her. She pressed her face into his neck and cried. The dog stood very still and whined a little until she let him go.

Lily went straight to Mabel's apartment. She didn't knock but threw open the door and said in a loud voice, "It's a doll." She saw Ed first, and then Mabel, whose earnest, drawn expression made Lily wonder if she hadn't interrupted an intimate conversation. Mabel's hand had been on the manuscript, and when she saw Lily, she had withdrawn her fingers quickly. But Lily didn't speculate on what had been happening between them. She had a story to tell, and she told it. Lily didn't know when she began talking that she would omit the part about the refrigerator, but she did. Had she been sure that Martin was lying about locking her up, she would have told it, but she had doubts. Martin thought she had died and come back to life. Could she have lost consciousness and then woken up while he watched? If it never happened, why did the story awaken in her a sense of having been bound and locked in? Why did she recall the panic of losing air and yet not remember any of the details? Kids lock other kids in cellars and chests and closets and even old refrigerators all the time. Hadn't she heard a story about a girl who died in one? When she had finished, Mabel said, "Should we call the police?"

"Is it against the law to make dolls?" Lily said. Mabel didn't answer this.

"You could charge him with assault," Ed said. His voice had more emotion in it than Lily had ever heard. He clenched his fists and leaned toward her.

Lily looked at her watch. Hank was at the police station. She shook her head. "It wasn't like that, really. Nobody's dead. That's the important thing."

"What did it look like?" Ed said. "The doll?"

Lily tried to describe the doll, but it didn't translate easily into words, and she couldn't remember the name of the material Martin had used and baked in his oven. She sensed that she had disappointed Ed a little.

"Was it well done?" he said.

"Yes," Lily said. She looked into Ed's face, pressed her lips together and then said, "It was very well done. He said that it took him a year."

Before Ed and Lily left Mabel, they checked her ankle. Lily squatted in front of the woman's naked foot. It was better, but still swollen and blue. It was an old foot with protruding veins and corns on the bent toes. Lily made an ice pack and when she placed it under the ankle, she looked up into Mabel's face, and for the first time asked herself how long the old woman would live.

Lily told Ed she wanted to sleep in her own bed that night. She said it was to be close to Mabel, in case she needed anything, but this wasn't true. Her neck was still sore from her struggle with Martin in the cave, and Lily felt vulnerable. She wanted to lie in her own bed with Ed, and she wanted to hear Mabel through the wall, wanted to know that she was there.

Ed smiled briefly at the poster of Marilyn when he walked into her room. He had seen it before, but he appeared to take note of it for the first time, and there may have been irony in the smile, but Lily wasn't sure. Then, without a word, he picked her up, carried her to the bed and made love to her. His touch was different that night. He paid more attention to her face than he had ever done before, stroking her cheeks and eyebrows and mouth with his fingers and then tracing the line of her neck. He reminded Lily of a blind person sealing a face in memory through its contours. And Lily was glad he didn't hold her too hard. Her skin felt sore and raw, and every muscle in her body seemed to have been strained. Even her bones hurt her, although she didn't know how that was possible.

And then later, when he stood naked in front of the window with a cigar between two of his fingers, and Lily lay on the bed watching the smoke move toward the ceiling, he told her he was going back to New York the next morning to see Elizabeth.

Lily didn't want to look at him, so she stared at the ceiling and said, "For good?"

"I have to come back. My things, my work . . . "

"You're going back to her?"

"She wants to try again."

Lily heard him inhale smoke, then blow it out.

"Aren't you going to look at me?" he said.

"No."

He moved to the bed and sat down. The only light in the room came from the streetlamps outside, and Lily turned her head away from him and studied the shadows on the rumpled sheets near her thigh. "Those things you said about her," Lily said.

"It's all true."

"I don't understand."

"I owe it to her," he said in a soft voice.

"Because you're guilty?"

"Something like that."

Lily couldn't say what came over her at that moment or why she acted the way she did, but she refused to cry or fuss, and that refusal freed her from herself. It had something to do with Martin and the doll and the cave, but she didn't know why. Maybe she was tired of drama. It wasn't only pride that kept her from throwing herself at him and begging him not to leave her, it was that she could imagine the scene beforehand: every stupid, sordid moment of it, just like a soap opera on TV, and Lily knew that if she acted desperate, she would never see him again, and that her only hope was her toughness. Whether that toughness was real or not didn't seem to make much difference. She said, "Okay."

"Okay?" Ed said.

"Yes, okay."

"Don't you have anything else to say?"

Lily shook her head.

Ed opened his mouth to speak, but Lily sat up and put her finger over it. "No," she said. "That's what you owe me. The last word."

Lily slept deeply. The rain came during the night, and she woke to a light spray on her face from the window. Ed was gone. He had left a note on her night table, and Lily switched on the light to read it: "Couldn't sleep. Went home to pack. I love you. Ed."

Before Martin Petersen walked into the Ideal Cafe at seven-fifteen the next morning, Lily's shift was uneventful. Vince was in a particularly good mood, as was Boomer, whose spirits rose and fell with his boss's. Boom gave Lily tidbits of gossip—the Hell's Angels were in town and rumor had it they would crash the dance at Rick's that night. Linda Waller was reportedly having an affair with Mr. Biddle, the high school basketball coach, and Lily's ex-boyfriend Hank Farmer was "sticking it to" Denise Stickle. Lily did not respond to this last bit of gossip but stared blankly at the image of Elvis on the boy's chest smudged with sausage grease and thought that Denise was the perfect choice for Hank's revenge, if it was revenge and not "true love," and it did occur to Lily that knowing that Hank and Denise were an item might give more punch to Hermia's fight with Helena onstage.

When Lily saw Martin through the screen door with a large grocery bag in one hand, she turned cold. She walked quickly into the kitchen, and standing behind the door, she put a hand on her chest to quiet her racing heart. Vince watched her critically but didn't say anything. She took a deep breath. Out of the corner of her eye she saw Boomer imitate her gestures. She ignored him and left the kitchen. Martin was sitting in his booth. He had placed the bag close to him on the seat. Lily imagined the doll's head inside it, then remembered Martin's arms around her neck and she touched the spot on her throat to feel for soreness, but it was gone. He can't do anything here, she thought. Lily walked over to his booth.

She waited for him to tap or speak or do something, but he didn't. Finally he looked up at her, and Lily took a short breath. The face Martin had lifted to hers looked waxy. His lips were red, too red, and it took her a moment before she understood that he was wearing makeup, not the drugstore variety, but stage makeup—a light-colored, heavy pancake—and that his mouth was touched with lipstick. She stared at him, and taking her pad from her pocket, she asked him what he wanted.

Martin did not tap. He did not stutter, and there was no music in his voice. "I want what I always want, Lily."

The ease of Martin's speech alarmed her, and she thought, Something's terribly wrong.

In the kitchen, Lily said to Vince, "Martin Petersen's wearing makeup."

Vince peeked over the kitchen doors and said, "Well, I guess he's come out of the closet. I knew there was something of the fruitcake about that guy."

"That not it," Lily said. "He's not stuttering either."

Vince shrugged. "Well, there's no law against weirdos, Lil'. This is America. We grow 'em fast and furious."

Lily nodded. Ed's gone, she said to herself. And then she felt it, the grief she hadn't felt last night. She had a sudden urge to run to the bathroom and start bawling in there, but she stopped herself and walked out of the kitchen.

The truth was that Martin had attracted very little attention in the cafe. If Mike Fox, Harold Lundgren or the others had noticed Martin's peculiar face, they weren't showing any signs of curiosity, and Lily thought this was a good sign. She served Martin his poached eggs, refilled his coffee and waited on Mr. Berman, who was in early with his *Minneapolis Tribune* and what looked like a sheaf of order slips. Mr. Berman was the only one who bothered to give Martin a second glance. He raised his eyebrows to register mild surprise for Lily's benefit, but then he settled into his reading material and didn't look up.

Lily cleared Martin's plate. He had eaten all his food.

There were lines of smeared egg yolk on the plate, but that was all. She spoke to him in a whisper, the plate shaking in her hand. "It isn't true, is it, Martin, that you locked me up? It's just a story, right? Please tell me."

He looked at her but didn't speak.

"I want you to understand," she continued, still in a whisper, "I want you to leave me alone from now on."

"I know what I know," Martin said. His voice had no stutter and no inflection to it. When she walked off with Martin's plate to the kitchen, she noticed Harold Lundgren watching her for a couple of seconds before he brought his coffee cup to his lips. On her way back from the kitchen, she breathed in Mike Fox's eighth Kent as she passed the counter and saw that Martin had the paper bag on his lap and was unrolling the top. By the time she reached the end of the counter, he had his arm inside the bag and was pulling out what looked like a ratty pink towel. Lily stopped and said, "Martin." She didn't say it loudly, and she said it more to herself than to him.

But Martin had carefully set down the paper bag and was now engrossed in unrolling the towel. Lily watched him work with both hands. His bandaged left hand didn't hamper his movements. Lily started walking toward him. When she reached his booth, she gasped, and the cafe went dead quiet.

Martin had unrolled a gun, an enormous gun she guessed was a forty-five, bigger than the ones at the police station and heavier. It lay on the towel for only seconds before Martin took it in both hands. Lily started speaking silently to herself, stating facts as if what she was seeing had to be affirmed. It's a gun, but it can't be loaded. Why does he have a gun? "It's not loaded?" she said to Martin aloud. Behind her, she heard shouts. Vince was yelling, "Lily! Move! Get down!" But Lily thought, I'm too close to it. I can't. I can't move.

Martin was pointing the gun at the ceiling now. His white face had no expression at all, and behind Lily Mr. Berman was saying, "Put it down, Martin. You don't want to hurt anybody." And then Lily thought she heard Boomer crying, but it might have been somebody else. Martin moved the gun down and turned it on Lily. He blinked, and she saw his head wobble for an instant. I'm going to die right now, she thought. He's going to kill me in the Ideal Cafe. Right now, these are my last seconds. Lily felt her face convulse. The glare of hazy sunlight from the window hurt her eyes. This is my death, she said to herself, and looking into Martin's placid face, she started to sob, "No! No!" but he held the gun on her, and she choked and cried and listened to the screaming behind her and the sound of someone dialing a phone. Urine ran down her leg inside her jeans. She hadn't felt her bladder give way. She felt only the warm stream that seemed to run on and on. "No!" Lily yelled through the blur of her tears. "Please!"

Martin did not speak, but she saw him look around the cafe for several seconds, and then he turned the revolver toward himself and pushed the barrel into his mouth. Lily watched him. She saw his red lips stretch over the steel and saw his pale blue eyes looking at her. She noticed the awkward position of his hands and elbows as he held the gun. She saw the dirt in the creases of his knuckles, and she heard the blast. Lily saw Martin lose his face, saw skin and bone and blood fly. She saw his ruined head thrown back against the sunlit window. She saw his body stop moving, and she saw the blood continue to run. There's so much blood, she said to herself.

Then the nausea came and Lily grabbed her stomach. I'm dizzy, she thought. I'm so dizzy.

It was Vince who carried Lily upstairs to Mabel's apartment, but by the time she regained consciousness, he had gone back downstairs. She saw Mabel, and for a moment didn't remember what had happened in the cafe, but when she looked down at herself, she saw that her chest was covered with blood and began pulling off her T-shirt. She examined her bra and noticed that a spot of blood had seeped through the shirt, so she yanked off her bra, too. Lily took off all her clothes. Without saying a word, Mabel stuffed every garment into a plastic bag, tied it, and put it into her garbage can. Then Lily took a long shower and scrubbed herself with a cloth. Standing under the water, she rubbed every part of herself methodically, looking closely at her skin as she moved the washcloth over it. Twice she thought she saw blood on her feet, but the stains turned out to be shadows. Then she dressed herself in clean clothes that belonged to Mabel and noticed how pretty the blouse was, but when she emerged from the bathroom, Lily discovered she didn't want the garbage bag in the same room with her and insisted on carrying it down to the bins in the alley. "Let someone else do it, Lily," Mabel said. "I would, but my ankle."

Lily did it herself. When she passed the back door of the cafe, she saw that it was open and heard voices, one of them Lewis Van Son's, but she did not look in. Every sensual detail of the walk outside into the alley—the light, the warm air, the shine of the silver garbage cans, the muscles in her arms straining as she pushed the bag firmly into the bin—was oddly distinct and measured. Then she turned and walked back up to Mabel's. The sight of her legs on the stairs moving through space, the pain in her elbows and knees, the stiffness in her neck when she turned her head were present to her, but also absent. She felt her body, saw it, but didn't believe in it.

She telephoned her parents in Florida from Mabel's apartment. She heard her voice telling them what had happened, heard her mother gasp, heard her father's horrified exclamation in the background. She did not tell them Martin had held the gun on her. She said she wanted them to hear it from her before anybody else. "I'm not hurt. Nothing happened to me." Her mother said they would fly back to be with her, but Lily said no.

Lily and Mabel didn't talk much after the call, except about what to eat. They listened to the hubbub downstairs, to the police cars coming and going and the noise of other cars, to official voices that barked orders and the exclamations of people who had stumbled onto the aftermath of a spectacular suicide and were getting the dope.

Lily knew what she had seen. She knew that Martin Petersen had shot himself to death while she looked on. This was a fact. She remembered the pink towel, the gun aimed at her and then at himself. She remembered his lips around it, but after the gun went off, she found no image of him in her mind. She couldn't see Martin dead. She knew there had been a lot of blood, because she remembered telling herself about the blood, and she had seen it on her clothes. Now that she had rid herself of the clothes, only the words remained. The picture had disappeared. Other than that, there was nothing in her. She didn't feel sorry or sad or even shocked. She did know she didn't want to say anything to anybody, and Mabel didn't demand conversation, so Lily kept silent. She sat on

Mabel's sofa and looked at her legs and wiggled her toes. She watched herself move. There was an urgency about this that captivated her full attention. At about five o'clock she suddenly asked Mabel what day it was.

"Thursday, June twentieth." Mabel was reading with her glasses on, and she pulled them down to look at Lily.

"It's dress rehearsal!" Lily said. "I've got to get ready."

"No, Lily. You're in no shape to go."

It was Mabel's tone that decided for Lily. It was incontrovertible. Lily was silent.

Mabel phoned Mrs. Wright and kept her voice very low throughout the conversation.

After dinner they heard the band at Rick's, not the music so much as the bass, a steady pounding beat that went on and on. Motorcycles roared on Division Street, and Lily remembered the Hell's Angels. It thundered, and then it rained.

At about nine o'clock, Hank knocked at Mabel's door.

Lily was sitting on the sofa looking at her knees under Mabel's pajama pants. Hank sat down beside her. She looked up but Hank didn't speak. A piece of hair had fallen across his moist forehead and stuck to his skin. It thundered again. She had nothing to tell him. Yesterday she had wanted to explain to Hank about the doll, but now she didn't.

"I'm sorry about what happened," he said.

"Is he at Swensen's?" Lily said. "Martin, is he at Swensen's?"

Lily saw Hank glance at Mabel. "Yes. The funeral's Saturday."

"The funeral," Lily repeated. She had forgotten about a funeral. Of course, there would be a funeral.

Hank hugged her, but Lily didn't hug him back. She

stiffened at his touch and turned her head away. He was trying to be nice, but she didn't care.

That night, the next night, and for many nights after that, Lily slept with Mabel in the woman's big bed, surrounded by bookcases on all sides.

Mickey Berner played Cobweb. He wore the clean and pressed costume Mrs. Baker found hanging in the wardrobe room Wednesday night. Mickey was bad, but then nobody expected him to be good. Martin Petersen had been the best fairy in the play, and everybody knew it. Lily was surprised when Mabel asked her if she wanted to go on after what had happened. Of course she did. She rode her bicycle to the Arts Guild and pretended nobody was staring at her when she walked through the doors. She had expected the cast to be upset, to be amazed by Martin's death, and they were. But more than that, the suicide seemed to have enlivened the cast like a stimulant. Oren pledged his performance to Martin. Gordon declared loudly that the play would "keep Martin's memory alive," and Denise cried in the dressing room. Lily didn't cry. She had been too close, and her closeness to Martin's death made the others circumspect and distant. Mrs. Wright had told her how sorry she was, but the awkward expression on her face looked a lot like shame to Lily. Only Mrs. Baker hugged her, and when the woman's arms came around her, Lily felt a quaking inside her and the threat of real sobs, but she did not give in to them and couldn't return the embrace. "I'm all right," she said. "Thanks."

When Lily put on her costume Friday night for the first performance and looked in the mirror, she lost Hermia and forgot her lines. She had often dreamed of such a moment, going onstage without a word in her head. But it didn't last. When she heard her cues, the lines came back to her and so did Hermia, who seemed to have changed again, to have become a little fiercer and more passionate, and when she fought Helena, the audience was very, very quiet. Mabel sat in the front row, and once when Lily looked down at her while she was speaking, she saw the old woman's lips moving without sound. And after that first performance was over, and Lily was cheered and congratulated, she kept Hermia inside her a little longer, and she and Jim held hands offstage.

Saturday, the weather was perfect. Winds from the Dakotas swept in a cloudless sky and low humidity, and walking up the church steps Lily thought to herself that her father would have seen it coming if he had been there. The church wasn't full, but it was almost full. Lily seated herself beside Mabel in a pew toward the back and noticed several people turning their heads to get a glimpse of the waitress who had served Martin Petersen his last meal. Ida came wearing a silver bow in her high hairdo. Mrs. Baker and Mrs. Wright came with their husbands. Jim, Denise, Oren and Gordon arrived together. Bert brought Boomer, but Vince stayed home. Lily recognized Martin's sister, Eileen, and his older brother, whose name she couldn't remember. Lily waited for them, but Frank and Dick never shuffled into the church. Dolores came. She wore a blue suit that hugged her figure and had put her hair up. The effect tamed her, Lily thought.

Pastor Carlsen avoided the word "suicide." She guessed she would have heard if he had said it, but the truth was that Lily didn't listen very closely. Martin's coffin was standing in the front of the church, and she looked at it very hard to focus herself. She imagined Martin inside the coffin, and then she tried to remember the doll. She had been worrying about that doll. She didn't want anyone to find it and recognize her in its face and body. Martin could have left it anywhere, and as she thought about the doll, she tugged repeatedly at the material of the black blouse she was wearing, the one Mabel had given her. She did this without thinking and didn't stop until she felt Mabel's hand close over hers. She lowered her hand and looked at Mabel's cane. It had a taupe rubber grip. If someone finds it, they'll know it's me, she said to herself.

Martin's sister was talking, and Lily tried to find Martin's face in hers, but she couldn't. Eileen had just finished saying, "My brother was a kind person," when she looked up, opened her mouth wide and emitted an odd, little noise. It wasn't loud, but it expressed amazement, and the congregation turned as one to look toward the back of the church and saw Tex charging down the aisle dressed like an outlaw from the old West, complete with black hat, six-shooters at his hips and spurs that jingled as he flew past Lily and Mabel's pew toward the coffin. Had it not been church, Lily knew that several people would have leapt to their feet immediately, but it was church and for a couple of seconds a horrified pause fell over the sanctuary. Then from the back a child started crying, and Lily saw Martin's brother leap to his feet and saw Pastor Carlsen with his hands raised and his mouth open. He was speaking, but Lily heard nothing through the din that had now broken out among the people in the pews.

Lily didn't move. Tex had mounted the coffin and was straddling it awkwardly. Big as he was, the coffin was too wide for playing horse, and the next thing she knew Tex was pounding on the lid, yelling, "Marty! Marty!" Four or five men near the pulpit, including Pastor Carlsen, threw themselves at Tex and dragged him off the coffin, but the huge man turned and heaved himself back toward the box, and for a second or so, no more, Lily thought she saw the lid of the coffin opening. Her face vibrated with what felt like electricity. She shut her eyes and imagined Martin sitting up in his coffin and climbing out. In her mind, he was wearing his costume but then she wondered how they had dressed him. In Webster, every male corpse she had ever seen had worn a navy blue suit—her grandfather, her uncle, Mr. Deerhoeven. When she opened her eyes, she saw Pastor Carlsen untangling his vestments from Tex's spurs. The coffin was closed.

After Lewis Van Son and Dick Shockley hauled off Howard Gubber to jail, everybody stayed for the end of the service. Lily could feel the collective determination in the room to finish what they had started. Eileen was shaking, but she continued her speech. She said Martin loved carpentry and books and animals. Lily didn't know about the animals, but she took his sister's word for it. It's all true, she thought, and it's all a lie. Eileen wanted to remember him, to say what was right, but Lily had a feeling you could dig and dig and talk and talk until doomsday and no "real" Martin would be found, that whatever had been there, you couldn't say it. When the pallbearers carried the hidden body out of the church, Lily fumbled for Mabel's hand without looking at her, and she held on to it through the benediction: "The Lord bless thee and keep thee. The Lord make his face shine upon thee and give thee peace."

The Ideal Cafe reopened the following Monday, and Lily started working her usual shift. For about a week the only people who sat at the booth by the window were from out of town. After that, nobody seemed to care where they sat, but Martin's death remained a hot topic. People were less interested in why Martin had killed himself than Lily would have thought. They said he was crazy or in despair, but that's all. As far as she could tell, they took it, as her aunt Irma used to say, "philosophically." It interested her, too, that Martin's pointing the gun at Lily wasn't included in the story. People in the cafe that day must have seen it, Lily thought, but nobody talked about it. Nevertheless, Lily sensed that there was talk about her and Martin, and that even if nobody blamed her for Martin's death, they knew she had been somehow involved in it. When people stared and whispered, she felt as if she had become an object to point at and say, "She was right there when he did it—only inches away. There was blood all over her."

For several days Boomer Wee gave tours of the "suicide booth," mostly to boys under twelve. Then Vince got wind of it and told him to stop. But while it lasted, Boomer charged a quarter for the "reenactment": "Had the weapon in a bag. Big sucker. Stuck it 'tween his teeth." That was Boomer's cue to bite down on his finger and throw himself backward toward the window while he continued his description, which came straight from the pages of a comic book: "Pow! Bang! Blew his head off!" Boomer had been in the kitchen when Martin shot himself. He had seen him die through the door. Apparently only seconds after the shot, Mike Fox had come barreling into the kitchen, and Boomer had thrown up all over both of them. Something about Boomer's performance fascinated Lily. She didn't mind seeing it, just as she didn't mind the abbreviated version of the story that was told again and again. "Martin Petersen walked into the Ideal Cafe and ordered his breakfast as usual. He ate it, every last bite, and then he took out a gun and blew his brains out." Neither Boomer's theatrics nor the little story misrepresented what had happened, and yet when Lily watched Boomer gyrating in the booth or listened to someone telling about the suicide, she experienced the gestures and words as evasions. She had forgotten Martin's corpse, but somehow that blank spot in her mind where his body should have been came closer to the truth than anything anyone could do or say.

A rumor began to circulate that had purportedly started at the funeral home. It was said that when Martin's body was being prepared for embalming, the bandage on his left hand was removed and that Lily's name had been carved into the skin of his hand below the knuckles. Bert told Lily one morning in the cafe to stop Boomer from spilling the beans first.

Lily said nothing. She looked at Bert for a moment, then turned away and stared at Division Street through the window.

Bert touched Lily's arm from behind. "He's dead, Lily. It doesn't matter anymore."

Since Martin's death, Bert had left groceries for Mabel and Lily, had baked pies and cooked casseroles and delivered them without waiting for thanks. She had called Lily every day to "shoot the breeze" and had pretended that Lily was holding up her end of the conversation.

"It will blow over, Lil'," she said.

Lily looked down at her apron. "There's something wrong with me, Bert. I can do everything—work, eat, sleep, talk— but I don't want to do any of it." Lily didn't look at Bert's face, but she grabbed her friend's hand and squeezed it. "It's like they smell the corpse on me, Bert. Sometimes, I think I smell it."

Bert looked down at her own hand.

Lily felt a shudder go through Bert's fingers, and she let go.

Later that day, the day she heard about Martin's hand, Lily covered the mirror in her room. She didn't explain this act to herself, but she draped her bathrobe over the mirror and left the medicine cabinet open in the bathroom so she didn't have to see herself there. She didn't spend a lot of time in her own apartment anyway except to change her clothes. She lived with Mabel now, although neither of them had said this in so many words, and she avoided Mabel's two mirrors rather easily. They were both small.

One evening, Mabel lifted her manuscript off her desk and told Lily it was time she read it to somebody, and that was how their nightly reading began. Mabel's book was much simpler than Lily had imagined. It began: "My first memory is of my mother. She is squatting on the floor with her arms open and I am walking toward her." Mabel's first memories were isolated fragments that she told in high detail—a tablecloth with green glasses on it, her brother naked in the outhouse and a dead cat. At about seven, her memories became more continuous, and she began to tell the story of her childhood in South Dakota and to recount early dreams she could remember. Lily liked the dream Mabel read to her about flying over a city and rescuing her brother from a witch who lived in a shack that was covered with newspapers.

Lily discovered that the reading was her favorite part of the day. Sometimes they read in bed. Mabel would sit up with pillows behind her, and Lily would lie with her head down and listen to the years go by slowly or quickly, depending on the events recorded. In the book Mabel often poked fun at her younger self, and she and Lily laughed together. Lily thought it odd that she could laugh at what was written in the book but found nothing in her own life funny anymore. When Mabel arrived at the page that told of her mother's death, Lily cried for the first time since the day she had found Martin in the cave.

The two women had gotten used to the business of sleeping together. At first Lily had held herself tightly against the edge of the bed, conscious even in her sleep of the old woman's body, but that awareness disappeared, and often they would wake up entangled in each other—an arm or a leg thrown over the other—and after the first few times, they didn't bother with apologies.

As it turned out, Mabel had been keeping a secret. The woman read the passage that revealed it in the same voice she had read every other page. In Chicago, when Mabel was eighteen years old, she had found herself pregnant, poor and alone after she had left Owen Hartwig at the courthouse. She gave the baby away—a little girl—and she had never been able to find her. She didn't know whether her daughter had lived or died or what her name was. "It's such an old story," Mabel read to Lily, "an old, familiar story, told over and over again, but that doesn't make the grief of it any less. I never gave away the things I salvaged from that room—the table, the keys and the bird's nest. That was where the woman from the adoption agency gave the speech that persuaded me to give up my daughter. It was a bad speech, full of clichés and tired rebukes. Even then, I knew how stupid it was, but I memorized it and have never forgotten it. As she talked, I fixed the words onto the various objects in the room and burnt them into my mind. It wasn't a long speech."

Lily turned over in bed and looked at Mabel. "What did you name her, Mabel?"

"Anna," said Mabel. "Anna Wasley."

"Isn't Wasley your married name?"

"I was a bluestocking, Lily," Mabel said. "I never changed my name."

By the second week of July, Lily realized that she hadn't menstruated. Ed had not written or called. His disappearance was so absolute that he no longer seemed real to her. Mabel told her that he had paid the July rent at the Stuart Hotel and that she expected him, but Lily did not. Still, there had been days when she had wanted to call him, when she believed he wanted to hear from her, days when she hoped. She had his telephone number and address on a little piece of paper that she kept on her night table, and once she had gone so far as to dial the number. But after listening to a single ring, she had hung up. Lily had been afraid Elizabeth would answer. She had started a letter to him as well, but when she had read it over, she hated every word she had written and threw it into the wastebasket. She felt her belly often, examined it for signs of some change, some indication of fetal life, but she couldn't tell. Although she stayed away from mirrors, she looked at her arms and legs and feet often and felt them with her fingers. Sometimes when Mabel read to her, Lily stroked her arm over and over or rocked herself in the bed. Mabel brushed Lily's hair before work and laid out her clothes. Once she put out lipstick and a small mirror on the table. Lily knew it was a hint, but she ignored it. She didn't go to the doctor. If she was pregnant, she wouldn't change it anyway. That was for other people.

Lily read the police log twice a week as soon as the *Chronicle* came out. She was waiting for someone to find the doll, but nobody did. There were three unusual sightings during the month of July, however: a UFO over Dundas, a ghostly cowboy running in the direction of the public pool and another angel. The angel was spotted in the Klatschwetter field, maybe by Mrs. Klatschwetter herself, although no name was mentioned, and it caused a rash of angel jokes in the cafe for about a week. Lily didn't believe a word of these reports, but it seemed to her that somebody out there was making fun of her. When Lily mentioned the angel to Mabel, she paused for a moment and said, "I think you should go to the cemetery and see Martin Petersen's grave, Lily."

"What?"

"Just as I said. I'll go with you if you like."

Lily didn't answer Mabel, but she started thinking about Martin's grave. Did it have a stone yet? Would there be writing on his headstone or just his dates? Had they put him beside his mother? Lily hugged herself and shut her eyes on Mabel's sofa. She remembered Martin talking about the doll as a thing "between." Why did she feel that his grave was between, too, that it was between her and Martin.

"They're casting for *My Fair Lady* at the Arts Guild, Lily. Auditions are in two weeks." Mabel's sharp voice cut Lily off from her thoughts. She looked at her.

"You should try out for Eliza Doolittle."

Lily eyed Mabel but said nothing. The woman seemed to age a little every day: her wrinkles looked deeper, her face more skeletal. She even seemed to have less hair.

The morning following that conversation, Ed walked into the cafe. Mike Fox paused from his Kents. Pete Lund looked up from his coffee, and Vince and Boomer stood watching behind the kitchen door. But Lily hadn't known he was there until she felt a hand on her shoulder and turned around and saw Ed standing beside the cash register. She remembered him with a sudden, violent rush of familiarity. He looked the same. But Lily had an urge to scream, the way people do in movies when they think someone is dead and it turns out they're alive.

He started talking to her in a low voice and tried to take her hand, but she held it back from him.

"I didn't know," he said. "I didn't know until just now when I ran into Stanley and he told me what happened. You should have called me, Lily. You should have written me. I would have dropped everything and come . . . "

It's too much for me, she thought. Seeing him now. I'll crack. What does he want?

Lily heard Vince clearing his throat behind her. She felt her face moving uncontrollably. She opened her mouth and shut it. She blinked and felt a gob of mucus in her throat.

Then Vince was behind the counter, Vince, who had been unnaturally nice to her since Martin's death. He was waving an accusatory finger at Ed, and Lily heard him say that maybe Ed should have bothered to check in with her, that she'd been through hell, and where the hell had he been all that time? Lily backed away from both of them until Vince threatened to "deck" Ed. She staggered forward and stood between them, looking from one to the other. "Stop it," she said, and as she looked up into Ed's face, she asked herself who he was, this man who had come and gone and then come back again, and why he thought he could pop in and out of her life like a jack-in-the-box. I'm really mad at you, she thought all of a sudden. Lily didn't look Ed in the face. "You never called me," she said. "You never called me once." She clenched her fists at her sides and grit her teeth. It seemed to her that if she strained every muscle in her body, she could hold herself together. "I'll come and talk to you after my shift," she whispered, addressing Ed's hands.

Vince, who had stepped back several feet, said to Lily that he'd get Bert to cover for her if she wanted, but Lily turned to him and in the calm, loud voice she had used for Hermia told him that she had promised she would never walk out on him again, and by God she was going to stick to it.

Vince, looking very red in the face, retreated, and after he had disappeared into the kitchen, Lily heard Boomer give a long, loud whistle.

Before she walked across the street to the Stuart Hotel, Lily went into the toilet and looked at herself in the mirror. The face she saw was younger, prettier and paler than she remembered, and she was glad she had looked at herself, because she wanted to know what Ed was going to see.

At Ed's, Lily saw a suitcase lying open on the floor, and she recognized his T-shirts and jeans spilling out of it. She had worn some of those clothes. The room smelled of paint, smoke and other nameless but familiar things, and when she sat down in the canvas chair, Lily felt afraid of those smells. They had come to mean Ed's body and sex with him in the little iron bed, and she wondered if she would dare to let him touch her again.

Ed sat across from her, but Lily found it hard to look at him, so she studied her hands.

"Stanley didn't say it in so many words," Ed said. "But he basically told me I'd been a shit when I ran into him downstairs. He stood there shaking his head and avoiding my eyes.

'You should have been in touch with that girl.' He said that several times. I'm sorry, Lily. I'm terribly sorry . . . "

"Why did you come back?" she said.

"Look at me, Lily,"

"I don't want to."

"Okay," he said. "Don't look at me. What you've been through is terrible. I wish I had known . . . "

"Why did you come back?"

"It's over with Elizabeth. She didn't really want me. She found out about you, and that's when she started pushing me to try again, but it didn't take me long to realize that nothing had changed. It felt like a sham."

Lily looked at the painting of Mabel, which was still standing in the center of the room with its empty story boxes, and asked herself why Elizabeth seemed so unimportant now. The word "sham" seemed to leave a trace in her ear. She repeated it aloud—"Sham."

"I'm sorry."

She knew he was. "I'm sorry, too," she said. It wasn't an apology. It was more like a comment on the world in general, the way things happen or don't happen.

Ed seemed to understand this, because he didn't say anything. She looked at him and noticed that although his body remained still, his face looked grim and set. He stood up, walked to the suitcase, and after riffling through some of the clothes, pulled out a sketchbook and brought it to her. "I drew Martin," he said. "I started drawing him after he left that day, and I've been doing sketches for a while. I want you to have them. You can do whatever you want with them—burn them, throw them away. I don't care."

She could hear the decision in his voice—the stubborn

will that she remembered. He opened the book and handed it to her.

Lily looked down at Martin. There was no background, no floor, no place in which he was standing in the picture. His body seemed to float on the page, and in his right hand he was holding a cowboy hat. He looked very young—like a boy. She closed her eyes. "You wanted to paint him," she said, understanding all at once what the sketches meant. "He was going to be the fifth one." She was whispering to keep away the tears.

"I thought about it," Ed said. "But I had decided not to. That's the truth." Lily noticed that Ed was jiggling his knee.

"Martin was afraid you were going to paint me, but you wanted to paint him. It's funny." Lily made a sound, half laugh, half sob, and handed the sketchbook back to Ed. "He . . . he . . . " She put her hand over her mouth so Ed wouldn't see her lips trembling.

He leaned forward. "I love you," he said. "I'm not sure that makes any difference now, but I want us to be together."

Lily sat back in the chair and waved him off. After he had pulled away from her, she met his eyes but didn't answer him. What are you saying? she said to herself. What do you mean? And then as she continued looking at him, she thought, I used to watch you early in the morning before the sun came up. I used to go to the window just to look at you, because I wanted to see you, no, because I had to see you. Why? she thought. Aren't you saying now what I dreamed you would say to me from the very beginning? It's strange, Lily thought. Everything is strange in the world. And she looked toward the window and without knowing why she remembered Oberon's speech near the end of the play: "I then did ask of her her changeling child; / Which straight she gave me, and her fairy sent / To bear him to my bower in fairyland. / And now I have the boy, / I will undo / This hateful imperfection of her eyes." And Lily felt her chin begin to shake, then her neck and shoulders. She didn't try to stop the shuddering. It seemed all right now, like a seizure that had been a long time in coming. It wasn't just that Ed was telling her that he wanted her or that she realized how terribly she had missed him. It was also that Vince had been ready to punch him and that Stanley had yelled at him, and it was the afternoon light coming through the window, and the happiness in Mabel's face on the painting. It was her own brown legs in Ed's chair and the warm tears falling on them. And it must have been Martin, too.

"I want you to come to New York with me," he said. "I want you to live with me."

Lily shook her head. She wasn't saying no. She just felt overwhelmed.

"If you don't want to live with me, I'll help you find an apartment. You can take acting classes there, and we can see each other every day. If not every day, as much as you want to. I'm not going to give you up, Lily."

Still she couldn't say anything. She looked at the floor and went on crying.

But she let him kiss her then, and she cried off and on through the hours they spent in bed together. Later, when he sat up and started reaching for his clothes, she stopped him.

"I want you to go to the window," she said, "and just stand there looking at me."

Without asking any questions, Ed walked quickly across the room. And then Lily lay on the bed and looked at him standing naked in front of the window and several long minutes passed before she told him it was all right to move.

Mabel told Ed about her lost daughter by describing the pictures he had to draw in the narrative boxes. In the first was a pregnant girl and the adoption agency woman in the room in Chicago. Mabel remembered the room in such detail that Lily found it uncanny. In the second, the girl sat in the same room alone staring out a window. In the third an old woman sat in the same position in Mabel's living room across the street. In this last room, the window was on the other side. She gave him these drawing instructions in the evening, and when she had finished telling him what she wanted, Lily felt that the room was drained of everything except stillness and twilight and Mabel's unseen grief.

During the days that followed, however, Mabel exhausted Ed with those boxes. She criticized his drawings ferociously. This thing and that were all wrong. She insisted he change the chair's seat and the table's legs until they satisfied her. "It's not naturalism," he told her. "I'm not drawing from life, don't you see? It's the story that counts."

"You're drawing from my life, damn it," she said, "and you'll listen."

Mabel won every point, and then Mabel and Tex and Stanley and Dolores were packed up, crated and shipped.

"Maybe someone will buy them when you show the paintings in September," Lily said as she sat with Ed and his suitcases in the empty room.

"I hope so," he said. "People are buying all kinds of shit in New York these days. I might get lucky."

"Some rich person will hang Mabel or Tex on their wall,

and they won't even know who they are. They'll say, I like that old lady or that naked cowboy, and they'll tell their friends they bought 'a Shapiro.' "

"And their friends will wrinkle their noses and say, 'Who's that?' "

"It's just funny, that's all." Lily looked at him. She hadn't told Ed that she might be pregnant. She wasn't sure, and she didn't want to say anything until she was.

Ed rubbed his face and lit his last cigar in Webster. "I know that you haven't promised me anything, but I've decided to be patient."

Lily looked at him and smiled.

"I'm going to call you every day."

She kissed him. And then he was gone.

About a week later, Mabel and Lily were lying beside each other in bed when Mabel sat up and said in a low voice. "Are you going to move to New York, Lily?"

"I don't know. What do you think?" Lily sat up and hugged her knees in the dark.

"I think you should leave here," Mabel said. "You shouldn't stay in Webster. I've come to like this town, and it's fine for an old lady who's coming to an end." Mabel grinned as if this were a good joke. "But you've got too much for this place, and after a while it will beat you down. And New York . . . " Mabel shook her head. "New York is the best city in the world and the worst city."

"You want me to go," Lily said.

"Yes." Mabel paused. "But I want you to go for yourself."

"Not for Ed."

"Not for Ed," Mabel repeated.

Through the window Lily could see the bricks of the Stuart Hotel. "I can't live with him," she said. "I can't live with anybody." She smiled when she realized what she had said. "Except you, I guess. I'm in love with Ed, but there's a lot I don't understand about him . . . "

"I was married to Evan for fifteen years, and I never knew him completely. I've been thinking about him ever since he died all those years ago, and I still can't explain him. But I adored him."

"Didn't you ever fight?"

"Of course we fought. I was a hellcat in those days—an impossible woman."

"If I go to New York, you'll lose your roommate."

Mabel turned her head away from Lily and looked at the wall. From outside in the street she heard the bus for Des Moines stop in front of the Stuart Hotel and then the hydraulic whoosh of the bus door as it opened to let in a passenger. Looking at the back of Mabel's head, Lily heard the woman say, "I think about her every day, about my Anna. If she's still alive, she's much older than you. She could be a grandmother. I could be a great-grandmother. Isn't that something?"

And suddenly Lily felt Mabel's child as someone very real, as a person who was living now or had lived, and in the same moment, she wondered if Anna wasn't turning her into a ghost, if she hadn't become in some funny way a substitute for the baby Mabel had lost.

Mabel turned her face toward Lily, and her voice cracked as she spoke. "I'd never ask you to stay here, you know, to hold my hand at the Dilly Home when I'm hooked up to some goddamned breathing machine. It's not my style."

Lily looked at the woman's face and touched her cheek. "I know," she said. "But sometimes people do things because they want to—things like holding a person's hand." Lily lay back on the pillow. "Now," she said, "read to me."

And Mabel did.

The first Saturday in August, Lily rode her bicycle to the graveyard after work. It was a hot, dry day and the grass had begun to scorch yellow-brown from too much sun. When she arrived at the cemetery, she didn't know where to look for Martin's grave, except to walk beyond the old graves toward the new. "He probably doesn't have a stone yet. I won't know which is his. Old Mrs. Knutsen was buried last week. She'll have flowers, and Martin won't, probably." Lily muttered these observations as she walked past one marker after another toward the treeless place at the edge of the cemetery that looked over the wide farmland flats of corn and alfalfa. There were three nameless graves, and Lily stopped beside one that had new sod over the earth and guessed it was Martin's. It occurred to her that it was expensive to die, expensive for your relatives. She wondered if the sod came with the deal or if you paid extra. She stood on the new grass, put her feet squarely on it and tried to feel something important like an ending. But the truth was she didn't feel anything. There was a hot wind, and in it the smell of a distant fire mixed with dry alfalfa and car exhaust. The wind blew onto her face as she stared at the line of the horizon.

Then she thought about the shoes and the stone she had marked them with. She thought about Dolores, too, her face in the car when she had driven Lily home, and her heavy thighs on the sheets of her bed. Lily lay down on top of the grave. The sod, after all, was man-size, and she fit inside the rectangle. She lay her cheek on the grass and opened an eye to look out for ants. She saw one on a fat blade of grass. Where there was one, there were more. Lily worked at feeling the dead Martin, because she couldn't see him in her mind, not dead. Then she dug her hands into the grass and, grabbing hold of some of it, yanked it up by the roots and cast it on either side of her. The hot sun baked the back of her legs and arms and neck. She could smell her own hair as it brushed her nose. When she sat up, she looked down at her thighs and saw that grass had made indentations in her skin and a few blades had stuck to her. She traced a faint red mark and spoke to the ground.

"Martin," she said. "I'm still alive."

Then Lily heard steps in the grass behind her and turned around. She didn't move off the grave. She saw that Dick and Frank were walking toward her, and she was glad to see them. In the sunlight she noticed how dirty the two men were all over again. Neither one made any sign that they saw her, but she supposed they did, and she watched as they slumped toward her and stopped.

Frank looked down at her from under the brim of his hat, his eyes the color of wet sand. "Guess you knew 'bout him all along," he said.

Dick stood behind his brother. He was looking at her with an expression Lily couldn't make sense of—a fixed but bright stare. She looked at Frank. "How do you mean?"

"That he'd hurt somebody—hurt himself in the end. That's bad enough."

Lily looked down at the grave and shook her head.

When she looked up, Dick's eyes were still fastened on her face, and he was nodding vigorously. Frank wasn't looking at Dick, but he seemed to feel the nods at his shoulder, and he spoke again.

"Dick wants me to tell you we took care of it."

Lily looked from one brother to the other. "Took care of it?"

Frank nodded. Both men were nodding at the same time. Dick's eyes didn't leave her face. "What Marty left behind."

Lily crossed her arms on her chest and rubbed the skin above her elbows. "You found it?"

Frank shook his head. "Nope, Marty came with it that morning. Said to burn it."

"And you did?" Lily had an abrupt, vivid fantasy of the doll burning in the trash bin outside the house and Dick watching it.

Again Frank shook his head. "Dick wouldn't allow it. Put her in a big long box, lucky we had it, had to fold her up a bit. Then he buried it back of the house. Dick took a shine to it—little slip of a thing, wasn't she?"

Lily looked at her feet on the grass. One of her shoelaces had come untied and lay on the browning sod. "He told you about the cave?"

Frank nodded but just barely—a single motion of his chin. "Knew we couldn't keep it round the house, not with Marty gone and his last wish bein' to burn it, but Dick said he wasn't gonna burn nothing' that looked like a girl."

Lily nodded. She bit her lip.

"Better to lay it down in peace on the property. Don't s'pose Marty'd really mind that. An' this way there's no talk, Miss Dahl, 'bout you and him"—Frank was mumbling now and his eyes had lost focus—"on account of the likeness."

The three of them didn't speak for several minutes. Dick moved away from his brother and stood over her. He folded his hands in front of him and looked down into Lily's face like a man who didn't fully believe what he was seeing. Their silence wasn't an awkward social pause in which all the parties are at a loss about what to say. It was the intimate silence of a shared secret, and Lily realized that the doll was merely the form the secret had taken at that moment. It wasn't the secret itself. The secret was somewhere else, always somewhere else, and as Lily said this to herself, she heard her own breathing and heard Dick's and Frank's and it made her feel happy.

Dick was staring at the ground now. Then very slowly, he began to bend, then to squat. Lily couldn't understand what he was doing. Once he had arrived at a squatting position, he let himself fall heavily forward on his knees, and then he grabbed Lily's shoelace.

"Oh, Mr. Bodler," Lily said. "I can do that." She bent down and reached for her shoe, but Dick batted her hand away and began to tie the lace very slowly. He made a good, tight bow and looked up at her before he righted himself.

"Thank you," Lily said.

Once he was on his feet, Dick took Lily's hand. She could feel the calluses on his palm and the oiliness of his skin. He pulled her away from Martin's grave and walked back through the stones with her as Frank followed them. Dick dragged his feet but moved with stiff determination, his fingers tightly around her own.

He took Lily to his mother's grave. The headstone was small and gray-white. It looked older than it should have and was stained green by moss near the bottom, but there were trees in this part of the graveyard, and the shade cooled Lily as she stared at the inscription: "Helen Bodler, born

December 6, 1899, died June 21, 1932. Beloved mother of Ethan, Frank and Richard Bodler." Ethan Bodler was buried beside his mother—born January 5, 1926, died February 11, 1926. Looking at the grave, Lily squeezed Dick's hand. She turned to read Dick's face. He had continued to hold her hand and was sweating into her palm, his grip so slippery she felt her fingers might slide out of his at any moment. Dick opened his mouth and laughed his noiseless laugh and moved his feet ever so slightly on the ground. Frank didn't interfere with him this time. Then he stopped and the three of them walked to the road together. When she pointed to her bicycle, Dick released her hand.

Lily didn't refuse their offer of a ride. She climbed into the cab beside Dick as Frank drove slowly into town and asked that they drop her in front of the Arts Guild. Dick leaned on Lily rather heavily, and the weight of his shoulder was uncomfortable. Why feeling him so close to her should have made her think that Dick had seen his mother killed many years ago, she didn't know. But Lily did think it. He might not remember, she thought, but I think he was there.

After Lily had hauled her bicycle from the back of the truck, and just before he started the motor, Frank looked out the window and spoke to her. Lily saw and heard him speak but didn't understand what he was saying until moments later, as though her brain lagged behind her ears. When the truck was pulling away and she saw only Frank's elbow sticking out the window, she realized he had said, "Dick wants ya to visit."

Auditions in the Arts Guild had already started. Lily heard a piano from the stage beyond the vestibule doors, but she saw no other rivals for the role of Eliza Doolittle. Mrs. Carter squinted at Lily. "Any later and you'd have missed the whole thing," she said.

She explained to Mrs. Carter that she'd be right back, raced down the stairs and into the little room at the end of the hallway. She dropped her jeans and sat down on the toilet. While she listened to the rush of urine, she noticed a spot of blood on her underpants. So, Lily thought, there it is, and then she felt tears warm the corners of her eyes. She drew out a long piece of toilet paper. She folded it, placed it on her underpants and hiked up her jeans. As she walked down the hallway, the coarse paper scratched the inside of her thighs, and Lily stopped, hastily sticking her hand into her pants to adjust the wad. She found herself outside the closed door to the costume room. Only weeks ago, Martin had been sitting in there on the floor scribbling down her measurements, quoting the play, asking her to go home with him. Lily imagined the inside of the room now, and saw Cobweb's costume hanging from a wardrobe rack labeled "DREAM."

Then from somewhere above her, she heard a woman calling her name in a high voice just like the one her mother had used to call her up from the creek for dinner. "Lil—y! Lily Dahl!"

"I'm here!" she called. "I'm coming."

The street Lily imagined in her mind as she leapt up the stairs was real, and the fog was real, too. She was singing loudly on a London corner in filthy clothes with a basket of flowers in her arms. I can be her, she thought suddenly. Then Lily straightened her back, lifted her chin and walked quickly through the double doors toward the stage.